D0228930

THE LIFE
SHE LEFT
BEHIND

For more information about Jessica Blair visit
www.jessicablair.co.uk

THE LIFE SHE LEFT BEHIND

Jessica Blair

piatkus

PIATKUS

First published in Great Britain in 2017 by Piatkus

13 5 7 9 10 8 6 4 2

A CIP catalogue record for this book
is available from the British Library.

ISBN 978-0-349-41127-9

Typeset in Times by M Rules
Printed and bound in Great Britain by
Clays Ltd, St Ives, plc

Papers used by Piatkus are from well-managed forests
and other responsible sources.

MIX
Paper from
responsible sources
FSC® C104740

Piatkus
An imprint of
Little, Brown Book Group
Carmelite House
50 Victoria Embankment
London EC4Y 0DZ

An Hachette UK Company
www.hachette.co.uk

www.littlebrown.co.uk

For my great-granddaughter
Imogen Raisbeck, born 20 June 2016

Also, remembering a happy life with Joan

And for Anne, Geraldine, Judith and Duncan

And for Jill, a dear friend,
whose interest in my writing has
encouraged me to keep going

1

'One last wave!' forty-two-year-old Glenda McKinley instructed her daughters as she drew her thick plaid shawl more tightly around her shoulders against the chill that had arrived with the lowering of the sun on this April day of 1878.

Her eyes were fixed on her husband John whose strong arms were sending the rowing boat scudding in the direction of the tiny island in the loch, near to its opposite shore.

He was still thin after a severe chest infection and Glenda now recalled the handsome strong, young man with slightly curled dark hair that had first won her heart. He was still relatively young at forty-two years of age but he was leaner and his hair and beard now had streaks of grey; his skin dark and tough with the wind and sun that also gave these Highland mountains their wonderful subtle colours.

'Just a little longer, Mama,' pleaded sixteen-year-old Caitlin.

'There's a lot to do before your father returns, and that

'won't be long with the light fading,' countered her mother.

'He should have gone earlier as you suggested, Mama,' put in nineteen-year-old Rosalind, a little tetchily.

Glenda knew what was upsetting her eldest daughter but, deciding this was not the moment to chide Rosalind, held back a reprimand. Instead she said, lacing her words with encouragement, 'Come on, let's see how Mrs Lynch is getting on with the cooking. When we've done that we'll go and dress ourselves in our best attire.'

'We'll give Papa the surprise of his life,' laughed Caitlin.

'Are you sure he knows nothing of your plans?' asked Rosalind.

'Yes,' replied her mother. 'He doesn't suspect we are doing anything special. The staff have been sworn to secrecy.'

'This is so exciting!' cried Caitlin quickly, putting aside any sorrow she felt on leaving.

'So don't you give it away by over-reacting,' warned her sister.

'I'm not stupid,' snapped Caitlin.

'Now come on, let's not bicker.' Glenda waved her daughters into the house and headed for the kitchen. Within a few minutes Mrs Lynch was reassuring her that the celebratory meal would be ready by the time the master was ready to sit down.

'So there is nothing more for us to do?' Glenda enquired.

'Nothing, Ma'am. You and the young ladies should go and enjoy getting ready.'

Glenda and her two daughters hurried up the stairs to their rooms. Twenty minutes later they all reappeared on the landing.

'Oh, Mama, you look wonderful,' gasped Rosalind, looking with both excitement and sadness at her mother's beautiful peacock-blue gown that complemented Glenda's Celtic red hair and emphasised a still trim figure.

'You do, you really do!' added Caitlin, not wanting to be left out.

Glenda laughed. 'You've seen this dress before. The present situation did not warrant my buying a new one.'

'I know, Mama, but you seem to glow and make it look special on what is really a sad occasion. Our last night at home.'

'Thank you very much.' She stepped back a little and took in her two daughters, Ros, so much like her father with her high cheek bones that were accentuated whenever she smiled and Cat, the young 'tom-boy', whose love of the outdoors had tanned her pale skin; but her real beauty shone from within, lighting up her hazel eyes. 'You two look just as lovely in those dresses; perfect to walk down the stairs with me when your father comes in.'

'Should I start my lookout now, Mama?' asked Caitlin, her tone filled with the expectation of how her father might react when he saw the three of them standing on the stairs dressed in their finest just for him and for the dream they were to follow.

'Why not?' replied her mother. 'We don't know exactly when he will leave the island, except that he won't be late.'

'I'll get the best view from here,' announced Cat, heading for the window seat at the end of the landing.

'A good loud shout when you first see him,' said Rosalind. 'Don't miss him by daydreaming about the future.'

'As if I would,' muttered Caitlin, as she ran to the seat and settled her gaze across the loch towards the castle that stood, a half ruin, on the tiny island a short distance away. She followed the sun's rays touching the mountain-tops with an ever-changing light that also took every opportunity to spread enchantment into the glens and, closer to home, the trees her father had planted when her and Ros had been toddlers. She smiled at the memory of them insisting that he should name them all. She must not miss the first signs that her father was heading home.

Glenda smiled to herself at her youngest daughter's determination to play her part in the surprise. 'Come, Rosalind, we may as well be comfortable while we wait.'

They went down the stairs and settled on to a comfortable, slightly faded sofa in front of the blazing log fire in the sitting room. Glenda looked at her daughter, staring at the leaping flames as if they were not there. The sparkle had faded from Rosalind's eyes recently.

'Still worried about leaving Scotland?' Glenda asked her gently.

Rosalind screwed up her face. 'Not exactly worried but I don't really want to go. I love this land. I love our Scottish mountains. I love my home, all our memories of every room in this house. I want to take them all with me.'

'So do I,' said Glenda. 'I'm locking them away in my memory so I'll have them with me wherever I go. You try and do the same, then you and I can share them whenever we want.'

'So why are we going?'

'You know the last few years have been difficult for us, Rosalind. Your father and I are getting older and have no son to take on such a large estate with challenging farming conditions. Your father's illness last year took a lot out of him and now he feels he wants a better life for us all and believes that we can find it in America. He has not taken this decision lightly. He has consulted your Uncle Gordon who's been in America for sixteen years now. He tells us there is good land available from which we can live well. We should be able to build ourselves a solid and profitable future. We are lucky to have his advice from which to profit.'

'I know, but life there won't be the same as it is here.'

Glenda smiled. 'It won't, but it might be better; Uncle Gordon believes so. After moving around he has now finally settled in Colorado. He also agrees with your father's decision not to sell up here, so that if ever any of us wishes to return, we can do so. That's why we are leaving the furniture, our best clothes and so on. We have to see what life in America is like before we make a final decision.'

'Is that a promise, Mama?'

'You know it is, and also that the estate is being placed meanwhile in the capable hands of Mr and Mrs Martins; Jessie will keep her eye on the house and Greg will look after the estate helped by his son. Your father has given Greg and Clive carte blanche to do as they think best to keep the estate a viable proposition. So, you see, you can be reassured once again that Pinmuir House, Loch, its castle and lands, are being looked after . . .'

Her words, which she saw were reassuring her eldest daughter, were cut short by a piercing scream that echoed through the house.

Glenda started. A chill ran through her at the sound of

further screams. The colour drained from Rosalind's face. 'Caitlin!' she cried, leaping to her feet. Her mother was close behind her as they reached the hall.

'Mama! Mama!' Caitlin, racing down the stairs, was shaking so much she could barely get the words out. She flung herself at her mother.

Glenda grabbed her by her upper arms and shook her slightly. 'What is it, Cat? What's wrong?'

Caitlin gasped, 'Fire ... fire!'

Glenda released her, turned and rushed to the front of the house. She yanked open the oak door and even as she plunged outside saw dark smoke and flames rising from the castle. She started towards the loch but after a few steps realised it was useless – John had their only boat!

'Papa!' gasped Rosalind, following her mother. She was aware of someone beside her, turned, grasped his arm and said, 'He's over at the castle, Clive! The boat is still tied up there. Get help ... quick!'

A shocked Clive acted immediately. Thankful that he had come from his home on horseback, he sent the animal galloping in the direction of their nearest neighbour, a mile along the shore of the loch.

There was still enough light to distinguish any movement on the island but all Glenda could see were the devouring flames, their macabre dance reflected in the still waters of the loch.

Caitlin clung to her mother, and Rosalind huddled close to them both. Glenda felt the weight of the inevitable settling over her, even though she tried desperately to cling to some last shred of hope.

2

Glenda waited on the shore. She resisted Mrs Martins' attempts to persuade her to return to the comfort of the house, and found strength in Rosalind and Caitlin's refusal to leave her side.

'Mama, will Clive be long?' The plaintive note in her youngest daughter's voice tugged at Glenda's heart.

'I hope not, love,' she replied.

'He'll be as quick as possible,' said Rosalind. 'I hope he finds Mr McBain at home.'

'Won't Mr McBain have seen the fire?' asked Caitlin.

'Not from where the family live,' said Glenda. 'The spur of the mountain protrudes into the loch and masks their view in this direction.'

'Come on, Clive. Hurry up, hurry up!' chanted Rosalind, half to herself, but Caitlin caught the words and joined in.

Glenda moved restlessly from one foot to the other, wishing there was something more she could do. She knew the people who had gathered by the lochside would wait until news arrived and be ready to help if needed. She wanted the McBains to arrive with their boat and then she could get to the castle, find John alive and unharmed, safe from the fire that still gnawed at the stone walls as if seeking their complete destruction.

The minutes passed by slowly with people speculating as to what the delay might be. Tensions were mounting. Then the sound of a galloping horse penetrated the gloom. The suspense eased and hope balanced on a knife-edge.

'The McBains are on their way!' yelled Clive as he hauled his horse to a halt. He swung out of the saddle and ran to Mrs McKinley. 'They shouldn't be long, Ma'am.'

'Thank you, Clive,' she returned, anxiety in her voice.

He glanced at Rosalind who echoed her mother's words almost silently, which he acknowledged with a small reassuring smile.

'How many boats are coming, Clive?' asked his father.

'Two,' he replied.

'Good,' said Greg Martins, who started choosing the men he would like to accompany him over to the island.

'I'm coming too,' Glenda announced firmly.

'No, Ma'am. You'd be better here, looking after your daughters.'

'No!' screamed Caitlin. 'I want to go too. I want Papa!'

'The wind is too strong for you to go. You stay here and look after your mother,' said Greg in a gently persuasive tone. 'You'll be doing an important job.'

His eyes met Glenda's and she nodded.

'You'll do that for Mr Martins, won't you?' her mother asked the girl.

Caitlin tightened her lips and bowed her head in acceptance.

'We'll do it together, Cat,' said Rosalind.

Jessie Martins stepped out of the group of people who had gathered in spite of the cold when news of the fire had spread among the estate workers. She turned to the cook. 'Mrs Lynch, let us go into the house. We'll make a warm drink for everyone.'

Glenda nodded her approval but she herself stayed close to the water's edge. 'Off you go and help, girls,' she said to her daughters.

'No, Mama. Mr Martins wants us to look after you,' said Caitlin.

'Very well.' Glenda allowed herself a little smile at her daughter's acceptance of her role.

With every passing minute their attention veered between the direction from which the boat would come and the spectacle of the burning castle nearly a mile away. Horror filled Glenda's eyes at the realisation that the timbers, supporting the stone walls, had started crashing to the ground, and without them parts of the roof had started to cave in also. Her eyes were now fixed on the disintegrating building and she saw the sudden leaping of flames and dust thrown up to the sky.

Glenda flinched. 'John, John . . . where are you?'

'The boats! The boats!' There was hope in the cries that went up, started by Caitlin.

Men rushed into the water, ready to grab and haul in the boats as soon as they reached the shallows. Shouts rang out, orders were willingly taken, the beach came alive with willing would-be rescuers, but then words of warning were uttered as the early-evening sky over the island filled with billowing smoke. Another castle wall had collapsed and the danger they faced was emphasised once again.

'No, Mrs McKinley. No!' Glenda had stepped determinedly towards the boats as soon as they touched the shore. Mr Martins' attention was on her at once. He reached out to stop her, stumbled but managed to grab her arm and hold on as he fell. Willing hands hauled them both to their feet.

'Take your daughters into the house. You can do no good here, Ma'am. The men will do their best.'

'Come, Mama,' said Rosalind, taking her mother's hand.

As Glenda felt her other hand taken by Caitlin and heard her younger daughter's sobs, she nodded towards Greg. They watched the boats leave and then walked slowly to the house.

Glenda sank on to the first chair she saw, took her two daughters in her arms and then succumbed to the ministrations of Mrs Martins, who said gently, 'You must be exhausted. I know it will be hard but go to your room and try and get some sleep, Ma'am. I'll keep my eye on what is happening here.'

Glenda nodded and reluctantly went to the room she shared with her husband. Her daughter followed her.

Two hours later a noise disturbed Glenda. She woke with a start, trying to grasp where she was and why. After a few brief moments realisation dawned with a sense of alarm and an intense desire to see John. So as not to wake her sleeping daughters she slid carefully from the bed. She threw a shawl around her shoulders and stepped over to the window. She eased aside a curtain so she could look out. There was no movement on the shore so she knew the men were still on the island. She still expected John to come back, striding in the side door of the house, casting off his old tweed jacket in the lobby to go and settle inside his study. Surely she would once again walk in to see him with a glass of whisky in his hand, turn to smile at her before he settled down to work. She would kiss him again, wouldn't she? Her wait would have to continue.

Clive and his friend Tim, with four other men, having quickly gathered provisions in case they needed to spend the night on the island, started to move along the shoreline away from the castle. Their knowledge of the loch and local conditions had led them to believe that if John McKinley had fallen into the water, in an attempt to leave the burning castle, he could have been washed ashore further along the lochside. With light fading from the sky they made camp in the shelter of some rocks and held on to the hope that a new day might yet bring success.

A bright morning sun heightened their expectation and they lost little time in renewing the search.

Clive called out, 'There's an outcrop of rocks ahead that should give me a good view. I'll push on and scale it.' With the approval of the others, he left them at a quick trot and, reaching the mound, started up it. From the top he signalled to the search party.

Clive surveyed the jumble of rocks beneath but nothing claimed his attention. He decided to move further to the right before continuing along the shore. After a hundred yards he stopped on the brink of a gully that dropped sharply to meet the waves of the incoming tide. His eyes

11

widened. Excitement gripped him. Was that a rock ... or clothing?

He yelled to attract his companions. 'Here, over here!' He pointed where he wanted them to go.

Tim signalled their acknowledgement. They closed ranks as they moved closer and closer to the gully. Clive held his position. If the bundle was not what he thought it was, his guidance might still be needed. Anxiety gripped him as he watched. He held his breath when he saw them reach the heap and bend down to examine it. One of them straightened up slowly. 'It's John!'

Then any hope Clive still had was dashed as two of the men gesticulated with their thumbs down. He scrambled back in a cascade of rocks, heedless of the danger. Suddenly he was on the shore and running towards the grim-faced group.

'Dead when we found him,' one of them reported. 'With the strengthening wind he's taken a beating on the rocks.'

Words lodged in Clive's throat at the thought of breaking the news to the McKinleys. How could he face Rosalind and Caitlin? What could he say?

As the boats neared the McKinley home the men saw Glenda and her daughters rush to the shore. Eyes met and held. That brief moment of time marked the last moment when there were still those who believed that John might yet be alive.

The men carried him carefully, a blanket over him, towards the group of onlookers on the shore.

Glenda felt her elder daughter's grip on her tighten and

knew Rosalind had guessed the truth: this could be no one but her father. A choking cry came from Caitlin as she too realised what lay so still beneath the blanket. All three of them stood without moving, frozen by grief.

A dreadful silence prevailed as the estate workers watched the rescuers approach Glenda McKinley and lower their burden gently to the ground at her feet.

Mrs Martins and Mrs McBain came close to Rosalind and Caitlin to hold them back. Turning and resting her head on Jessie Martins' shoulder, Caitlin sobbed uncontrollably for the father she had loved.

Glenda, with tears streaming down her face, fell to her knees and folded back the blanket from his face. There was a moment's pause. Then, as she took her husband in her arms, the cry of a haunted soul reverberated across shore, loch and hillside. 'Oh, John, why? Why, why, why?' There was no answer, only shuddering sobs from Rosalind and Caitlin.

After a few minutes Glenda kissed him, laid him gently down, and stood up. The men dropped the blanket over him again but as they lifted his body one edge slipped and, in the seconds that it took to re-cover him, Caitlin turned and saw a horribly deformed face, covered with lacerations and bruises, and barely recognised it as belonging to her beloved father. She tried to cry out but no sound came. She was transfixed by the horror of what she had seen. Then she was aware of her mother holding out her arms and indicating to her daughters to walk beside her. They led the sad cortège to the house where Glenda directed them to lay John on his bed.

*

Tears stained the paper on which Glenda wrote to her husband's brother in America.

Dear Gordon,

It is with an aching heart that I write to tell you that John died yesterday. He had gone to the castle in the late afternoon. It seems that he fell and probably injured his leg knocking over an oil lamp that started a fire from which his only escape lay in the loch. Sadly that and the rocks were too much for him.

The tragedy is still too recent for me to write more now, except to say that, our American dream is shattered and will remain unfulfilled.

God keep you at this tragic time.

Your loving sister-in-law,

Glenda

3

'It has been a hard day, Ma'am,' said Mrs Martins as Glenda and her daughters came into the house after seeing the last of the mourners leave. 'I told Mrs Lynch to prepare some tea for you. I'll let her know you are ready for it.'

'Thank you,' said Glenda, weary after a day when she had been obliged to act with composure despite the wrenching sorrow inside her.

As they were settling themselves Caitlin asked, 'Mama, don't you think your relations could have come to Papa's funeral?'

'I agree with you, Cat,' put in Rosalind indignantly. 'You and I don't know them but they could have come, for Mama's sake.'

Glenda gave a weak smile. 'I didn't expect them to, not after all these years.'

'Why? It's not as if they live far away – only ten miles or so as the crow flies.'

'The rift has become too wide. Your grandfather was adamant that if I married your father, I would be an outcast as far as the rest of my family was concerned. I was cut off without a penny. No one else dared to contest that, and they were all banned from contacting me in any way.'

'But you didn't obey him,' pointed out Rosalind.

'I loved your father too much to lose him.'

'What exactly happened when you said you would marry Papa?' asked Caitlin.

'I had to leave home immediately, with only what I stood up in.'

'That was cruel,' said Caitlin in disgust.

'What did you do then, Mama?' asked Rosalind, who had always wondered about her scarcity of relatives.

Glenda paused. She had never told her daughters the full story but now felt it was the right time. They were older and needed answers to the questions she had previously shrugged aside.

'Your father was angry when I told him that I had been cast out. He was all for confronting my father there and then, but I persuaded him not to. It would only have led to more trouble.'

'What happened to you then?'

'Your father persuaded me to go home with him.'

'To this house?'

'Yes. Your uncle Gordon and your father were living here together. Immediately your uncle was aware of the situation, he invited me to make my home with them. I have ever been grateful for that invitation. Your father and I married immediately, to avoid any scandal, and were very happy.' Her voice caught in her throat at the thought that her life could no longer be the same.

'If you were all happy together, why did Uncle Gordon leave?' asked Rosalind.

16

'Didn't he like children?' Caitlin suggested.

'No, no, no!' Glenda protested quickly. 'He loved the two of you; spoiled you as if you were his own.'

'So why did he go?' pressed Rosalind.

'Your uncle believed that if he left, life would be easier for us as a family. We tried to persuade him to stay but he was adamant. He insisted on signing over the estate to John so that your father was free to work it as he saw best. And, well, you know the rest. Gordon found himself a new life in America, worked hard to make it a success. You've read in his letters how he moved around, always seeming to do well for himself in spite of the harsh conditions. He is now settled in Colorado where his cattle ranch is thriving. He realised from your father's letters to him that our estate here was stagnating and advised us to follow him. He believed we could make a good life in America.'

'Can we?' asked Rosalind.

'I don't know.' Her mother shook her head from side to side, and fought back further tears as she added, 'We will have to see. There will be much to decide, but for now we have to observe mourning conventions. You two will wear black for a year . . . two years for me.'

The sisters pulled faces. 'Do we have to?' moaned Caitlin.

'Yes. We do from respect for Papa.'

'Does that mean we'll be staying here now?' asked Caitlin.

'Certainly for the present. For now I think it best if we follow the plans your father left for the estate. Because we were going to America, he put a lot of thought into them.'

'Does that mean we might still go?' asked Rosalind.

17

'Not necessarily, but it does mean we have time to grieve, sort ourselves out and consider our next move. The Martins will look after the estate for now. Neither of you should worry. We will see how life works out for us.'

Seeing her daughters were reassured, Glenda left them to mourn in their own way. She went to her own room craving silence and memories, knowing the future would seem for ever empty. Lying on her bed, her face in the pillow to silence the racking sobs and tears, she fought back screams until she felt exhausted but she arose knowing her first task was to inscribe the date of John's death in the family bible. She brushed down her black skirt, went to the study and took up her pen. Once that was done she decided she would write to Gordon. It was the next day before she composed the final script.

Dear Gordon,

I thought you would like to know that John was laid to rest in a simple service conducted by Rev. Kintail, whom you won't know as he came to Gartonhag long after you were gone. He could not have been kinder or his address more apposite. The weather was warm and dry. I'll swear the hills and mountains remembered how you and John enjoyed sharing their beauty and put on a special display for him. A lone piper played a lament that I will hear again every time I stand at the grave side.

The girls and I miss him as we missed you when you left for America.

Keep us in your thoughts – we face an uncertain future.

Glenda

After finishing the letter she sent for her daughters. When they entered the room a few minutes later Glenda remarked, 'Those mourning dresses suit you, they fit well.'

They both pulled faces and muttered, 'Black, ugh!'

Glenda, recalling how she had felt at their age when having to wear black, gave them no reprimand but merely said, 'The time will soon pass but it is up to you to live your lives as normally as you can. Enjoy yourselves, in fact – I place no restrictions on any activity, except to say you should wear black whenever you are in company.'

'We will, Mama,' they both promised.

'Good. Now, we should settle back into our lives here. It is fortunate we have only our personal belongings to see to. I suggest we do that straight away.'

'May we go riding, Mama?' asked Caitlin.

'Get your things unpacked and you can go tomorrow morning.'

'Good, good!' cried Caitlin excitedly. 'Are you coming too, Rosalind?'

'Of course. Let's see to our clothes now and then we'll find Clive and tell him to have your Pearl and my Freya ready for us in the morning.' She enjoyed Clive's company. They had been brought up together, her father having no son had taught him to shoot and hunt. He found himself the envy of the other boys at the local school. Afterwards John had taught him further on subjects while his own father instructed Clive on all practical estate work. He had grown into a handsome, young man of twenty-one with ambition to become a gentleman.

*

19

On returning from their ride the next day they led their ponies to the stable where Clive commented, 'I'm so pleased you are able to exercise your fine pair of Highland ponies. They are strong and sure-footed, but need more daily exercise than I am able to give them with all the other work I have to do.' Looking at Rosalind he added, 'I thought your riding might be restricted at present.'

'I think Mama sees it as a way for us to take in some fresh air and be out of our black for a while.'

'I'm glad she does,' said Caitlin, screwing up her nose as she added, 'I really don't like black. We must keep to the estate, though, for our rides.'

'I'm sorry I can't accompany you. Father's already drawing up a plan of work now your mama has left the running of the estate to us.'

'Are you pleased about that?' asked Rosalind.

'More than pleased,' replied Clive enthusiastically. 'I think we can make improvements even though we are restricted by the lie of the land. But we'll see.'

'You really do like working here then?' queried Rosalind.

'Yes.'

'Wouldn't you like to work on a bigger estate, with better land?'

'Not really. I can see the potential here. Your father had ideas but his illness restricted how much he could do himself.'

'And your father and you believe you can make improvements?'

'We'll try, as a tribute to him.'

'That is very thoughtful of you. Papa would have been touched,' Rosalind said.

'We'll do our best for him. And, of course, for you.'

She smiled to herself when she saw Clive was embarrassed by having made this last observation aloud. 'Thank you,' she murmured.

'And if we do go, you'll take good care of Pearl and Freya won't you?' asked Caitlin.

'Of course.' Clive smiled at her. 'Haven't I always?'

'Yes. I didn't mean you hadn't,' she added with embarrassment.

'Come on, Cat, we'd better be getting back,' Rosalind told her.

As the sisters turned away, Clive caught Rosalind's eyes. 'I'm glad you aren't going to America now,' he said.

She gave a little nod of her head in acceptance of his remark without making any verbal acknowledgement of it. After they were out of earshot, Caitlin said in a hushed tone, 'I think Clive has a crush on you. You'd be a fool to pass him up!'

Life gradually slipped back almost to the normal, though they were acutely aware of the yawning gulf left by John. Glenda found great comfort and support in her daughters' company and in the loyalty of her staff, especially that of the Martins who all worked hard to keep Pinmuir a successful estate. But Glenda realised that, sooner or later, she would face some difficult decisions about whether or not this place was the best one for a widow and her two unmarried daughters. And when she did, she must take these decisions alone.

A letter arrived from Gordon.

Dear Glenda,

Thank you for your correspondence and particularly
the information about John's funeral. I am glad it
was a fine, typical Highland day. I could picture it
all so vividly. I remember such days when the three
of us were together walking in the hills. Those were
wonderful times.

Of course you are ever in my thoughts and you
know if I can be of help to you, despite the distance
that separates us, you only have to ask. Or if you wish
to resume your plan to visit me here, maybe even
consider making the move permanent, you will always
be welcome.

Yours with brotherly affection,
Gordon

Glenda replied:

Dear Gordon,

I thank you for your offer of help. The distance
between us is a hindrance but it is comforting to know
that I can seek your advice if I can't cope or make a
sound decision by myself. I fear nothing can be decided
about the possibility of coming to America until after
our mourning period is over.

The Martins have sought my reassurance about their
future. I've told them to carry on in the way agreed
with John. I was sure you'd approve of that, even
though you relinquished any right in the estate when
you emigrated.

I am still prepared to contemplate a move to America

in due course, subject to whatever the future may hold for Rosalind and Caitlin. As you know, the Martins are devoted to us and that makes things here a lot easier. We will allow ourselves a period of calm reflection before making any definite plans.

Ros and Cat send their love.

I hope you are well and that life in America continues to suit you.

Glenda sat for a moment with her thoughts drifting to her brother-in-law, wondering if Kirsty McLain was the reason he had left his beloved Highlands so suddenly.

Then, annoyed with herself for wasting time speculating about something that did not concern her, she picked up her pen and signed the letter with a decisive flourish.

4

Glenda gathered the four small stacks of papers from the top of her desk and secured them together. She breathed a sigh of relief that this, the fourth of the quarterly accounts she had supervised, had been completed. She was thankful that the first yearly report since John's death showed the estate was financially stable; previous accounts had showed some disturbing losses. Although she would have preferred to record a profit, she was satisfied. So long as things remained stable she could see their lives taking a satisfactory course. But dare she hope there would be no further upheaval? Could she really expect that? She placed the papers in a folder, secured it with a green ribbon and placed it in a drawer of the desk that she locked.

Believing she had earned a cup of chocolate, Glenda went to the bell-pull to summon the housemaid.

'It is a pleasant morning, Paula. I'll be on the veranda.'

'Yes, Ma'am.'

Glenda strolled outside and paused to enjoy her first

glimpse of the sun. It was warm and comforting, seeming to draw a special beauty out of the green clad hills, displaying them to advantage against the majestic backcloth of the harsher slopes beyond.

She sighed as she sat down and drove away the sorrow that dogged her. The sense of loss she felt was almost overwhelming, but she knew that she could not afford to succumb to that feeling – John would not want her to, and she had her daughters and their young lives to consider.

Rosalind and Caitlin had gone riding as they did most mornings. She was pleased they had this interest; it gave them something on which to focus and enjoy in the fresh air, some comfort for the loss of their father. Her own loss was eased somewhat by the way her children were coping and their solicitude and support for her. So, in spite of the shock that had almost overwhelmed her, Glenda concentrated on living day by day.

She stirred her hot chocolate, took a sip, pursed her lips in approval and picked up the novel she had started yesterday, believing it would refresh her mind after the figures she had been dealing with. She settled down to prove that *The Scarlet Shawl* by Richard Jefferies would do just that.

She had read four pages and drunk half her chocolate when she was disturbed by the sound of a galloping horse approaching the house. Alarmed, she rose from her chair and moved to the balustrade from which she could gain a better view of the rider.

Caitlin! Panic seized Glenda. Where was Rosalind? Seeing her mother, the girl veered Pearl away from the track to the stable yard and made for the front of the house, bringing the horse to an abrupt halt.

'Where's Rosalind?' Glenda asked, her eyes expressing concern.

'She's with the lady!' gasped Caitlin, trying to get her breath.

'Lady?' Glenda frowned in surprise.

'Yes! Yes!' snapped Caitlin, with marked irritation.

'Calm down, Caitlin! Who is she and what does she want?'

'I don't know who she is. She wouldn't tell us, but she asked to see you.'

'Me? Didn't she give a name?'

'No, she wouldn't, but she obviously knew you because she said she wanted to give you a surprise.'

'Surprise? Who would want to give me a surprise? Is Rosalind with her?'

'Yes. Ros signalled to me to ride ahead and tell you that you are going to have a mysterious visitor.' Caitlin revelled in emphasising the word 'mysterious'. 'Who can it be, Mama?'

'How should I know?' Glenda responded. 'I haven't even seen her yet.'

'Someone bringing us lots of money perhaps.' Caitlin's eyes widened in anticipation.

'I shouldn't think so, and we are perfectly well provided for,' Glenda reproved her daughter.

'I wish they'd hurry up,' said Caitlin, steadying Pearl, who was scraping one hoof over the grass. The moments seemed to drag by, testing their patience. Then, 'Mama, they are here!' announced the girl.

Curiosity overtook Glenda. The riders were still a little way off. She shaded her eyes against the sun.

'Oh, my goodness!' she gasped. The surprise of what she saw drained her face of colour. The woman, riding side-saddle, held herself with perfect poise, and her gentle touch on the reins had sufficient control to lead the grey to do her bidding. Glenda knew the new arrival would be revelling in the impression she made and enjoying showing off her eye-catching blue velvet riding habit; she suddenly felt drab in her mourning black. How she wished she could throw it off and meet the other woman on an equal footing. Then Glenda stiffened herself against such frivolity in a widow.

As she brought her horse to a halt in front of her mother, Rosalind said, 'Mama, Caitlin and I met this lady and she asked where she might find you. I requested her name but she would not give it nor reveal why she wished to come here. I thought it best to accompany her and send Caitlin ahead to inform you that someone had requested to see you.'

Sensing her daughter was wondering if she had done the right thing, Glenda reassured her. 'You acted perfectly properly, Ros. I suspect the lady in question held back information in order to surprise me completely. And she has certainly done that. Rosalind, Caitlin ... meet your Aunt Fiona.'

The two young sisters looked aghast. '*Aunt* Fiona?'

They saw little resemblance to their mother, Fiona having fair hair and a pale complexion with pink cheeks rather than the freckles of their mother. Only their eyes and proud demeanour showed a family resemblance.

The stranger laughed as she slid from the saddle and settled her feet firmly on the ground. 'Yes, your mother's sister.' With her eyes fixed on Glenda, eager for a reaction,

27

she held her arms wide. Glenda hesitated for a moment then, cautiously, stepped into her sister's embrace.

'Relax, Glen. I come on a mission of peace, with news that should please you,' Fiona whispered close to her ear. 'Let us have a private word and then I'll officially meet my nieces.'

Glenda gave an almost imperceptible nod and said to her daughters, 'Go and tell Mrs Martins that we have a surprise guest for lunch. And we would like another pot of chocolate now.'

The girls were moving off when they were halted by their aunt. 'Tell Mrs Martins, whoever she is, that I will have a whisky instead of the chocolate.'

They looked questioningly at their mother. 'Chocolate only!' Glenda commanded.

Rosalind turned to Caitlin. 'You tell Mrs Martins. I'll tell Clive to see to the horses.'

Once the girls were out of earshot, Glenda bristled and glared at her sister. 'I don't know why you are here but never, if you come again, countermand any order I give to my children. And certainly don't indulge yourself in drinking spirits or wines at this time of day.'

'I'm sorry,' muttered Fiona, though her apology carried little real regret. 'I thought they looked old enough . . .'

'Maybe they are but John and I set them an example about drinking. I won't have that undermined. They are approaching an age when they will be able to make their own judgements on these matters and I don't wish any of their decisions to be influenced by bad examples.' Glenda left a slight reproving pause then added, 'Now, Fiona, let us begin again. Why are you here? It must be over twenty years since we saw each other so I don't believe this is a social call. You wouldn't dare do that in case Father heard of it.'

'He won't hear of it because he can't – he's dead!' replied her sister crisply.

For a moment Glenda did not respond to the news in any way. Then she said calmly and precisely, her eyes never leaving her sister, 'Why should that interest me after what he did to me?'

'He was your father, after all.'

'True, but he destroyed any love I had for him when he refused me permission to marry John. When I defied his order he cut me off completely, and none of you had the courage to disobey his ruling, which, as you all knew, was breaking my heart. None of you gave me any support. I was cast out because I went against his wishes and authority – I lost you all and any right to a share in the family fortune, part of which should have come to me on my marriage. Father changed everything between us by annulling that right. Did you even dare to challenge him about it?'

Fiona answered her. 'We tried, Glenda, we really did. But you know Father would brook no opposition to his authority.

'Once I became the only girl I bore the brunt of it, Roger helped me as best he could and, for a while, I blamed you, but I gradually realised if the same chance came my way I'd have done the same thing.'

Glenda recalled John as he took her away ashamed and penniless to become his wife. He often told her it was the best decision of his life when he made Pinmuir her home. Would she really ever leave it?

Paula appeared with the pot of chocolate and cups, placing the tray on the table that Glenda had been using and removing her mistress's dirty cup; a simple, everyday action that allowed the two sisters a moment in which to reflect.

'Would you like your drink here or inside?' asked Glenda.

Fiona gave a little shrug of her shoulders. 'Wherever you wish, but I would definitely like to see my nieces again.'

'You shall, but first tell me: why are you not in mourning for Father?'

'Black is so drab; it does nothing for me,' replied Fiona in an offended way. 'I'll follow convention when necessity demands it, but otherwise I'll please myself.' The shrug of her sister's shoulders told Glenda that was the end of the matter, so she asked, 'When is Father's funeral?'

'It is two months since he died. You missed it.'

'And no one thought to let me know?'

'It was mentioned, but Roger was adamant that Father would not want you there. Besides, would you have come? None of us thought so. Neither you nor John tried to make amends or get in touch with us, even when Mother's grandchildren were born. Estrangement works two ways, Glenda.'

She stared hard at her sister but decided there were things they would never agree on.

'So why are you here, Fiona?'

'I heard a rumour that you were leaving for America but had lost John. I heard no more until a couple of weeks ago when a question about you arose at a dinner party I was attending. I wasn't able to give an answer, but the query set me wondering.'

'And you thought you'd like to know the truth,' said Glenda, a chill in her voice.

'You'll remember I was always noted for my curiosity,' replied Fiona, twitching her lips with a trace of amusement.

'You always were like a dog with a bone: holding on for all it was worth. Well, I'll tell you – it's no secret. When John died we were preparing to visit Gordon at his invitation, to sample life in America.'

'From what I remember of him, he was always seeing opportunity in unlikely places. What scheme was he filling John's head with this time?'

'John was always cautious; he would never be drawn into any unsound proposition,' snapped Glenda defensively.

'So this one was good enough to draw you into the unknown?'

'Don't insinuate that Gordon was seeking to profit from our move. You may not know this, or have dismissed the information in a fit of jealousy, but my brother-in-law has done well for himself. He owns a big ranch in Colorado and runs a large herd of fine cattle.'

'And this is what he used to tempt you all to America?'

'There was no temptation involved.'

'You were all going?'

'Only on a visit, to see if we liked what life there had to offer.'

'And I suppose that plan has been set aside after John's death?'

'Not completely. We may still consider it.'

Fiona's look of surprise could not disguise her interest. 'You would still go without John? Without the company of a man?'

'It would only be a visit. At first. We could review other options when we were there.'

There was silence for a few moments before Fiona announced: 'Well, if you do decide to move to America after a visit there I would be most interested in buying this estate and all its assets.'

Glenda gasped at this unexpected offer. She gave her sister a doubtful look.

Fiona picked up on her incredulity. 'You look as if you don't believe me?'

'Well ... how ...'

'The offer is quite genuine. I have the means to honour it. You see, Father left me a sizeable fortune that includes a part of what you surrendered! Glenda, I'm a very rich woman.' Her sister gave a delighted chuckle. 'If you accept my offer, you'll get part of what could have been yours by right, if by a different route ... a smack in the face for Father after his treatment of you.'

'I'm not interested in that aspect of the offer,' countered Glenda sharply.

'But you are interested in selling?'

A door had opened unexpectedly and widened the possibilities for Glenda's future and those of her children. Who wouldn't be interested in such a proposition? She thought of John – what would he want her to do?

At that moment the terrace door opened and Rosalind and Caitlin came out.

'Hello, girls,' Fiona greeted them brightly. She caught the glance Glenda shot her and read in it a request not to divulge her offer. She gave her sister a reassuring nod.

The girls returned their aunt's greeting, then Rosalind

added, 'As we came into the hall, Mrs Martins saw us and asked us to tell you Mrs Lynch will have lunch ready in five minutes.'

'Very good,' said Glenda. She rose from her chair and Fiona did likewise. 'I'll show you where you can refresh yourself,' Glenda told her sister.

Ten minutes later they were all enjoying vegetable soup, freshly made to the special recipe of the McKinleys' cook.

The two girls were soon at ease with their newfound aunt and Glenda marvelled at the way in which her sister, who had never had any children of her own, was totally at ease with them. Would it be a good idea for them to get to know Fiona better? Could it lead to reconciliation with the rest of the family? Glenda decided she could test the attitude towards her if she made the first tentative moves through her sister. But was that a good idea? Fiona had been the only one to make contact after their father's death. Could anything worthwhile be built on that or was she seeing light where there was very little? Were Fiona's pleasantries based solely on her desire to own what was currently her sister's? Glenda wanted to know but deemed the best way to find out was to extend the olive branch.

'Fiona, do you have to be back home today?' she asked tentatively as lunch was drawing to a close.

'No, I'm a free spirit. I come and go as I please. But I am careful not to overstay my welcome whomever I visit ... then I can visit again.'

'So why not stay with us for the night?'

Fiona turned to her nieces. 'Would you like that?'

'Yes, yes!' they both agreed, excitement in their voices and smiles.

'It isn't every day that we discover an aunt we did not know,' added Rosalind.

'Then we'll make it a memorable event. You'll be able to show me around. I saw two men planting trees about half a mile along the road to the house.'

'That would be Mr Martins and his son Clive,' said Rosalind.

'We are doing some afforestation along that hillside,' said Glenda. 'Something Greg ... that is, Mr Martins ... suggested a couple of months ago. The Martins are a loyal family. Mrs Martins ... Jessie ... is my very efficient house-keeper and amanuensis.'

Glenda felt herself thawing towards her sister and sensed that the feeling was reciprocated. The two of them took a walk in the afternoon during which Fiona learned more about the Pinmuir Estate.

'This may be an indelicate question but I have to ask it. Have you ever thought of demolishing the castle after what happened?' she asked.

'No. I haven't found it troubling even though its destruction took my beloved John from me. In some strange way, I find it a fitting memorial to him and what he was doing here.'

'Do the girls talk to you about him?'

'Rosalind, yes. Caitlin very, very, rarely. You see, she was the one who first saw the fire and raised the alarm.'

'Is that why you still entertain thoughts of what Gordon can offer – a life completely different from the one you lead here, a new life that could help erase the bad memories?'

'Yes, and to fulfil John's last dream, but I think it wise

to hang on to the estate meantime, just in case I or the girls should wish to return.'

'Very sensible,' agreed Fiona. 'But may I ask, should the time ever come that you wish to sell, will you give me first refusal? You could always retain the house – I shan't need that.'

Before Glenda could answer, the strains of music from a piano flowed through the house. Fiona looked at her sister. 'Who's playing?' she asked.

'It will be Cat,' replied Glenda. 'They both play but Cat has the most delicate touch and she loves Chopin.'

The sisters sat quietly listening, enjoying the impromptu recital that seemed to put the finishing touch to their reconciliation. But Glenda also wondered whether she had done the right thing in involving Fiona so closely in their lives.

5

Glenda did not sleep easily that night as her mind dwelt upon the many aspects of her life that had been thrown into question by the unexpected visit from her sister.

Twenty years since they had last met, Fiona seemed still to have the same effervescent personality, one that would kick over the traces if it suited her, though always cautiously and in such a way as to preserve her safety and status. She could be a rebel but was able to control the tendency if it meant her actions might rebound on her. Glenda sensed her sister was still a good judge of character from the way she'd spoken to Rosalind and Caitlin and elicited information without causing offence. She always had an eye out for the main chance, though. Now Glenda wondered if Fiona's tacit support of her defiance of her father's objections to her marriage had been purely for her sister's own ends; after all, hadn't she admitted she had inherited part of what would have been Glenda's?

Unable to sleep she lay wondering how she would tell Rosalind and Caitlin of their aunt's proposal to buy the estate. What would they have to say to that? After all, it would affect their lives and, as young as they were, she knew she should listen. But that would have to wait until after Fiona had left. With that thought Glenda finally fell into a shallow sleep in the early hours of the morning.

She awoke with her soft feather bed encouraging her to enjoy its warmth a little longer, but the sunlight streaming in across her room called to her to enjoy the day out of doors. Since the previous year when she had reduced staff numbers, Glenda had done without a personal maid and so she dressed herself. Twenty minutes later, when she entered the dining room, she was surprised to find Fiona, Rosalind and Caitlin already enjoying breakfast.

'Good morning, Glenda,' Fiona greeted her brightly. 'I peeped out when I woke, saw it was a lovely morning and decided to go riding.'

'Aunt heard us moving, poked her head into our rooms and invited us to accompany her,' explained Caitlin, excitement gleaming in her eyes.

'Come with us, Mama,' put in Rosalind. 'It will do you good.'

It took Glenda only a moment to consider this. 'Thank you, I will. I'll have a quick breakfast, get changed and join you at the stables in forty minutes.'

'I'll go and tell Clive to have your horse ready,' said Rosalind. 'I've already told him about ours.'

Forty minutes later they were all taking charge of their horses while Clive oversaw the stable boys, to make sure everything was as it should be for the riders. He paid particular attention to adjusting Rosalind's stirrups to her liking.

'Comfortable, Miss?' he asked.

'Yes, thank you, Clive,' she answered with a smile.

'Where are we heading?' asked Fiona.

Glenda looked thoughtful.

'Can you still get to Eishken Loch?' Fiona queried.

'It's a long time since I've seen it,' Glenda replied.

Before she could add to that, Caitlin said, 'Ros has been there.'

Her revelation brought her a sharp glare of hostility from Rosalind, who hoped her sister's disclosure would pass unnoticed. It did not.

'I warned you of the dangers of the terrain around Eishken Loch and forbade you to go there alone,' said Glenda, coldly critical.

Before Rosalind could offer any explanation, Caitlin explained, 'Clive knew you had told her that, so Ros asked him to accompany her.'

Glenda raised an eyebrow but refrained from further comment. Her look was reprimand enough for Rosalind and her mother did not wish to spoil the day for them all, so when Caitlin said, 'May we go, Mama? I've never been?' Glenda could do nothing but agree.

'Very well, but don't stray. Follow the rest of us carefully and keep close. I remember there are some tricky stretches to negotiate.'

'If the way is as I remember it, your mother is right,' agreed Fiona.

'You've been before?' asked Caitlin, somewhat surprised.

Fiona gave a little laugh. 'Oh, yes, when we were younger. In a group that included your father.'

*

38

After securing their horses, they all walked to the lochside, found some flat rocks and sat down to chatter and enjoy the sunshine.

After a while, seeing her mother and aunt absorbed in conversation, Rosalind stood up and said, 'I'm going to have a walk. Want to come, Cat?'

She scrambled to her feet, saying, 'Yes, I want to see the ruined kirk.'

'Very well,' said Ros. 'Let's go. We will be back soon, Mama.'

'There's no rush,' said Glenda. 'Your aunt and I are quite happy here.'

She received a nod of approval from Fiona, who realised her sister had seized on this chance for them to have some private time together.

Once the girls were out of sight Glenda asked, 'Fiona, you want first refusal on the estate ... are you genuine about your offer to buy it at the price you quoted me last night?'

'Yes. That was a serious offer, should you decide to settle in America.'

'I must point out that the estate was barely paying its way before John's death, though there are signs that the Martins are turning things round again. I don't know how I would have managed to get through this last year without them. I would wish for reassurance about their continued employ-ment here should I ever decide to sell to you.'

'You may have that. I am sure that something could be written into the articles of sale to guarantee their continued employment. And, as I said, if you do not wish to sever all connections with Pinmuir, you could always retain the house for a lesser sale price.'

'This is a very generous attitude you are taking.'

'If that is a trace of suspicion in your voice, you can eliminate it. I seek only to salve my conscience for what Father did to you.'

Glenda nodded thoughtfully then said, 'I will speak to Rosalind and Caitlin and let them know of your offer. This is their home and they should be consulted.'

'That suits me,' replied Fiona.

'If you are not tied to any other engagement, why not stay on for a few more days?' A teasing twinkle came to Glenda's eyes as they met Fiona's. 'It might give you time to change your mind.'

Fiona smiled as she said, 'I don't think I will even though staying on would give me the chance to get to know my delightful nieces better. I hope to see them again.' Then a more serious expression returned to her face. 'With what I'm offering you, you would be free to follow in John's dream.'

'You mean I could live it for him ... be reunited with Gordon?'

'Yes, and get away from the stark reminder of John's death that stands still in Pinmuir Loch.'

Glenda tightened her lips thoughtfully for a moment, gave a little shrug of her shoulders and said, 'We shall see.'

Fiona nodded. 'Think carefully. Any decision taken now will affect my nieces' future. Especially Rosalind, who, it seems to me has a particular interest in Clive.'

Glenda looked startled by this then gave a dismissive smile. 'They've been friends since childhood. Besides, Ros has always said she will marry a rich laird.'

They heard laughter and saw Ros and Caitlin coming back from the loch.

'Have you had a good time?' asked Fiona.

'Lovely,' replied Caitlin. 'The old kirk is so mysterious.'

'I'm glad you enjoyed it,' replied her mother. 'Now we must get back. Your aunt must be away.'

They lost no time in reaching the house where Ros asked, 'When do you want your horse, Aunt? I'll tell Clive to get him ready.'

'Thank you.' Fiona glanced towards her sister and gave a knowing smile that was answered by a shrug of the shoulders.

A few minutes later Clive appeared. 'Your horse is ready, Ma'am.'

'Thank you for looking after him, Clive.' Fiona could see how attractive he was, having an air about him that generated confidence and trust; Rosalind could do worse, she thought.

Fiona hugged her nieces. 'Look after your mother,' she said meaningfully.

'Please come again,' Caitlin requested.

'I shall.' Her aunt smiled at her.

'Yes, do,' said Rosalind.

As Fiona embraced her sister she said quietly, 'Thank you for having me. A bridge has been repaired; it has taken us a long time. Don't let us be parted again.'

'I won't,' replied Glenda, 'but what about the rest of the family?'

'I can't speak for them but I'll do my best to cauterise their minds of the bitterness Father instilled in them.'

'Thank you. It is good to have your friendship again,' Glenda conceded. With her daughters beside her she watched her sister ride away.

'Did you like your Aunt Fiona?' Glenda asked her girls.

'Yes,' said Rosalind. 'She's very agreeable.'

'I liked her too,' put in Caitlin. 'I wish she had stayed longer.'

'She might come again,' said Rosalind.

'I hope so,' added Caitlin with enthusiasm. 'Do you think she will, Mama?'

Glenda hesitated for a moment. Was this the right time to put Fiona's offer to them? Why not? Her sister required a decision, so why not seek the girls' thoughts?

'Let us stroll beside the water. I have something to ask you.'

'That sounds mysterious,' said Rosalind as she fell into step with her mother.

'Your aunt has offered to buy the Pinmuir Estate if we went to America and decided to stay.'

Caitlin raised an immediate objection. 'Even the horses? She can't have Pearl! She can't!'

'It would give us a chance to carry out the plans your papa made for us all, and we'd have the help and support of your uncle so would not be alone.'

'What do you want to do, Mama?' asked Rosalind.

Glenda gave a little smile but said only, 'I want what is best for all of us.'

Ros quickly added, 'I'm sure Cat will agree with me that we want you to be happy in whatever we do.'

'That is very thoughtful of you both. If we decide to follow your father's dream, we need the decision to be unanimous.'

In the thoughtful silence that followed Glenda thought

she saw doubt overcoming her younger daughter. 'What is troubling you, Caitlin?' she queried gently.

The girl bit her lip and then, with a sorrowful look in her eyes, said quietly, 'I don't want to leave Papa.'

'Oh, Cat, nor do I. But we must believe that, whatever we do, he will be watching over us.'

Cat pursed her lips thoughtfully, then gave a nod of acceptance. 'If that is so, I don't mind if we stay here or go to America.'

Glenda glanced questioningly at Rosalind. She saw that this daughter too was grappling with doubts. 'I love where we live. I love the mountains, the lochs, the wild country-side. Like Cat, I don't want to leave Papa but I can accept your explanation that he will be with us wherever we are, if we keep our memories of him strong and try to do what he would want us to do. I'm sure he'll keep us safe and guide our lives.'

'And what would you miss most if we left this life behind?'

'Lots, but along with the usual things it would be the Martins. They have become much closer to us since you included them in our household after Father died. I know they had been involved with the estate and our lives before that, but now they seem part of the family don't they? I'll miss them all, but if we are making a visit to America merely to test how we like it, then I am in favour of going for a limited period.'

'And I!' shouted Caitlin.

Rosalind watched for her mother's reaction.

Glenda nodded slowly and then smiled warmly as she said, 'We won't rush into a decision. There is no need.

Besides, I still have nearly a year's mourning to observe.'

'Do you have to, Mama?' asked Caitlin. 'Ros and I are free from that now.'

'Yes, I must,' replied Glenda firmly. 'The time will pass quickly and it will give us the opportunity to consider the merits and demerits of a journey to America.'

6

'Off to sleep, young lady.' Glenda swept a rebellious strand of hair from her daughter's forehead. Cat returned the smile and nodded. Glenda gave a tug on the eiderdown; her heart was full as she straightened up and turned to the door. One year and one week since the fire had taken John from them. During the past seven days Ros and Cat had refrained from mentioning the tragedy, and Glenda knew they had done so for fear of upsetting her. Her throat tight with emotion, she turned the oil lamp lower and slipped quietly from the room, leaving the door slightly ajar.

A lamp burning at one end of the landing cast shadows along the dark red carpet, contesting the slow movement of those created by the pale moonlight shining through two mullioned windows. Glenda paused at the first one to look out at the moon coating the lawn and a stand of firs with a silver sheen. 'Oh, John,' she whispered, allowing a tear to run down her cheek as she recalled nights when they had needed no words to express how much they loved each other. She stood lost to the immediate world, minutes passing by, until a slight movement from the next room along the landing attracted her attention.

She stepped over to the door and pushed it open gently, at the same time asking, 'Are you awake, Ros?'

'Not in bed yet, Mama. Come in.'

Glenda stepped into the room, closing the door gently behind her.

'I was engrossed in this book,' said Rosalind.

'What is it this time?' asked Glenda, pleased that her eldest daughter's love of reading complemented her love of the outdoors.

'*Far From The Madding Crowd.*'

'Are you enjoying it?'

'Oh, yes,' replied Ros enthusiastically. 'Hardy is such a good writer, I get totally engrossed in his characters and drawn into their story.'

'Good. I'm pleased you are enjoying it. I wish Cat was as interested in reading as you are.'

'It will come, Mama.'

'I hope you are right. Now, put the book down and come and look at the wonders of the night with me.'

They crossed the room together and each drew aside one of the velvet curtains, allowing moonlight to bathe the room with its bewitching glow. Gazing out into the garden Ros commented, 'I'm sure the fairies will dance for us tonight!'

'I wouldn't be surprised at ...' Glenda's sentence was left unfinished, cut off by the unearthly scream that shattered the peace. Painful memories were instantly revived.

'Cat!' Ros was already heading for the door. Glenda was

only a stride behind. They burst into Cat's room to find her standing stiffly near the window, her wide eyes drenched in terror, screams issuing from her lips.

'What is it?' Glenda asked, dropping to one knee beside her daughter.

Ros put her arm around her sister's shoulders, hoping the contact would reassure Cat.

Caitlin gulped and trembled. 'Mama ...' Tears streamed down her face.

'What is it, love?' asked Glenda.

'The fire!'

Glenda automatically glanced out of the window. Puzzled, she said, 'There is no fire, Cat.'

'There is, there is!' Her voice rose higher with every word.

'No, there isn't,' added Rosalind firmly.

'There is! There is!' screamed Cat.

'All right, Cat.' Glenda hugged her daughter close. 'You've been dreaming, that's all. There is no fire, I promise you. Now calm down. Ros will get you a hot drink.' She glanced at her eldest daughter, who nodded, rose to her feet and hurried from the room.

Glenda smoothed Cat's hair as she held her, humming a gentle tune and hoping that the soothing sound would combat her distress.

'There is a fire, Mama,' insisted the girl. She raised her head to look into her mother's eyes. 'I saw it very clearly. I was trying to warn you but you ...'

'Hush, hush. You were dreaming.'

The last three words were delivered with a firmness that made them lodge in Caitlin's mind. She gave a deep sigh.

47

Glenda seized her opportunity. 'Come and see.' She eased her daughter to her feet and, hand in hand, led Cat to the window. 'See, there is no fire.'

Cat shuddered. Bewildered, she said, 'But there was, Mama.'

'Yes, there was, but that was a year ago. For some reason it came to your mind while you were asleep and you thought it was real and happening now.'

Before Caitlin could comment further the door opened and Ros came in, carrying a tray with cups of chocolate on it.

'Here you are, this will help you sleep,' she said with conviction. She placed the tray on a table near Glenda for her mother to take charge. The chocolate and biscuits began their soothing effect and the scare that had woken Caitlin was not mentioned again.

Twenty minutes later she was warm in her bed once more and hardly responded to the gentle kiss Glenda placed on her forehead.

Ros stopped her mother when they left the room. 'I'll sit with her in case she wakes again. You get some sleep. And don't worry, I'll stay with her.'

'Thanks, Ros, but wake me if she is disturbed again.'

'I will. I don't suppose it will happen a second time.'

'I hope not. Strange that it has taken over a year for her to be disturbed by dreams of the fire. Let's hope there is no repetition.'

Two days later when Glenda said goodnight to Caitlin she was relieved that the day had ended with a warm smile from her daughter and no mention of any bad dreams haunting her. Cat seemed relaxed, chattering about the day's activities and especially their morning ride.

'Can we do it again tomorrow, Mama?'

'If the weather holds good,' replied Glenda.

'Then I'll ask God to make it so.'

Glenda kissed the now seventeen-year-old Caitlin on the forehead and said, as she had done so many times throughout her daughter's life, 'Sweet dreams.'

Glenda and Rosalind were both fast asleep when the grandfather clock in the hall struck midnight. Used to it, neither of them heard it, but they did hear the scream that followed the last stroke. They were awake immediately and knew that the scream had come from Cat. They scrambled from their beds, pulled robes around themselves and ran from their rooms. Neither of them spoke as they burst on to the landing. A few strides brought them into Cat's room where they found her standing, looking out of the window. Her wide-open mouth screamed in alarm at what she was seeing.

Glenda dropped to her knees beside her and put her arms around Cat in a protective way that she hoped would ward off whatever was alarming her. 'What is it?' she asked, trying to sound gentle and not cause any further alarm.

Cat pointed at the window. 'There! Someone's trying to take Papa away. I can't stop them!'

Ros looked out. 'There's no one here, Cat.'

'There is!' snapped the girl. 'Stop them! Please stop them!'

'I can't,' returned Ros. 'I would if I could but I can't even see them.'

'You've let them get away!'

'I couldn't see them.'

'Let's you and me look,' suggested Glenda. She eased Cat closer to the window. 'There you are. There is no one.'

Cat shuddered and tears rolled down her cheeks accompanied by great gulping sobs. Glenda held her tight and stroked her shoulders. As Ros left the room to fetch warm drinks she wondered what had caused the nightmare to erupt again. Would her sister ever escape the horror she had witnessed?

7

Rosalind, disturbed by the same noise, came half awake. For a week now she had heard the movement of padding feet coming restlessly from Caitlin's bedroom in the early hours of the morning. This latest disturbance had started a week after her sister's last nightmare, at a time when Rosalind and her mother had believed the horrors in Caitlin's mind had finally been conquered. Now Rosalind wondered if the sound of her sister walking the floor was a forerunner of a new cause for concern. Not wanting to spark off any untoward reaction, Rosalind lay still, listening to the movement in her sister's room; always the same rhythm, step after step, then a short pause that Rosalind judged to be in front of the window. Finally the pacing stopped, bringing silence to the house except for the creaks and night sounds that were familiar to them all.

When her mother did not speak about hearing Caitlin's footsteps, Rosalind decided to remain mute about them. But after another week, in which the pacing became more agitated and on two occasions she heard her sister whispering something in an argumentative tone, Ros decided to mention Cat's disturbed nights.

'Mama, I've finished,' said Caitlin, moving her breakfast plate away from her. 'May I be excused?'

'Are you riding?'

'Yes, Mama.'

'Are you going too, Ros?'

She was quick to seize her chance. 'I've not finished my breakfast yet. You go, Cat. Stay in sight of the house and I'll join you when I'm ready. Then we'll take a ride into the hills.'

Cat gave her a grin, eyes widening in anticipation of the pleasure ahead.

'Off you go then,' said Glenda, 'but wait around for your sister.'

'Ask Clive to saddle Freya, please,' called Rosalind as Caitlin ran from the room.

'I will,' called Cat. 'He'll like doing that.'

Ros automatically glanced at her mother and the eye contact caused her to flush.

'Do you like Clive?' Glenda asked.

Ros's colour deepened and she answered shyly, realising what her mother was implying, 'Yes, Mama. I don't meet many men my own age, and of course he's always so helpful.'

'So he should be,' replied Glenda. 'You've known him all your life. You've played together, grown up together. Your Aunt Fiona thought there might be more to it than that, but I said you were intent on marrying a rich laird.'

Rosalind said nothing but looked at her fingers resting

52

on the table. Glenda knew it was best to say no more at this moment – the ice had been broken. She took a sip of her coffee and Ros did likewise.

As she placed her cup back on its saucer, Rosalind asked, 'Mama, have you heard Caitlin during the night recently?'

Glenda's expression immediately grew alarmed. 'No. Have you?'

'Yes, but I'm next door to her and you are further along the landing.'

Glenda nodded. 'Go on.'

Rosalind quickly told her about Cat's disturbed nights.

'You should have come to me before this,' her mother said.

'I didn't want to alarm you. The nightmares seemed to be over, but I thought you ought to know when this carried on for so long.'

'I'm glad you have.' Glenda pondered for a moment or two. 'I think I should consult Dr Hamley, merely as a precaution so that he will be forewarned if there are any further developments. You are going riding with Cat so I'll go to see Dr Hamley while you're out. Don't say where I have gone. Tell Cat I decided to take the opportunity to see Mr McBain about repairs to our boat. It's time we started using it again.'

Glenda usually enjoyed the ride to the small neighbouring village and, whenever she came this way, resolved to do it more often. Today, though, she barely observed her surroundings, too worried about Caitlin.

The doctor's house was set at the opposite end of the village so there was no evading the questioning gazes and whispering tongues of folk not bothering to hide their curiosity about the presence of this widow still in mourning black. Glenda kept her back straight and her eyes fixed firmly ahead; she did not wish to be drawn into idle conversation.

'Soon be there, Bess,' she whispered to her horse.

A few minutes later they reached the last house on the street. Trees had been cleared from the hillside so as to build the doctor's residence. Dr Hamley had had the plot landscaped to a design drawn up by his wife, blending it in with the rising ground as if it was part of the mountain.

Glenda slid from the saddle, tied Bess to the nearby posts especially placed for patients visiting the doctor, brushed her skirt and then walked briskly to the front door. Her tug on the bell-pull was soon answered by the housekeeper, neatly attired in black skirt and white blouse, her hair pinned carefully at the crown of her head.

'Good day, Mrs McKinley,' she said brightly.

'Hello, Iris. I would like to see the doctor, please.'

The housekeeper moved aside to allow Glenda to step in. After closing the front door, Iris opened one that revealed a comfortable waiting room.

'I'll let Dr Hamley know you are here, Ma'am. As you see, there are no other patients so I'm sure he will be with you in a few minutes.'

Within three he had joined her.

'Mrs McKinley.' The doctor, while speaking brightly, was making his private assessment of Glenda. He stood tall in his grey tweed suit, extending one hand to her. As she took it she felt his comforting touch. 'It is good to see you. I hope your visit is not of a serious nature,' he said.

'Thank you. I am very well,' she replied.

'Good, good. I am pleased you seem to have got over your terrible ordeal but I do know how much you suffered, both bodily and mentally. You have done exceedingly well to recover so fast.' He indicated for her to sit down as he asked, 'What brings you here?'

'It isn't for myself, Doctor, it's about Caitlin.'

He raised his eyebrows to query this.

'She started having nightmares a while ago,' Glenda explained.

'She's the youngest girl?'

'Yes.'

'Are these nightmares related to anything specific?'

'The events of just over a year ago; the fire in particular.'

He nodded thoughtfully. 'Describe to me what happens. And does anything you know of bring them on?'

'I really don't know. She goes to bed quite happily and then wakes up screaming. It takes some time to calm her down.' Glenda went on to describe the nature of her daughter's nightmares and what she and Rosalind had to do to calm her. 'Yet the following morning she never mentions the terror she felt. It is as if she doesn't remember anything at all.'

'Has that continued to be the pattern?'

'Oh, no.' Glenda went on to describe how the disturbances had taken a different form recently.

When she had finished Dr Hamley looked thoughtful for a few minutes. Glenda remained silent and still while he reflected.

'Little is understood of the mind and its workings. I have read some of the new theories and drawn my own conclusions, whether right or wrong I do not know. I can only outline to you what my opinion is and from that offer a suggestion of what you can do . . . no, no . . . I should say what you can try to do, because I cannot offer any guarantee that it will be the solution to your daughter's problem.' The doctor paused, his eyes fixed on her. Glenda knew he was weighing up how much hope he could give her that Caitlin's nightmares would stop.

Dr Hamley went on to explain what he thought might help Caitlin. 'Having a change of environment might be beneficial . . . in fact, probably will be. Removing her from the scene of the trauma should help her mind adjust to other things, though when she returns home again I cannot say what her reaction might be. I'm sorry, Mrs McKinley, you will need to remain vigilant and then act in the best interests of your daughter.'

Glenda considered his words.

'Thank you, Doctor, you have been most helpful.'

'I don't know what I have done except to talk. I wonder if I even made sense?'

'I think you did. I will take what you have said into consideration and act upon it.'

'I hope you do, Mrs McKinley. You deserve to find peace again. And if you . . . no, when you do . . . I will rejoice with you.' He took her hand as she stood up. 'God go with you and with your family, Mrs McKinley. When you find the solution, let me know.'

'I certainly will, Doctor.'

'Better still, when you decide on the path you will follow let me know and thereafter keep me informed of any progress you make – you could be doing a service to others.'

*

On the ride home, Glenda turned her thoughts to all the aspects of what the doctor had termed 'Caitlin's illness'. She pulled Bess to a sudden halt. Why hadn't her husband suggested the obvious remedy? 'John, why didn't you speak to me before now?' Glenda said aloud. She eased herself on the saddle and cast a glance at the gathering rain clouds. She patted her horse's neck. 'Come on, Bess, beat the rain home.'

The horse interpreted the urgency of her tone and in a matter of moments was stretched into a gallop along the track for Pinmuir House. Because the weather had taken a turn for the worse Glenda knew her daughters would have returned early from their ride.

The sound of a fast-approaching horse brought Clive and Rosalind hurrying from the stables.

'It's your mother. I'd better make myself scarce,' he commented.

'No need,' answered Rosalind quickly. 'I'm sure she suspects there's more than just friendship between us. Stay. She'll need you to look after Bess.'

'If you say so. I've never seen her arrive home at this speed. Something must be wrong.'

'It can't be Caitlin, she's inside playing the piano,' Rosalind pointed out.

Anxious about what such haste might herald, they watched her approach.

Glenda pulled Bess to a halt that tore up the ground. Clive ran forward to grasp the bridle and counter the nervousness he detected in the animal.

'Thank you,' called Glenda.

Ros took her arm and ran with her into the house. Glenda

changed out of her wet clothes and seated herself in a comfortable chair in the drawing room.

'I'll ask Mrs Martins for some tea,' said Caitlin, who had come to see what had caused the commotion.

As the door closed on her, Glenda straightened and took hold of Ros's arm. 'I might have a solution to stop these nightmares of your sister's.'

Ros was about to say something but was stopped when Glenda said, 'It concerns Cat so let's leave it until she comes back.'

'Mrs Martins has told Cook, who promised us some biscuits she has just made,' Caitlin informed them on her return.

'Now you can hear what I learned,' Glenda announced. She looked at Caitlin. 'I have been to see Dr Hamley about your nightmares.'

'Why, Mama? They've stopped,' Cat said, a touch of indignation in her tone.

'You haven't thrown them off completely, Cat. Ros has told me you wake every night and walk about your room, sometimes for as long as an hour.' She saw Cat frown and give her sister a hostile glance.

'Don't blame her for telling me. She did the right thing. In view of the more violent nightmares you had, I thought it wise to seek help from the doctor.'

Caitlin looked sullen. 'What did he tell you?' she asked grumpily.

'He was very helpful even though he could not guarantee a full cure, telling me that in the medical profession little is known about the mind and how it works. He suggested possible avenues to go down. Of these there is one I think should help you.'

Glenda paused for a moment as if considering carefully what she should say next. 'He suggested we should move away from the area where the tragedy occurred since it acts as a constant and generates bad memories for you.'

'But I don't want to leave,' Cat objected.

'Nor do I,' Ros pointed out, 'but if it will do you good, I'll go.'

'I don't want to be done good to,' Cat snapped.

'Of course you do,' countered Glenda. 'Don't you see that the doctor's suggestion is an attempt to make you better? To rid you of these nightmares and let you lead a normal life? Besides, not long ago you were excited by the prospect of going to America. Please let us give it a try.'

Cat did not reply immediately but continued to look down at her hands, resting in her lap, then said, 'Will these fingers ever play a piano again?'

A little surprised by this question, Glenda seized on it. 'Of course they will. We'll come back here with you fully recovered and those keys will ring to joyful, triumphant notes.'

Cat looked thoughtful then said, 'All right,' though still a little reluctantly.

'Good, I'm sure you have made the right decision,' said Glenda enthusiastically. 'I think we should take up your father's plan to visit your uncle Gordon.'

'But didn't Father want to settle there?' asked Rosalind, seeing the possibility of the ties between her and Clive being torn apart. With a sudden jolt she realised the true extent of her feelings for him. It wasn't just flirting and friendship, but something much deeper. Would that last with her in America? What would a different life there bring?

Ros quickly turned her attention to her mother as Glenda said, 'Settling there was a possibility, certainly. It can remain a possibility. I have decided to keep the estate for now.'

Rosalind seemed satisfied by this. She and Caitlin exchanged quick glances of approval.

'Very well, Mama, if going to America honours Papa's plan for us and helps Cat, then we both agree.'

Glenda looked relieved, a new light in her eyes. 'I'm sure your decision is a wise one and will help all of us. And I promise, if anyone wishes to return home they can do so.'

8

Rosalind went to her room deep in thought. America? A new life? The enormity of her decision to accompany her mother and sister struck her anew. Her future was turned upside down when all she had wanted was for her life here in the Highlands to endure. Clive! The coming separation struck even harder now she had realised her love for him. She was overwhelmed by the prospect of telling him of the impending visit to America and the other changes it might bring about. But there was no point in putting it off; she didn't want him to hear it from anyone else first. As she crossed her room to the wardrobe she glanced out of the window. The rain was ceasing and the clouds were breaking, allowing the sky to brighten – could she take this as an omen for her future?

She slipped her feet into her black leather boots, quickly laced them up, shrugged on a green calf-length coat and left her head uncovered for Clive, who loved her flame-coloured hair. She tripped quickly down the stairs, out of the front door and over to the stables. Her hope of finding him there was answered.

'Clive, walk with me,' she said.

His surprise gave way to joy but he had to admit, 'I must finish this grooming first but it'll only be a few minutes. I'll see you in the usual place.'

'All right, don't be long.' Ros left the stable. Once outside she turned away from the house and took a familiar path on which she was soon out of sight of Pinmuir's buildings. She walked briskly to the top of a rise from which she headed into a small, secluded valley where a dilapidated stone building nestled close to the mountainside. A well-worn wooden door still hung from its iron hinges. It creaked when Rosalind pushed upon it. She smiled to herself, recalling the day she and Clive had found this place, and her recollections continued to the occasion when they had made it a little more comfortable with some hay ... Here they had talked, laughed and shared dreams. Now she nervously settled to await his arrival.

Clive speeded up his grooming without neglecting it. Satisfied with the result, he grabbed the jacket he had thrown over the partition between two stalls. He swung it round his shoulders and slid his arms into the sleeves as he walked outside and took the path after Ros. Eager to be with her and discover what lay behind her request that was unusual for this time of day, he lengthened his stride.

Ros recognised his footsteps and was on her feet when he pushed the door open.

She crossed the stone floor quickly, flung her arms round his neck and kissed him fiercely on the mouth in a way she had never done before. His hands, broad from outdoor work, spanned her waist and held her tightly to him when she would have broken away. They swayed together, enjoying the sensations that coursed through them, until finally Clive pulled away a little and asked hoarsely, 'What did you want with me?'

A mischievous twinkle came into her eyes as she replied, 'Couldn't you tell?'

'I meant, why did you want to meet today?'

'It may not be what you want to hear,' she replied.

Alarm bells started to ring when he saw her serious expression. 'What is it, Ros?' he asked.

She tried to stop the tears from coming but failed. It was no good holding them back. The truth had to be told. 'I'm going to America.'

Clive's shock was total. 'No! No, Ros, you can't!'

She gave a little nod. 'I'm afraid it's the truth, and I can't alter it.' She felt as if her dreams had been torn out of her heart and now lay scattered across her beloved mountains. There was no solace left for her.

'When? Why?' he cried.

'Mother has talked to Dr Hamley about Cat's troubled condition and he suggested a change of environment would help, so Mother thought it a good idea to visit Uncle Gordon as Father planned before he died.'

'But why do *you* have to go? *Why*?' he protested.

'I can't let Mother travel alone with Cat, who truly is not well. There might be problems. I would hate myself for not accompanying them if anything happened to either of them.' She hesitated, to let the words sink in. 'Please try and understand.'

Grim-faced, he sighed. 'I don't want to, but I do,' he said with obvious sadness. Clive felt his whole world was collapsing just when it had been beckoning him on to a joyous future. America! The name thrust insidiously into his mind.

It settled there, mocking everything that had been born with the realisation that this beautiful girl had become much more to him than a childhood sweetheart.

Ros saw distress tearing him apart. Now was the time to show him what he really meant to her. She reached out, took his hand in hers and drew him to her. She kissed him. She felt his lips tremble and then they were both swept away by a passion they had never felt before. They lingered, not wanting to interrupt the sensations that flowed through them and imprinted on their minds another kiss they would treasure forever.

'The memory of this will remain with me until we meet again,' he whispered close to her ear.

'As it will with me,' said Ros, then added, 'and there can be other things to remember.' She leaned back against his arms so she could look into his eyes and seek agreement.

She found it. Together they sank down upon the hay.

As they were leaving the house she pulled on his sleeve and smiled at him. 'Don't look so solemn, Clive. I'm not going yet. There is a lot more we can do first.'

'I suppose so, but you *are* going.'

'And I'll be coming back.'

'Who knows? America might change your mind,' he said doubtfully.

'My heart is with you, here in the mountains that I love as much as you do. I will carry our love in my heart, and America won't steal it from me. Let us make the most of our time together until I have to leave.'

Clive looked wistfully at Ros. 'I don't want you to go but I understand why it has to be.' He kissed her, not with the passion that had recently flared between them but with regret that they were having to part. They must keep alive the flame of the love they had kindled today.

They shared a silence as they started to stroll again until Ros said, 'I expect Mother will tell your parents of her decision, so please don't mention it to them before then.'

He met the pleading in her eyes. 'My lips are sealed,' he said.

Glenda's mouth tightened in an attempt to stop her head from buzzing with all the things that needed to be done before they left for America, but there was one thing that must be tackled first. She went to her desk picked up her pen and began to write:

Dear Gordon,

I will come straight to the point of this letter and the request it contains.

Since witnessing her father's death, Caitlin has been suffering from bad nightmares in various forms. I have consulted our doctor and he has suggested a change of environment might help. A move of that sort would take her away from daily reminders of the tragedy and hopefully let her see that life must go on without dwelling on the past. Colorado might provide the answer and I wondered if you would allow us to resume John's old plan? I intend merely a visit, though should life there suit us I do not rule out the prospect of settling there permanently.

If you have to refuse my request for any reason, please say so. I will understand.

I hope all is well with you.

With respect,

Your sister-in-law

Glenda signed the letter, read it one more time and, in the hope that the answer would be favourable, sealed it in an envelope that she had already addressed, thankful for the new speed with which letters to America travelled since the Transatlantic crossing time had been improved.

At lunch she told Ros and Cat what she had done, then added, 'Please don't tell anyone else what we intend until we have Uncle Gordon's agreement. Only then will I break the news to the Martins.'

'Oh, Mama, I've already told Clive,' Ros blurted out guiltily, but quickly added, 'I did ask him to keep it secret until you had told his family yourself.'

'I hope you didn't mention my nightmares,' said Cat.

'Of course I didn't,' replied Ros, crossing her fingers.

'I'm sure Clive is honourable enough to keep your secret,' Glenda told her. 'I suggest we live our normal lives until we hear from your uncle. It is no good making plans until we know with certainty whether he is still agreeable to our going to Colorado.'

They waited anxiously for his letter in reply. When it came three weeks later Glenda opened it in front of her two daughters.

Dear Glenda

Of course you must come. All of us must do our best to enable Cat to regain full health without any worries. Start making your arrangements to come as soon as possible. I will do the same here. When you have your sailing date and the name of the ship, please let me know so that I can be at the port to meet you.

Looking forward to seeing you again, Glenda, and to meeting my grown-up nieces.

Gordon

'Now we can really lay our plans,' she said as she put the letter aside. 'I will tell the Martins this evening, and tomorrow I will write to the shipping company.'

'Which one is it, Mama?' asked Caitlin.

'It was founded by Samuel Cunard and is commonly known as the Cunard Line. It is noted for its punctuality, comfort and safety so we'll be in good hands.'

'How long will we be at sea?' asked Cat.

'I think the crossing will take thirteen days from Liverpool to New York,' said Glenda, 'but I will get all the information when I write to Cunard's. We must decide on a date as soon as possible so I can let Uncle Gordon know the crossing details.'

Glenda, who had begun to have some doubts as to whether she was doing the right thing, was gratified by the reaction of her daughters. 'It's getting exciting now you are going to apply for berths,' said Caitlin.

'And we'll be able to see the mountains Uncle Gordon says are bigger than our Highlands, unless he's teasing us,' said Rosalind.

Glenda laughed. 'I don't think he's doing that, Ros, and I'm just as eager as you to see them.'

The following day Glenda made it her first job to write to the Cunard Line supplying possible sailing dates. Excitement took over at Pinmuir when, ten days later, she received word from the shipping company.

'Hurry, Mama,' urged Cat as her mother took up a letter opener to slit the envelope.

Ros watched intently, knowing that the letter's contents would announce the day she must part from Clive.

Glenda withdrew a sheet of paper and scanned it quickly. 'We sail from Liverpool on the twelfth of July in the *Malta*,' she announced, her voice trembling a little. 'I must write to your uncle immediately.'

Glenda grew anxious when July arrived with no further communication from her brother-in-law. Finally a brief note arrived that she was able to read to her daughters: 'I will meet you at the *Malta*'s berth in New York. Regards, Gordon.'

Brief though this was, Glenda found it reassuring.

Ros felt the void that had been deepening in her grow almost overwhelming.

The thought that Ros seemed to be moving out of his life worried Clive as the day of their parting drew nearer. With only their pledges to hold them together, could they stand the strain of parting?

Caitlin hid her worry. She was so tired of the long nights spent lying awake dreading the images that might penetrate her sleep if she dared to close her eyes. Her only hope lay in the doctor's suggestion, but would the unknown that lay ahead be enough to save her?

9

After the arrangements were made the enormity of her departure for America with her daughters had begun to weigh heavily on Glenda's shoulders. Leaving her beloved home for an uncertain future was so hard. If it hadn't been for the need to help Cat perhaps she would have changed her mind. She felt in need of some relaxation and good company away from Pinmuir.

She hurried to the stables and called, 'Clive!' sending his name echoing through the building.

'Ma'am,' he called back as he lowered a horse's hoof that he had been examining. He stepped out of a stall.

'Clive, have my horse ready in half an hour, please. Not side-saddle,' Glenda said briskly and hurried away.

As good as her word, she reappeared at precisely the time she had indicated.

'Bess is in good shape, Ma'am.'

Glenda patted the horse's neck. 'So you are,' she said lovingly.

Clive held the horse steady as Glenda swung into the

saddle. Taking the reins, she brought the animal under her control. 'Clive, if you see my daughters, tell them I've gone to see their Aunt Fiona. They can expect me back when they see me.'

'Yes, Ma'am.'

He watched her ride away, admiring the way she handled the horse. Wondering where Rosalind might be, he picked up a stiff broom and started to clean out the stall just vacated by Bess.

Five minutes later Caitlin interrupted him. 'From my window I saw Mother leaving; did she say where she was going?'

'Yes. To your Aunt Fiona's.'

'Thanks,' said Cat. 'That gives me the opportunity to start packing my bags for America, without Mama breathing down my neck. If I see Ros I'll let her know and she can do the same.' Cat didn't wait for any comment from him.

As he watched her hurry off in the direction of the house, Clive thought now would be a good time. He cast his eyes across the valley where they had agreed pre-arranged signals that meant only one thing: I am here. There was no such signal yet.

He stamped his foot in frustration and brushed the ground harder. Nearly ten minutes later he saw the desired signal. He threw down the brush in its usual place, acknowledged Ros's sign to him and rushed from the building. There wasn't a moment to lose! She would be waiting at their secret rendezvous.

Ros was standing in the doorway when he came in sight.

Her heart beat faster with desire. She opened her arms wide. He did not slow his pace. She braced herself but allowed him to carry her down with him, tumbling into the hay.

When they finally lay quietly in an atmosphere of joy, Clive gave Ros the message from her mother and told her that her sister was packing. These messages sobered them both until Clive raised himself on one arm so he could look into her eyes.

'I love you, Ros, so very, very much.'

She reached up and touched his lips with her fingers. 'I will lock away those words in my heart until I return. I will think of them every day.' She kissed him. 'And you can do the same.'

'Your kiss and your love are already imprinted on my heart,' he whispered as he ran his fingers down her neck.

Their lips came together again and they allowed time to stand still.

Glenda slowed her horse to a walking pace when she caught her first glimpse of Fiona's house, which she remembered in her childhood days being a lodge for the gatekeeper. The front façade was much as Glenda recalled it: a central front door with sash windows to either side. There were three windows on the upper floor, set symmetrically. She could see an extension had been carefully matched to the existing building and now included a round tower of two storeys with a conical slate roof. The additions had, to Glenda's mind, improved the look of the building, which now had the air of being truly cared for.

'Who can this be?' muttered Fiona, and added a curse as she laid her book down on the small table beside her wing chair, placed to catch the light streaming in through the bow window. 'Just when I was enjoying *Barchester Towers*.' Hearing the horse's hoofs slowing, she added to her displeasure with an uncomplimentary, 'Front-door visitors too! I'm not expecting anyone who merits that!' She went to the window, peeping out so she would not be seen.

'Glenda!' Fiona's tone changed completely; the day had even brightened! Her sister's visit could only mean that they had set aside the bygones that had marred much of their lives. Once more she darted a glance out of the window. What was Glenda wearing? Fiona gave a short gasp. A beautifully cut dark green riding habit with split skirt ... 'Oh, my goodness, she has been riding astride!' Not that Fiona was being critical. She knew Glenda had flouted a great many polite conventions after their father had disowned her. She strode out of the room and was at the top of the stairs just as her butler was opening the door to Glenda. 'Good day, Ma'am,' he said, politely curious.

'Mrs McKinley calling on Miss Copeland,' Glenda informed him.

'Thank you, Ma'am. I will see if ...'

'No need, Charles,' called Fiona, running down the stairs.

The butler kept his surprise under control, as he replied, 'Yes, Ma'am.'

He stepped to one side to allow Glenda to enter the hall, saying, 'Please come in, Ma'am.' He closed the door behind her and moved quietly away to the rear of the house.

'Glenda! My dear, this is a pleasant surprise. It is so nice to see you again. You look ravishing. That colour suits you and the cut of that riding habit is just right for you. And not side-saddle, I note!'

72

Glenda laughed at her sister's enthusiasm. 'It's good to see you so approving.'

'Anything my little sister does I approve of, even shedding widow's weeds a little early.' Fiona linked arms with her. 'Come in. Sit down. Fancy a drink?'

'Chocolate, please.'

'Nothing stronger?'

'No, thank you.'

Fiona went to the bell-pull, calling over her shoulder, 'Make yourself at home.'

Glenda slipped out of her jacket and sank on to the settee, thankful to have thrown off the need to make any decisions for a while.

'You've made a few changes to the old lodge as I remember it,' she commented.

'Roger inherited Father's house and moved in with his family so I decided to move out, though he tried to get me to stay. He was seeing me as an amanuensis to his wife. Unpaid naturally.'

'Typical,' commented Glenda. 'He always tried to boss all of us about when we were children.'

'Well, I was not having that. I don't like his wife anyway, and his children are all snobs, really stuck up.'

The chocolate arrived and as the door closed behind the maid, Fiona, whilst filling two cups, said, 'I hope this visit will take us even further along the road to reconciliation and we can smooth the future ahead of us.'

'Me too,' returned Glenda. 'But it may have to wait awhile.'

Fiona looked startled. She paused with her cup halfway to her lips, then returned it slowly to her saucer and settled her eyes on her sister as she said, 'Why?'

'We are going to America!'

Fiona sat up, eyes wide with the desire to know more. She sat enthralled without interrupting Glenda's flow of information as she told of her consultation with the doctor and his recommendation for a change of environment for Caitlin.

'It could be just what Cat needs,' Fiona agreed.

'I hope so.'

'You are going to Gordon's then?'

'Yes. It was what John had planned and Gordon has welcomed us to take up his offer.'

'Your plans are thrilling,' said Fiona. 'Are you looking forward to your adventure?'

'I don't know that I am really,' said Glenda with a doubtful grimace.

'Oh, come on,' returned Fiona, disbelief edging her words.

'I'm doing it for Cat. I'd do anything to rid her of the horrors she witnessed. If this is what it takes then I'll do it.'

'What about Ros?'

'She is in agreement, for the sake of her sister.'

'But what about her relationship with Clive? Surely that is blossoming into something serious?'

'I think you are seeing more in that than there really is. I grant you that there is a stronger feeling than I first thought when you mentioned it to me, but Ros was all for helping Cat. If strongly in favour of coming back again!'

'And she's willing to risk a new life in America changing her mind?'

'Look, Fiona, both Ros and Cat are young women now and what they make of life is up to them.'

Seeing how firmly decided Glenda was about this, Fiona let her opinions about her nieces' future go unspoken. 'And you?' she said to her sister. 'What might the future hold for you when you see Gordon again?'

Glenda bristled. 'What are you implying?'

Fiona shrugged. 'You two were always so close as children.'

Glenda responded sharply, 'Yes, as children. Then I grew up and fell in love with John and married him. He will always remain the love of my life.'

Fiona gave a little smile. 'We'll see what America does for you all.' She changed the subject quickly before Glenda could make any retort. 'Have you given any further consideration to my offer to buy your estate, except for the house and the small parcel of land on which it stands?'

'Yes. The answer is still the same: I'm not selling anything. The house remains with the estate. As I have indicated before, we want somewhere any of us could live if we chose to return.'

Fiona nodded. 'I'm disappointed, but I understand. I will say it is a wise decision. If ever circumstances change and you decide to sell, I would still like first refusal.'

'You have it,' said Glenda firmly, rising from her chair to shake her sister's hand, a gesture that sealed an unwritten contract.

'Thank you,' said Fiona. 'You can be certain that I will keep my eye on the house and property.'

'I don't mind that but I will brook no interference with the Martins family whom I am putting in charge, as of now. You must understand that. They have supported me, with understanding and loyalty, through the loss of John. I am leaving them in full charge. They can make any decisions they see fit for the betterment of my property. I will draw up an agreement between them and me, officially signed. Copies for them, for me and for you.'

Fiona looked thoughtful then after a few minutes' consideration she agreed. With the situation settled, Glenda accepted her invitation to stay for lunch.

The sisters enjoyed their time together. It was obvious to both of them that they were trying to make up for their lost years.

When the time came for Glenda to leave Fiona said, 'As we have been talking, I have been considering your sailing date from Liverpool.'

'Yes, the twelfth of July.'

'I will accompany you there, to see you off. You will have no one else to do that, will you?'

'No. But there is no need for you . . .'

'I must do it. I cannot let you leave without someone being there to see you off,' Fiona interrupted. 'You can leave the organising of getting us all to Liverpool to me. I will arrange accommodation there for three nights, and an extra one for myself before I return here.'

'This is so generous of you but I shouldn't accept.'

'Of course you should,' Fiona insisted. 'Say no more. I will see to that side of your departure. You will be busy with all the other things you have to manage.'

'This is so very generous of you,' returned Glenda. 'It will be more than comforting to know that accommodation in Liverpool is taken care of. Your presence as we set sail will be a tremendous boost. I am sure Ros and Cat will appreciate your kindness too. May I ask that you book them a double room at the hotel in Liverpool? It is what I have done with the shipping company for our berths on the ship, just in case Caitlin can't settle.'

'Of course. It shall be done,' replied Fiona.

10

'Mama! Aunt Fiona's here!' Caitlin's cry rang through the house.

'I'm coming!' Glenda's acknowledgement was accompanied by a quicker footfall as she crossed the hall to meet her sister. She opened the front door and stepped outside, to see Fiona's head-groom driving the coach along the road that swept the side of the loch. Today it was ruffled by small waves that seemed to lap against the shore with a melancholy sound. The groom turned into the driveway and almost before he had brought the vehicle to a halt an under-groom had jumped down from his seat and was opening the door for the passenger. Fiona gave him a nod of thanks then turned to her sister whose arms were held out in welcome.

'The great day is here,' said Fiona as they embraced. She turned to Caitlin. 'Are you ready for this big adventure?'

'Yes, Aunt,' replied Cat. 'I am.'

Fiona was pleased to detect excitement in her niece's voice, and hoped this would be Cat's attitude to the whole expedition.

'Where's Rosalind?' she asked as they were walking into the house, leaving the servants to see to the luggage.

'Saying goodbye to Clive somewhere, I expect,' replied Cat.

'She'll join us soon, no doubt,' said Glenda, without further comment.

Clive's fingers were entwined with Rosalind's. Their sadness was mirrored in each other's eyes. 'I'm going to miss you terribly,' he said, a catch in his voice.

'And what am going to do without you?' she replied. 'I so wish I hadn't to go.'

'I know,' he said, 'but I suppose you must help Cat, and be there for your mother. You'll remain in my thoughts every day.'

'And you in mine.'

Their lips met in a kiss that expressed their feelings for each other. They lingered, not wanting to separate, not wanting to part and place thousands of miles between them.

Tears dampened their eyes as she went to the house, and he to the stables. They paused and looked back at each other. The temptation to cross the space that separated them was almost overwhelming. As the one who was leaving, Ros knew she had to be the one to stay strong. She blew Clive a kiss, turned away and disappeared into the house. He stood staring at the blank space where she had been and only became aware of his tears when he felt them streaming down his cheeks. He was startled by the emotion that burned through him. Grown men did not cry! He brushed away the tears and walked into the stables.

Ros dried her eyes and hurried to the room where she knew her mother, Caitlin and her aunt would be. Recognising there had been tears, Glenda gave her daughter a hug of understanding but made no comment, allowing the activity in the house to divert Ros's mind from the sadness of parting. First love was always hard.

As the servants carried the hand luggage to the coach, where the groom oversaw its packing, Jessie Martins said to her husband, 'I hope all those trunks that have already been sent are safely stored away in the ship's hold.' The groom also saw that the coach was being made as comfortable as possible for his passengers. Mrs Martins fussed over her employer's needs, making sure that nothing was left behind, while her husband helped with the luggage that had been packed for the journey.

Finally all was ready and farewells had to be made. Glenda looked across the loch and the rising mountains, and recalled John's love for them and for her. Caitlin wondered what might lie in store for her in a foreign land. Apprehension cast a shadow over her enthusiasm for the journey so that she had to force it from her mind and concentrate only on her hopes for a cure. Ros could hardly bear this parting from everything she held so dear but kept telling herself it might not be for too long. They all took their places in the coach.

The groom called to his team of two and flicked the reins. The carriage lurched forward. They were on their way. Good wishes were finally called and hands waved in goodbye.

Hurt stabbed at Rosalind's heart. Clive had not appeared for the final parting, to wave them off. She had seen the look of disapproval on his mother's face. Ros felt limp with disappointment. Her whole world was crumbling around her. Had the kisses of a few minutes ago meant nothing? She sat quiet through all the commotion. The roadway dipped along the lochside then turned towards the valley, striking up through rising terrain, but Rosalind was seeing none of it through her damp eyes.

'Ros, look! Look!' Cat's shout startled everyone. They sat up, staring in the direction she was pointing.

'Clive!' Ros's voice was joyful. 'He came.' Her expression was radiant with relief. 'And he's brought Freya to say goodbye!'

'And he has my Pearl,' enthused Caitlin, seeing her horse held on a long rein by Clive's side.

He matched the pace of his two horses to that of the coach and stayed there for half a mile before he signalled that he must return to Pinmuir. He gradually dropped behind, waving until the track turned a bend and the coach was lost to his sight, leaving him with one thought. I wonder when I will see Ros again . . . if ever.

'That was a wonderful thought of Clive's bringing Freya and Pearl to say goodbye,' commented Glenda with an approving smile that lightened Ros's grieving heart.

The girls settled down for what to them would be a journey of discovery. Fiona knew a great deal about the way to Liverpool so was able to keep up their interest in what they were seeing. Glenda was glad she had at last chosen to make the passage to America; by doing something John had set his heart on, she felt closer to him.

The miles sped away; Fiona made sure no one felt bored or overwhelmed by the travelling. She had purposely split the journey into three stages with very good nightly accommodation to ease its rigours before their final destination, the Adelphi Hotel in Liverpool.

As they moved into the outskirts of the town Cat uttered her surprise. 'Mama, so many houses!'

Fiona smiled. 'You'll see many more before we reach our hotel, Cat. At the moment we are in one of the better parts of Liverpool.' They passed close to a development that was a maze of streets with rows of houses facing each other, making Cat ask where all the people were and what they did for a living.

'There is a part of this town that is known as Sailors' Town, so that tells you what some of them do,' answered her aunt.

'Will we see Sailors' Town?' asked Rosalind.

Fiona shook her head. 'No, your mother wouldn't thank me for taking you there; it's a rough and rowdy area. You'll maybe catch a glimpse of it when you embark the day after tomorrow. I don't know what quay we will be using but that information will be waiting for us at the hotel.'

Their coach came to a halt and they heard the groom asking for directions to the Adelphi. A moment after receiving these they were moving on and in five minutes were at their destination.

'It looks as though the hotel has had some work done recently,' commented Glenda. 'In fact there's outside work still awaiting completion.'

Their arrival had drawn a plethora of liveried hotel employees to greet them with offers of help. Luggage was brought inside, the coach and horses taken care of, registration completed efficiently, bell-boys were called and handed keys to the rooms the new arrivals would occupy. The head 'boy' supervised the care being given to the new guests and oversaw them being directed to their allocated rooms. He efficiently passed on any information he thought necessary and finally wished them an enjoyable stay.

Rosalind and Cat excitedly conducted a quick examination of their room and ran into their mother's and aunt's, giving them the seal of approval.

With the stage set, Glenda and Fiona joined in the excitement, pleased that both young women seemed to be taking pleasure in their future.

That continued the following day when the four of them perused Liverpool's shops, relaxed after tea, and finally retired after an exceptional evening meal that seemed to be especially for guests sailing for America the following afternoon.

At breakfast Fiona announced, 'I have asked reception to hire a cab to take us to the dock from which the *Malta* is sailing. You have to be on board by two for a three-thirty sailing.'

'Fiona, thank you for that. In fact, I cannot thank you enough for all the trouble you have taken in organising everything for the first stages of our journey.'

'Please don't. It is something I have enjoyed doing, and a gift from me to see you on your way. Remember me to Gordon. I hope you find him well and thriving.' She left a slight pause then added, 'All I ask is that you keep in touch regularly so that the bond we have reforged won't be broken again.'

'You have my promise,' Glenda assured her.

*

Although there had been some doubts in the McKinleys' minds when the visit to America had first been mooted, now the time for leaving England was close, excitement was beginning to replace any other feeling; even Ros was now looking forward to this new experience.

Glenda bustled Ros and Cat when she poked her head round their door. 'Get those bags shut, *now*! The porter will be here any moment to take them to the cab your aunt has hired. Then come down, ready to leave.'

An air of rising excitement was palpable as several other people assembled for the cabs they too had ordered. A few minutes later the commissionaire announced, 'Cab for the McKinley family!' Waiting bell-boys whisked their luggage away, leaving the family to follow them. Once outside they were in the hands of a cabbie, who quickly had them settled in their seats. A moment's check satisfied him that they and their luggage were all ready to leave. He climbed on to his box, took the reins and called to his horse. The animal responded and was skilfully guided through the traffic that was almost filling the way to the docks. The hustle and bustle of central Liverpool changed to the more industrial aspect of a town thriving on its growing wealth.

'Mama, look at all those ships!' called Caitlin when she saw the docks seemingly choked with so many vessels; sailing vessels, some with sails furled, others with them ready to try and make their way among the throng needing to sail down the Mersey before heading for their destination. There was movement on all the quays as cargos were dealt with by beehives of men, whose shouts were barely recognisable in the general cacophony of sound that swept over the quays.

84

'It's unbelievable,' gasped Ros. 'How can they ever tell where things should be put?'

Fiona laughed. 'They find a way. Any ship held up here is losing its owners money, and time spent idle in port does not put wages in its crew's pockets.'

'How on earth do we find our ship?' asked an incredulous Glenda.

'The cabbie knows which quay is being used by the American packet ships,' Fiona reassured her.

A few minutes later they turned on to a quay alongside which was moored a three-masted ship, with its sails furled.

'Why the sails if we have a funnel?' asked Caitlin, a little indignant at the thought that they might use an old-fashioned method of locomotion – the wind.

'For added speed,' said Rosalind. 'The captain will order their use if he thinks the wind will help.'

The minutes ticked by relentlessly until the order 'Ten minutes to sailing time' rang through the ship.

Fiona said, 'Well, this is it,' as she turned to Rosalind and took her into her arms. 'I should have known you long ago, but from what I know of you now I am pleased you are my niece.'

'And that you are my aunt.'

'Take care of your mother and Cat.'

'I will.' A tear trickled down Ros's cheek. 'Give Clive my love.'

'It is as good as said,' replied Fiona. She turned to Cat and hugged her. 'Enjoy yourself, and get better.'

'I will, Aunt, I will.'

Glenda looked deep into Fiona's eyes. 'Look after yourself.'

'I will, and you do so too.'

Their eyes spoke so much to each other that they both knew there was no need for more, except an extra hug when the words 'All ashore that's going ashore' rang out. The ship became alive with people heading for the gangways as the crew supervised the exit. The quay once again became crowded, as did the rail of the ship. Shouts filled the air with orders for the crew competing with passengers' goodbyes.

When the powerful engines were engaged the ship began to move slowly away from the quay. The McKinleys waved vigorously and Fiona responded with equal zest.

Under the captain's supervision, the gap between ship and shore widened steadily. She took to the sea as if that was the place she needed to be, and, with each passing moment, as she ploughed steadily through the Atlantic waves, the time came nearer and nearer when she would dock in New York.

11

They stood watching the great city draw closer. 'Will Uncle Gordon be on the quay, Mama?' asked Caitlin when she saw the line of docking places assigned to passenger vessels.

'I would have thought so but maybe not; his last message to me was merely that he would meet us in New York.'

Caitlin's brow furrowed. 'We won't know where to go if he isn't here, and from what we have seen of all those buildings he will be difficult to find.'

Rosalind smiled at her sister's doubt. 'I think Uncle Gordon will be more considerate than to leave us high and dry, wondering where we are supposed to go.'

'I'm sure he would have left a message somewhere if he was not able to be here,' Glenda added to reassure Cat. 'Look, even from here, we can see lots of people gathering on the quays in use, especially the one we seem to be heading for. Let's keep a lookout for him.'

'But I don't remember him,' moaned Cat.

'Then I'll look out for him,' said Glenda, crossing her

fingers behind her back and hoping that her brother-in-law had changed little in twenty years.

The quays drew nearer and nearer as the *Malta* was skilfully manoeuvred under the watchful eye of her captain, now dressed in the official Cunard uniform for the ship's arrival in her home port.

The number of people on the section of the quay allocated to those meeting passengers was growing all the time. They all strained to identify relatives and friends and readily gave way to their feelings when they saw anyone they recognised. The McKinleys felt lost in the welter of sound that sprang up from the passengers at the ship's rail.

Glenda's attention was caught by a hansom cab coming at speed on to the quay. It was turned and backed into a special area for cabs. A sense of relief flooded over Glenda when she recognised the passenger who sprang out of it. 'There he is, there he is!'

'Where, Mama?' Ros and Cat chorused together, excitement mounting in their voices.

'He's getting out of that cab that's just arrived.' Glenda's eyes fixed on the figure, now searching the people crowded along the ship's rail. Then an arm was raised.

'There he is,' said Glenda. 'The man who has removed his hat and is waving it at us.'

'Seen him!' called Ros.

'So have I,' added Cat.

Their waving became even more vigorous. They were rewarded by an equally energetic response, accompanied by a broad smile.

Oh, John! The words stayed silent on Glenda's lips as

her eyes fixed on the man whose presence was reviving so many memories for her of his brother.

The gangways were dropped. 'Mama, Mama, people are being allowed on board,' said Caitlin.

'Gordon's heading for our nearest gangway,' said Glenda. 'We had better stay here, he's seen where we are.' She tried to disguise the tremor of nervousness that accompanied her last observation but she need not have worried: each of her daughters was determined not to lose sight of him.

They watched Gordon stride up the gangway and slip past anyone who appeared to be blocking his way. When he reached the deck below them he disappeared from view momentarily only to step on to their deck a moment later and start towards them with a broad smile of welcome on his face.

'Gordon!'

'Glenda!' He took her in his arms and embraced her. 'It's so good to see you. After all these years, you bring a breath of Scotland to me.' He slackened his hold to turn to his nieces. 'And you two also. Ros, you were only a wee lass of three years when I left ... and Caitlin, the little babe, has already grown into a young lady.' He hugged them both and they held on to him a shade longer than was usually deemed polite, but nobody worried; they were all smiling happily, feeling that surely they were not strangers to each other even though, for many years, they had met only through the letters they exchanged.

'There is so much we have to say to each other, but that will all have to wait. We must get you settled into your hotel first.'

'I'll have to find one,' said Glenda.

89

'It is already taken care of,' Gordon assured her.

'How?' she asked.

'When you gave me the name of the ship I checked it out at the Cunard offices where I am known. They have always been very helpful. They made the hotel bookings for me. You have no need to worry about anything. It is all paid for; you are my guests for as long as you are in America. The bookings are for a week's stay. I thought you might like to find your land-legs again and see something of New York before we head West.' To lighten the moment and ease the tears he saw forming in Glenda's eyes, he added, as he turned to Ros and Cat, 'You'd like that, young ladies, wouldn't you?'

'Yes, please, Uncle Gordon,' replied Cat.

'This city looks so big,' commented Ros recalling the interest it had stirred in her as they approached the docks. 'It looks different from anything I've seen before.'

'It's a little bigger than Pinmuir,' said Gordon with a teasing smile. 'It's an interesting, vibrant place, but I'm always glad to get back to my ranch and see the mountains. I think you'll like those too, but for now we had better get you settled in your hotel.' He led the way down the gangway but on the quay diverted them away from the officials supervising the queue of passengers. He had a brief word with the officer in charge, who nodded and, with a smile, said to Glenda, 'I hope you and your daughters enjoy your stay in America. You are in good hands with Mr McKinley.'

'Thank you,' replied Glenda. She was about to ask about their hand luggage when the officer raised his hand. 'Ma'am, if you are concerned about your luggage it has been taken care of. Hand luggage is in your cab and that which you sent on from England is already on its way to Mr McKinley's ranch. It should be delivered before you arrive.'

'Thank you,' replied Glenda, feeling dazed by what was happening to them and thankful she had someone here who was familiar with the city and its ways; many travellers on the boat weren't so lucky. As she started to look around Gordon appeared beside her. 'Just follow the man heading for us. He's the cabbie who will soon be depositing us at the Grand Union Hotel.'

'Good day, Ma'am,' the cabbie said, touching his forehead with his index finger, but it wasn't his politeness that caught Glenda's attention.

'You aren't from these parts,' she commented with a smile.

'No, Ma'am, I originated near Kelso. Do you know it?'

'Ah, the Scottish Borders. What brought you here?'

'Seeking a better life for my wife and four bairns. A lot of Scotsmen came over at that time.'

'Have you found it?'

'It was hard when we first came. There was some antagonism but we stuck it out and managed. I was lucky to find a job here as a cab driver, then our luck changed completely when Mr McKinley hired me by chance. A Scot helped a fellow Scot. He set me up with this cab, recommended me to his friends and hires me himself whenever he is in New York. I've never looked back.'

'Good luck to you,' said Glenda.

'Don't forget, a week today, Sam,' Gordon reminded him.

'I'll be here on the dot,' he replied, and helped his

passengers into his cab. In a matter of moments Sam was showing his expertise as he drove them through the crowded streets to the Grand Union Hotel.

As they progressed there were constant expressions of surprise and interest from Ros and Cat, and the same disbelief in what she was seeing from their mother.

'I never expected New York to be as big as it is,' she commented. 'Who runs it all?'

Gordon was pleased with their reactions for it meant their minds were diverted from the tragedy that he felt sure still shadowed their lives. With so many more new experiences that he knew were coming their way, he hoped the past could be left behind in the country across the sea.

Sam guided the carriage into a drive and through formal gardens that fronted a huge building of four storeys. Four rectangular towers, one on each corner, dominated the hotel's façade, one of which was a floor higher and topped by a rotunda. Eye-catching flags flew from each tower.

'What a wonderful building,' commented Rosalind, in awe of what was to be their home for nearly a week.

'It was constantly improved and enlarged by its owners, the Leland Brothers, who bought it in 1864 and changed its name five years later to the Grand Union Hotel.' Sam was slowing the cab down as they neared the front of the building.

'Well, that's enough of a history lesson for today,' said Gordon. 'Now it's time to enjoy yourselves.'

'I like hearing all these facts,' said Ros.

'With everything so different and ever-changing as you cross America, you'll hear plenty more while you are with me.'

'Ros loves reading,' explained Glenda, 'She has a good memory too. They both ride but it is Caitlin who is a natural in the saddle.'

Conversation faded as Sam brought his cab to a halt. He jumped down from his seat as several bell-boys hurried from the hotel to take charge of the newcomers' luggage.

Sam bade his passengers goodbye and left them in the care of the hotel where the receptionist greeted the new arrivals.

'Good day, Mr McKinley. It is swell to see you again and to have you and your relations staying with us.'

'The only place in New York for me,' he replied with a smile, and went on to introduce Glenda and his nieces.

'Your first time in America, I believe?' said the receptionist.

'It is.'

'Then I hope you enjoy your stay. I am sure Mr McKinley will be a wonderful host.' He dealt with the necessary registrations quickly then signalled to two bell-boys who were standing close by. 'Suite Three,' he said, handing over the necessary keys.

The bell-boys took charge of the luggage and led the way to the lift.

Caitlin paused warily at the small box-like room she was to step into.

'Come along,' said Glenda. Cat frowned and gave a slight shake of her head.

'It's all right,' said Ros, gently persuasive.

Cat still hesitated but a quiet, 'Excuse me, Miss, may I help?' delivered politely by one of the bell-boys, dispelled Cat's wariness. She gave the boy a little shake of her head as she said, 'I'll be all right, thank you,' and took her mother's hand to step confidently into the lift.

Within a matter of moments the luggage was loaded and then, with everyone inside, a bell-boy closed the door.

It was the first time both girls had been in an elevator and they felt mixed emotions of fear and enjoyment.

Glenda smiled at them and silently mouthed the words, 'It is only a short ride.'

As if on cue a bell-boy set the lift in motion. Nervously Cat glanced at him. He gave her a warm smile and winked. Embarrassed, she blushed, but her attention had been diverted and she was unaware that the lift was coming to a stop. The door slid open. One bell-boy stepped out and assisted his passengers to their suite while the other saw to their luggage.

On stepping inside the room Glenda had to stifle a gasp; it wouldn't have been lady-like to reveal her surprise in front of a hotel employee. The room, part of a suite, was large, far bigger than she had expected. Two long sash windows flooded it with light and each had heavy velvet curtains held back by matching cords. Armchairs were placed near each window, leaving the centre of the room dominated by two sofas, with small tables conveniently placed at each end. Potted palms were placed to give maximum effect to the light oak woodwork and walls of subdued blue.

'Would Madam like me to show her the other rooms?' A query from the bell-boy refocused Glenda's mind.

'Yes, please.'

Rosalind and Caitlin, equally astonished, followed the bell-boy's tour. 'Your room, Ma'am.'

The large double bed looked so comfortable, Glenda want to flop on to it and stay there. A mahogany wardrobe with matching chest of drawers, and dressing table with mirrors and chair, did not diminish the feeling of space and yet there was everything to hand for a guest's comfort.

The bell-boy indicated a door. 'For the convenience of you all, Madam, and this other door leads into your daughters' bedroom.' The atmosphere became charged with excitement when Rosalind and Caitlin expressed their delight while simultaneously trying to choose the bed they particularly wanted. The room was furnished similarly to their mother's except that it had twin beds.

'If there is anything you need during your stay there is a bell-pull beside each bed and a porter on duty all night. A maid will be with you shortly to help you unpack.'

Their luggage was brought in and they were left to express their delight at the luxury all around them.

They had arranged to meet Gordon in the Palm Court in an hour and were pleased to see he was already seated at a table. Ros and Cat were fascinated by the foreign plants that stood by so elegantly, like soldiers keeping them safe.

'I have ordered tea for you. It was the first thing I missed when I came to America, but now I can't be without coffee. Is everything to your liking?' Gordon enquired.

'It's wonderful,' replied Glenda, 'and your nieces are overwhelmed and excited about the luxury of everything, as am I. We didn't expect this sort of reception. You shouldn't have gone to so much trouble, and in such a fine hotel.'

'You three deserve it and I am more than satisfied that you like it. It is so wonderful to have you here. Now I thought you might like to ask me about the city before you see it tomorrow, and of course anything else you would like to know.'

They asked him about the hotel that seemed like a palace to them, what they could and couldn't do, and Ros wanted to know more about the city and its inhabitants. After they finished their warm and very welcome drinks, Gordon said, 'Just get yourselves settled here for now. We'll talk more after our meal this evening, if that suits you?'

'Of course it does. Whatever you think best; we are in your hands.'

'Good. I'll call for you at six.'

'Thank you so much, Gordon. I just wish John was with us.'

'So do I,' he replied, with feeling in his eyes. 'It was one of my dreams that we would be together here, and I was thrilled when he said you would all come and see what you thought to my proposal.'

Glenda, giving a wistful smile, said, 'But now we must make the best of what life has brought us.'

Gordon nodded. 'You always were the wise one.'

She gave a little shake of her head but made no comment.

They rose from the table and Gordon, indicating where the elevator was, said, 'I will leave you in peace.' He allowed them to step inside and, before the bell-boy pressed the button for their floor, said, 'Remember, I'll call for you at six.' Then he was gone and the door closed.

For a few moments Glenda stood deep in thought. Gordon was so like John in his looks but she wondered how much life in America had changed him. Gordon certainly hadn't left anything of their arrival to chance she thought, slightly irritated by his efficiency, confidence and display of pride in the way he was known in this city. She remembered him as a carefree boy that just let life take its chances; something her quiet John had still managed to do alongside his estate work.

12

'My three young ladies look very glamorous this evening,' commented Gordon as soon as he set eyes on them.

'I don't know about that,' replied Glenda, 'but we thank you all the same.'

Ros and Cat echoed the remark and Ros added, 'We only had our travelling clothes, the others are in our trunks somewhere in America.'

'Heading for Colorado,' put in Gordon, and then added, 'I hope!' He screwed up his face thoughtfully. 'Maybe we'd better go shopping tomorrow.'

Cat's face lit up with surprise and hope. 'That would be thrilling,' she commented.

'It would be good to buy some new clothes,' Glenda agreed, 'but let us enjoy this evening first.'

'Are we ready to go down now?' Gordon queried.

They all nodded, and, when they reached the sweeping curve of the wide staircase, Glenda gratefully took his proffered arm. Ros and Cat followed.

A young footman met them at the bottom of the stairs.

'Good evening, Mr McKinley. It is a pleasure to have you with us again and to meet your lovely ladies. I see you are dining with us this evening. Would you like to go to your table now?'

Gordon cast a questioning glance at Glenda.

'Yes, please,' was her reply.

The footman escorted them to the restaurant where a waiter, immaculately dressed in white shirt and black suit, took over. Once again Glenda noted the respect the staff showed to Gordon at all times. 'You seem well known here and the staff are quick to respond to your requests.'

He smiled. 'I have always maintained that people in service are better on your side; they are a wealth of knowledge about who is who and what is going on. Treat them kindly, but keep them in their place without appearing to do so, and you'll always be well thought of. I put that into practice from my very first step on to American soil and it has paid dividends ever since. It has helped me to move up in the world in all sorts of ways and enabled me to occupy the place I have today. But you don't want to hear about me.'

'I do, but perhaps not just now.' Glenda cast her eyes in the direction of her daughters, which Gordon interpreted as meaning she wanted to speak to him on her own. He met her gaze and gave a little nod to show that he had understood.

At that moment the head waiter came forward and showed the same pleasure that other members of staff had expressed on seeing Gordon again. He presented the four of them with menus.

Ros and Cat were flattered by all the attention. Finally they had all made their choices, which, as the evening wore on, proved to be more than enjoyable. Gordon used the time to get to know about his nieces and was delighted that they were of a lively disposition, with interesting and enquiring minds. Remembering what Glenda had told him, he talked about riding, reading, and had his own questions ready to elicit further information on their interests.

As they left the dining room, Ros said to Caitlin, 'Let's you and I go to our room and have a game of cards, leaving Mama and Uncle Gordon to have a chat. They must have such a lot to talk about.'

'Let's,' Cat agreed.

When they had gone Glenda and Gordon settled down in comfortable chairs in the lounge and she said, 'I'll come straight to the point while we are alone.' He made no comment. 'I am concerned about the cost of our visit,' she went on. 'Everything so far has been paid for by you. This cannot go on.'

He held up his hand to stop her. 'Glenda, don't scold me for something I want to do. When you indicated that you wanted to come, I was delighted. It gave me a chance to do something for you and hopefully to help find a cure for Caitlin's problems. I want to be part of that. In the short time I've known her I can see she has a wonderful personality. So has Ros. I would like to be part of their lives even if you are not going to make a permanent home here. I don't want you to have any financial worries. Let me start by paying for this visit, no strings attached.'

Glenda sat assessing this proposal.

'I am more than grateful to you, Gordon,' she said finally. 'We all are; I appreciate what you are doing for us, but if we are to be here for any length of time we need to be able to pay our way in some form or other. At the very least let me look after your house and do some cooking. In the last year

Jessie Martins has taught me a great deal. My daughters would like to help, too, and it would give us the opportunity to weigh up our futures.'

Gordon looked slightly uneasy as he said, 'You have every right to be cautious. You are a very astute woman, John would be proud of you. Now, let us have a glass of champagne and drink to the future.'

They raised their glasses in the hope and belief that all would be well.

Caitlin stared at her cards with a vacant expression and yawned.

'I think it's time you went to bed,' said Ros. 'Shopping tomorrow is likely be a long and tiring day.'

Cat nodded and wearily answered, 'Are you going to bed too?'

'Shortly. First I want to write a letter to Clive so that it will leave tomorrow. Goodness knows when I'll have an opportunity to post another once we leave New York.'

Cat nodded and mumbled, 'Don't wake me up when you come.'

'I won't. Sleep well.'

'Say goodnight to Mama and Uncle Gordon for me.'

'I will.'

Ros settled at the card table and wrote:

Dearest Clive

I am writing to you before we move on from New York, which we will be doing in six days' time. It seems strange to be writing to you from this distance. The whole journey has been a wonderful experience but my heart ached because I was leaving you behind. The sea voyage was invigorating and it was a blessing that none of us were seasick, though some of the other passengers were very poorly.

Thank goodness Uncle Gordon was here to meet us, knowing exactly where we would be; he had a cab organised to take us to ... the largest hotel with the finest reputation in New York! It is all very interesting, though I am looking forward to moving on. I want to be where I can see the open views and big skies they talk about. I want to leave all the city people behind; they jostle and bump into one another because they seem always to be in a hurry.

I am looking forward to seeing Uncle Gordon's ranch in Colorado. He won't tell us anything about it. I think he wants it to be a surprise. It is hard to imagine we will be travelling for at least four days before we get there and will be still in the same country!

Mama is in good spirits and Cat is coping well. I think the new experiences are keeping her mind occupied. On the ship she had restless nights but no real nightmares. Who knows? Perhaps we will return sooner than we thought. Oh, how good it will feel when we are together again.

I am missing you and still picture you with Freya, watching us leave. It brings tears to my eyes, and will be with me every day until I see you again.

Take care of yourself and look after Pinmuir and Scotland for me.

My love as always,
Ros

The following morning a sharp knocking on the door woke Ros and Cat at the same time.

'Who on earth . . . ?' Ros muttered as she pushed the bedclothes back. Then she saw the time. 'Oh, my goodness!'

'Are you two up?' a voice asked from outside the door.

'Yes, Mama,' Ros responded.

'Breakfast's in forty minutes, don't be late.'

Footsteps faded away down the corridor.

'Come on, Cat,' Rosalind urged. 'It's dress-buying day!' Her sister swung out of bed. 'Can't keep Uncle Gordon waiting.'

They prepared themselves for the outing whilst speculating what attire they might look for. Ros kept her eye on the clock and, within a few minutes of the time appointed by their mother, they headed downstairs and into the dining room, where some of the hotel guests were already eating their breakfast.

The sisters saw Gordon coming towards them to take them to a table where their mother was already seated. Greetings were exchanged.

'Did you both sleep well? Were you comfortable, Cat?' asked Glenda, but glanced at Ros who quickly nodded and said, 'Yes, Mama. I woke only once and Caitlin was sound asleep.'

Cat put in, 'No nightmares last night, Mama,' clearly in a jovial mood, ready for their day out.

'I have been in touch with Sam, and hired him to be with you until you have finished shopping for your dresses and anything else you may want,' said Gordon.

'Won't you be with us?' asked Glenda, a touch of concern in her tone.

'No. I have some business to see to before we leave for Colorado. Sam is hired for the day, so make the most of him for your shopping; he knows where I have accounts. He'll drop you here at the hotel when you finish and I will see you for our evening meal at the usual time. I shall expect the three of you to be looking glamorous in your new purchases. Have a happy shopping day.' Smiling, he rose from the table and bade them good day.

'I think I've nearly had enough of New York City,' said Ros as she placed her purchases on the floor and flopped on to the bed with a deep, contented sigh.

'So have I,' agreed Cat, kicking off her shoes and rubbing her feet. 'New York pavements are a bit too hard. Thank goodness for Sam driving us the longer distances.'

'I have enjoyed it but the buildings seem to be crowding in on you. I like more space,' said Ros. 'I'm looking forward to seeing the wide open prairies.'

'Hopefully from a horse.'

'Definitely.'

'And giving it its head.'

'The thrum of its hoofs! With wider spaces than we had in Scotland, we will get a really good gallop.'

'We'll have to wait a while for that. Uncle Gordon has planned some sightseeing.'

'Five days to get there, if we don't run into any trouble.'

Cat raised her eyes to the ceiling. 'I just want to be there now!'

'The sooner the better.' Ros's words faded away. Cat covered her sister with a blanket, seeing she was already asleep.

*

Caitlin stirred. Her eyes flickered and then closed again. She could make no sense of anything except that she was lying in a comfortable bed – but where? For a few moments she tried to answer her own question. She was getting nowhere with the answer when suddenly her mind cleared. Cat sat up, caught sight of the clock and quickly rolled out of bed. She shook her sister, still sound asleep, and called, 'Ros! Ros! Get up!'

She woke in an instant and was thrown into panic. Was her sister having a nightmare? She flung her blanket aside and was on her feet before she spoke. 'Cat, are you all right? What's the matter?'

'Nothing. But it's time you and I were dressing for dinner or we'll be late.'

Cat quickly dressed and was soon priming her hair in front of the dressing-table mirror. Ros cast off her clothes but had difficulty deciding on which new outfit to wear. 'That one,' said Cat impatiently. 'Now hurry.'

Ros was just pinching her cheeks for the last time, to give her skin a healthy glow, when there was a tap on the door. Cat hurried to open it.

'Come in, Mama.'

'Are you two ready?'

'Nearly,' called Ros. She swung round on her stool. 'There. It's been a rush but will I do?'

Glenda gave them both a critical glance then said, 'Stand together.'

As they shuffled towards each other, they smoothed their new clothes to make a few last adjustments.

'You both look wonderful. The ideal choices for wearing both here and at the ranch,' Glenda told them. 'Your skirts fit perfectly. The green suits your complexion, Cat. And you, Ros, look very engaging in that deep blue.' She smiled at her eldest daughter and said, 'I wish Clive could see you now!' Her pride in them both was obvious.

They were flattered by their mother's compliments. 'You are too kind, Mama,' said Ros. 'That scarlet blouse of yours is sure to attract attention.'

'And I love the beautiful red shoes peeking out from underneath your skirt,' said Cat. 'You outshine us, and I'm sure Uncle Gordon will think the same.'

When he saw them coming down the stairs he was briefly struck silent.

'I shall be the envy of every man dining here this evening,' he said finally. 'I am privileged and delighted to be your escort. You have certainly had a good day, choosing these flattering outfits. You'll have to tell me all about it as we enjoy our meal.' He escorted them into the dining room where some of the other guests turned their heads in admiration.

'No one can match you,' Gordon whispered to Glenda as he sat down beside her.

Once Cat had nearly finished her main course she asked, 'When and where do we eat on our way to Colorado?'

'On the train,' replied Gordon. 'We have a Pullman compartment. Let's save the details as a surprise for you.'

'But we are going soon?' asked Cat.

'Yes,' replied her mother. 'And Uncle insisted we had the best means of travelling so that we can enjoy everything about our journey into a country we don't know.'

'It sounds so exciting,' said Cat, with an enthusiasm that Glenda saw as a blessing. She hoped her daughter's recovery continued.

But first they had New York City to explore.

The McKinley women were not used to sightseeing and though they were over-awed by the new Statue of Liberty, the mansions of the Robber Barons and a night at the ballet, it was the open-topped carriage drive through Central Park that they enjoyed the most, an anomaly in the centre of such a bustling city. It was good to feel the breeze freely blowing on their faces again.

After five days they found they had grown tired of the jostling people with their long drawling accents and, sometimes, uncouth ways. It was hard to get used to city life as well as the change in culture. Colorado beckoned.

13

'Just a few instructions before we set out on our adventure,' said Glenda when they were nearing the end of their breakfast a few days later. A glance from her told Gordon to take over.

He cleared his throat. 'Today will be the start of a long journey for you – in the region of two thousand miles, which will take maybe four days on the train. There will be plenty to keep you interested, though the prairies can become monotonous so have something to do with you, a book to read or cards to play. However, I think you will find plenty to hold your attention. As I told you, we will be travelling in a special Pullman carriage that I have booked. It will be exclusively ours, to sit in comfortably and take all our meals, served by attendants employed by the rail company. It will be just as if we are in a first-class hotel. Enjoy it.'

'Will other people be travelling in Pullman coaches?' asked Ros.

'Yes. At what grade depends on how much they pay. Other passengers travelling first- or second-class use a separate part of the train. They are not allowed to enter the Pullman coaches, though those travelling like us have the freedom of the whole train. However, I will say it would be best to keep to our carriage. The rest of the passengers will be a very mixed lot. There will be people from all walks of life: salesmen coming to peddle their goods in the rough, raw West, cowboys looking for employment, professional gamblers, wives going home after visiting relatives in the east, soldiers returning to their posts, miners and their families hoping to change their circumstances. There will be a whole galaxy of the people who make up this expanding country.'

'You make it sound so colourful,' said Rosalind.

'It is. America has unlimited potential that makes it truly exciting. You're going to love it.'

The pointers on the hall clock were nearing one-thirty when the McKinley party assembled in the hotel's ornate entrance hall.

'Everyone happy?' Gordon asked breezily.

Responding to his mood, the women chorused, 'Yes.'

Sam appeared in the doorway and started to gather their luggage. Two bell-boys hurried to take the rest of their belongings to the cab. With tips in their hands they bade the party goodbye. After checking that his passengers were comfortably seated Sam climbed on to his seat, took the reins and, with a call familiar to his horse, sent it on its way. As they approached the station the road became more and more crowded with passengers due to take the same train as the McKinleys.

'Coach three,' called an official, when the driver asked which coach his party was to take.

Sam drove alongside the train until he reached Pullman car three.

Seeing the cab slowing, a smartly dressed steward instantly stepped out to open the cab door for them. He assisted the new arrivals to the ground and waited while they made their farewells to the driver.

'According to the information I have been given, Mr McKinley, you have exclusive use of the whole of this carriage, and we are all ready to serve you at any time,' the steward said.

'Thank you,' replied Gordon, while Glenda and her daughters offered friendly smiles.

'I will let you get settled in,' said the porter, going to the door. 'Make yourselves comfortable and enjoy your time with us.'

'I'll leave you to it, if you don't mind,' said Gordon to the women. 'I'd like to get a couple of business letters off before we leave. I'll ask our steward to give you a conducted tour of the carriage. I'll be in the next compartment and will rejoin you shortly.'

'Very well,' Glenda told him.

Once the door closed behind Gordon, Glenda, Ros and Cat let their excitement spill over.

'This is simply out of this world!' Once again Glenda wondered how her husband's brother had made this amount of money; but he had always been more ambitious than John, she thought.

'This is so unexpected – it's magical! How can I describe it to Clive?' said Ros.

Cat flopped into one of the four armchairs arranged so they did not impede passage through the car or the use of the window seats. 'Ooh, that's so comfortable,' she said as she reclined against the back of the chair.

'So is this,' said Ros, who was trying one of the window

seats. 'Imagine sitting here and watching miles and miles of countryside go by.'

'No expense has been spared to make these cars special,' commented Glenda as she glanced around and stretched her hand towards the wall. 'These mirrors must be French plate and they shine as if new.'

'Excuse me but you are quite right, Ma'am,' said the steward as he came back into the compartment. 'I just caught your comment. The three chandeliers will interest you too. All of these delicately coloured fittings are especially created for the particular carriage in which they hang. The furniture and its coverings have all been made to Pullman exclusive designs. Some of the individual seats are swivelled so passengers can swing round to see the view on both sides of the train.' He demonstrated and smiled at the expressions of amazement on their faces. 'The next car, towards the front, is similar to this, and beyond that is the kitchen car. Your meals will be served in this, your exclusive carriage.'

'What about other passengers, where do they eat?' asked Glenda.

'First- and second-class passengers can take their meals in what we call hotel cars, very similar to dining in a static hotel. Those travelling in the lower-class accommodation take meals as they can, buying something from the refreshment services at stations where we stop; that can be a bit of a rush and a crush though.'

'I can imagine that, having seen so many people gathering on the platform,' commented Glenda.

The steward continued his conducted tour, allowing his passengers to pause to examine the black walnut woodwork and luxurious red Brussels carpeting.

As he brought his tour to a close in the main room of their car Glenda pointed out, 'You haven't shown us our sleeping accommodation.'

'No, Ma'am.' The man gave a little smile. 'It is here, in the full length of your car.'

The three McKinleys looked a little confused.

'Here, Ma'am.' The steward reached up to the carriage panelling and pulled down a section to reveal what could be used as a bed.

'How ingenious,' commented Ros.

'Wonderful!' said Cat, but at the same time wondered if she would be able to sleep when the train was moving.

'Privacy?' questioned Glenda.

'The hanging curtains at each bedhead can be drawn to make that complete.' He showed them.

'Thank you,' said Glenda, and added, 'whoever thought all this out deserves a medal. It is marvellous, so much thought for passenger comfort over long distances.'

'Mr Pullman was the brains behind it and other railway companies clamoured for the carriages. Mr Pullman built more, leased them to interested companies and made a fortune.'

Gordon had caught his comment as he returned to their car. He corroborated the steward's information and thanked him.

'No trouble, sir. It is good to show people around who are interested. I will bring you a menu and return for your order after you have seen what the chef is offering this evening.' He glanced at his watch. 'We should be leaving in fifteen minutes.'

111

14

Dearest Clive,

We are on our way in a Pullman train after leaving New York at 3 p.m. today.

You would not believe the luxury of our carriage (or car to use the American term). Uncle Gordon booked the whole carriage so we have it to ourselves: a living room with sections that let down to make comfortable beds although Uncle Gordon has a small private bedroom to himself, of course. We dine here on meals supplied from a special kitchen carriage. The stewards on the train are very attentive and eager to please. It should all make for a pleasant journey.

The land we have seen so far reminds me of the border country between Scotland and England, gentle and undulating, mostly cultivated fields but some woodland. From what I hear the drama in the landscape will come later.

How I wish you were here to share everything with me. It would make life so much more delightful. I try to make it so by holding you in my thoughts and remembering the days we spent amongst our beloved Highlands. I look forward to the day when we can do that again.

My love,

Ros

She addressed an envelope and made it ready to post at the next opportunity.

That came the following morning when passengers who were travelling with no eating facilities were informed there would be an hour's stop for refreshments at the next station: 'Ladies have their own refreshment room. Gentlemen, please observe that distinction. If you don't you will be ejected and thrown in the caboose!' Female cheers rippled through the train at this threat.

Ten minutes later metal clattering on metal announced that the train was slowing. This brought many of the passengers travelling without dining facilities to their feet. The train jerked as brakes were applied. People stumbled, grabbed the nearest passenger or sought the back of the closest seat for support. Everyone wanting to be first at the serving points started to claim their supposed right before the train had stopped. As soon as it did people spilled out on to the platform, eager to appease their hunger.

The McKinleys watched it all and enjoyed their tasty lunch from the comfort of their own carriage, ignoring a group of five urchins who pulled faces at them through the window, until a railway official scattered them with a swirl of his heavy cape.

'He's done that before,' commented Rosalind with a smile.

The platform had become a moving stream of people making sure, in one way or another, that they would be prepared for the next stage of their journey.

Ten minutes later three unmelodious blasts from the train's whistle signalled that they would be moving out in fifteen minutes. Some passengers from the first class carriage rushed to reclaim their seats, causing confusion when they sat themselves in the wrong places. Arguments that made the air blue ensued until a railway official cooled tempers and set the mistake right. Two more blasts warned passengers that their train would leave in ten minutes. This brought even more panic when a mother and father announced that their three young children were missing, causing confusion and a hasty search until someone shouted, 'Here ... they are here!'

A waiter from the cafe appeared, leading the children who were innocently eating ice cream. Their parents, scolding them mercilessly, bustled them back on to their carriage, their ice-cream cornets scattered in the dust. The next hoot startled everyone still immersed in the uproar. Three young men, a little unsteady on their feet, grabbed at the iron railings on the end of the final carriage. Amidst a crescendo of encouragement they managed to haul themselves on board. They rolled over the railings, grasping the flailing hands of their friends. Their success brought cheers from those who had witnessed it.

'That was a close call for them,' said Ros, laughing as she leaned out of the window to watch.

'Is this journey always as exciting as this?' queried Cat.

'It might get even more so.' Gordon smiled.

The train, puffing hard from its unusually shaped funnel, picked up speed, leaving a plume of black smoke marking its passing.

Once more the McKinleys settled down to enjoy the luxury of their carriage and relaxed as the train ate up the miles towards Colorado. While they were enjoying their evening meal Gordon informed them, 'Tomorrow we will see the prairies.'

'Will there be buffalo?' asked Cat.

'We might see some but there won't be the large herds there once were.'

'Why? Did the Indians kill them all?'

'No. They killed only what they required for their own livelihood, but that was always a sustainable kill because there were so many buffalo. The coming of the railways caused the real slaughter and decimation of the herds. The large numbers of workers needed to be fed as they laid the railroad tracks, and the buffalo were a handy food supply.'

'I hope we see some.'

'I hope you do too. They are fine animals and a large herd of buffalo, and I mean large, is a wonderful sight, especially if they are in a full stampede. The ground will shake, as you've never felt it, and clouds of dust rise so thick that you don't want to linger near them or you'll choke.'

'Ros, we must keep our eyes open tomorrow. I want to see a herd of buffalo!' called Cat, in a manner that said there would be disappointment if her wish were not fulfilled.

She went to sleep that night recalling the excitement of a day she had thought might be dull. And tomorrow, with any luck, could turn out even better – buffalo!

*

115

A shrill scream fought against the rhythmic clatter of the wheels. The dim night-light sent shadows dancing across the carriage in time with the swaying of the train.

Glenda woke abruptly, aware that Cat was in trouble. She flung off the bedclothes, sending them tumbling to the floor. Someone beside her was also struggling to their feet. 'Ros!' she called.

'I'm here, Mama.' Ros reached out to her mother, just as another scream split the air.

'Buffalo!'

Glenda slid her arms protectively around her younger daughter.

'It's all right, Cat, Ros and I are here.'

'You've just been dreaming,' Ros tried to reassure her, rubbing her arm gently.

Cat gave a deep sob that ended with the muttered words, 'The buffalo!' She eased herself away from her mother to look at her with baleful eyes. 'The buffalo were coming. I couldn't escape.'

'But you did. You are safe here with your mother and sister. It was only a dream.'

There was a tap on the woodwork. 'Is everything all right?' asked a worried voice.

'Yes, come in, Gordon,' replied Glenda, and slid the curtain back for him. 'Cat's had a nightmare.'

'I was being charged at by a herd of buffalo, Uncle Gordon.'

'Only a dream, my dear. Remember, I told you there weren't any on this part of the prairie,' he said, with such conviction in his voice that she nodded her head meekly.

'Now, back into bed, Cat,' said Glenda, gently persuasive.

She scrambled between the sheets and Ros tucked her in.

'Sleep soundly,' said Glenda, kissing her daughter on the forehead.

Cat nodded and gave her uncle a sheepish grin, saying, 'Silly me.' He pressed a reassuring hand on Glenda's shoulder. 'She'll be all right, but call me if there is a any cause for worry.'

'Thank you,' Glenda replied. 'Ros and I will sit here until she's asleep.'

'By the look of her that won't be long,' said Ros, noting how her sister's eyelids were drooping.

The next morning, as planned, nobody mentioned Cat's nightmare. Nor did she display any adverse reaction to it. In fact, it appeared as if nothing had occurred.

They finished their breakfast and settled down to observe the passing landscape, which rolled away into the distance broken only by oak savannahs and anaqua trees seeking water from the occasional stream.

'Is this the real prairie, Uncle Gordon?' asked Ros.

'Yes, as far as your eyes can see.'

'Clive would love the carpets of flowers and all the colours in the different grasses; he would look in wonder at how thick and tall they are.'

'Then he would probably be struck by the wealth of game there is here too: quail, turkey, deer and antelope.'

'I'm sure he would,' said Rosalind, 'but he'd also miss our deer, game birds and mountains.'

Glenda tried to divert Ros's thoughts. 'When you first came to America, Gordon, you wrote now and then but we learned very little of what you were doing. It was only after you had started ranching that you told us more, when you were trying to persuade John that there was a good life to be made for all of us here if we joined you. But what did you do before ranching?'

Gordon gave a little smile at her curiosity. 'There's no secret about it, Glenda. I wasn't a good correspondent, I know, and I'm sorry for that now; perhaps if I had been John would have been persuaded to come here sooner.' He gave a little shake of his head and tightened his lips for a moment. 'I was a stranger in an unfamiliar land when I first arrived. It was so different from everything I had known in Scotland. To be honest, I nearly came straight back, but that would have made me look foolish and I told myself there was a big adventure ahead of me if I wanted it. Eventually I decided to go West, probably believing that if I put as much distance as that between myself and Scotland I would be less tempted to give in and return. I worked here and there as I moved on. I lived frugally but in most places food came with the job because generally people were open hearted towards strangers. Of course there were those who tried to get more out of me than I was being paid for, and others who just didn't like a Scotsman. I stood up to them. Either I got the sack or I told them I was moving on.'

He paused, but seeing he had a rapt audience, went on. 'I reached the Mississippi and got work on one of the steamers plying its trade as a passenger and goods boat. Its captain and owner was Ed Berry, getting on in years but reluctant to give up. The river had been his life. He had lost his wife and young son in an accident I was told wasn't his fault, but Ed blamed himself. I had been with him three years when he told me he was dying and that he was leaving his boat to me. He hoped I would still run it in his memory for at least two years. I think he limited it to two because he saw I had the wanderlust, but also that I desired to better myself. After that time I sold the boat and all its trappings for a very good price and headed West, over the Rockies into Colorado, which wasn't a state then, and on to Denver, a rough town at the time. Because of the proximity of the silver mines in the mountains, I saw there was a good chance to make money there. That is exactly what I did.

'Four years ago I sold everything I had in Denver and bought land and started ranching – longhorns – beef cattle for the markets back east. There are a lot of mouths to feed there and they love a good juicy steak.'

'But how do you get the beasts there?' asked Caitlin.

'Drive them.'

'What? Walk them all the way?'

Gordon smiled at her incredulous expression. 'Not all the way, but to one of the railheads, which has a direct link to the eastern stockyards handling cattle.'

'Don't you lose any on the way?'

'Yes, but that is inevitable. Generally it doesn't affect our profits because most of the cattle survive. They eat well and actually put on weight during what can be a thousand-mile drive.'

'Just a bit different from driving cattle at home,' commented Ros. 'Clive won't believe me when I tell him.'

'And that is it?' said Glenda. 'That is what you are still doing at your ranch?'

'Yes. It has been a profitable move, but I've been wondering if I'm wise being so committed to cattle trading with the eastern market. I've always left myself something in the bank to fall back on in case of a setback to what I'm doing.'

119

'Can't you do something about that?'

'Yes. I could scale down my cattle business a little and replace it with horse-trading.'

'Why horses?'

'They are easier to work and control when driven on the trail, as they would be if I raised horses to sell. There will always be a market for them if you analyse their main uses, such as Army needs and ranch work, as more and more smaller ranches are appearing.'

'Would you consider no longer ranching cattle?'

'Oh, no. There'll always be money to be made feeding the population in the east. I suppose I am looking to expand into horse-dealing because they are always needed and I just like horses.'

'I'm glad you do, Uncle Gordon,' said Caitlin with a joyful smile.

'When you get to my ranch you shall have your pick of my horses.'

'What?' Cat's eyes opened wide in disbelief.

'You can choose the one you want and it shall be yours for as long as you are with me. That also goes for Rosalind and your mother.'

'Gordon, you really should stop spoiling us,' Glenda chided him.

'I'm not spoiling you. The horses cost me nothing: they were wild on the prairies, a large herd that I was able to round up, break-in and sell at a good profit bar those I chose for ranch work. So, you see, I lost nothing and gained a great deal. We always have mustangs at the ranch that are already broken in and well trained, so you can have your pick of those. Apart from that there are two things you will also need to consider. First, they are used to being ridden astride; and secondly, you'll have to learn to use the American saddle.'

'The first won't be a problem. We have all ridden astride,' said Glenda.

'I prefer it,' Rosalind supported her mother.

'I do too,' agreed Cat. 'Much more control, especially at full gallop.'

'Good,' said Gordon. 'And my cowboys will soon have you weaned away from the saddle you have been used to. They are a good crew and loyal to me. Perhaps that's because I treat them as equals in work and in play, but they know the consequences if they step out of line. I listen to their suggestions and opinions and sometimes use them. They appreciate the recognition.'

'It sounds as though you are a good man-handler,' commented Glenda with an admiring smile.

Gordon gave a little smile and a dismissive shrug. 'Maybe born in me, but I reckon I learned as I went along. But whatever, it has paid dividends. I am not boasting about my achievements; other men have done the same and more. All the land you can see from this train now is mine and all that we have travelled through for the last three hours. What you will see until we are an hour from Denver also belongs to me.'

Mother and daughters stared at him in disbelief.

'But . . .' began Glenda.

'There are no buts about it, Glenda. It's here to see and can be verified in the Land Office in Denver.'

'Are you driven to want even more?' she asked.

'In the beginning I was, but since I have achieved all I

wanted to, I am contented as I am. I love being a cowboy, if I can consider myself one.'

'I am sure you can,' commented Glenda. 'The amount of land you have, the herds of horses, the huge herds of longhorns you mentioned plus the English cattle you have introduced, could never have come about if you hadn't worked your way up from learning the life of a cowboy and immersing yourself in it.'

'Maybe,' he said casually, 'but you need luck as well.'

'But you've got to grasp luck as soon as you recognise it and make it work for you,' said Rosalind in admiration, 'otherwise it will pass you by.'

'Very true, young lady. You are wise beyond your years.'

'I heard my father say something like that to a young Scotsman once. It stuck in my mind and I recalled it when I was listening to you telling us how you achieved your dream.'

'If you would allow me to add something – I would say, in working towards your goal, don't let anyone else get hurt. Rather, offer them a helping hand towards achieving their dream. It is up to them if they accept it or not.'

'Yours was a good dream, though,' commented Caitlin, who had listened intently to all that had been said. 'Not like mine.'

'You'll soon be rid of yours,' said Glenda, her eyes flooding with sympathy. 'Don't think about that. Let it go. Replace dreams with thoughts of what Uncle Gordon is bringing to our lives.'

Caitlin nodded her understanding. 'I will try, if he will tell us more about life at his ranch.'

'I will, my dear,' he said. 'We will be there the day after tomorrow unless there are any delays. And if there are, we'll take them in our stride.'

As they settled down again, Rosalind's mind drifted back to her uncle's life and she wondered if Clive, given the same chances, would have achieved all that Uncle Gordon had.

15

'Did you finish your letter?' Gordon asked Rosalind the next day after they had enjoyed a tasty breakfast.

'Yes and no,' she replied with an impish smile.

'Yes and no! What's that supposed to mean?' chided Cat.

'It means I'm not sure; if I get time to add a note I will, if I don't then the letter can be posted in Denver as it is.'

Gordon gave a silent curse, but added for all to hear, 'I should have told you – it will be best if you post any letters at Cheyenne. They will leave there sooner than from Denver. We change trains at Cheyenne because Denver was missed out of the direct north–south line, which means, unfortunately, we have to interrupt our schedule and change trains. There is talk of putting this right, but as yet nothing has been decided. So, if you let me have your letters, I'll see they are taken at Cheyenne.'

As the train slowed on approaching the station, he took their letters and told them on which platform they would board the train for Denver. Their train awaited them and when they found their new carriage and all were settled,

Gordon said, 'The good thing is that this line between Cheyenne and Denver gives you better views of the Rockies.'

'How close will we get to them?' enquired Ros.

'The nearest is about twelve miles away, when we are at Denver, which lies at the confluence of Cherry Creek and the South Platte River. Just remember, although there are plans afoot for its development, Denver is still very much a mining town, rough and tough; a boom place that attracted all manner of people eager to dig a fortune in silver out of the ground.'

'Did they?' asked Cat, with an excited gleam in her eyes.

'Some did, some didn't. Many left, some stayed. A town built on mining is a town built on luck.'

'Did you ever try it, Uncle?' asked Ros.

'Yes, I did, but I soon realised it wasn't for me. Underground has never attracted me; give me wide open spaces any time – that's what I chose and they were kind to me, and still are. I hope you won't be disappointed by what you see later today,' he said.

Thoughts about what the ranch would be like were pushed to the back of their minds when Gordon announced, pointing his finger, 'You can get a good view of the Rockies now.'

The silence that enveloped their carriage was palpable, not even the rhythmic rotation of the train's wheels marred it. The distant mountains, forming a jagged skyline, were holding all their attention.

Glenda wondered what John would have made of this new land. Would it have taken a hold on him and never released him? Would the Rockies have triumphed or would the memories of their Scottish Highlands have been too powerful? And how would the magic of these mountains, already reaching out to her, influence her own future?

Ros's reaction was tempered by a feeling of resentment. Even from this distance she saw them as a formidable foe, trying to drive a wedge between her and Clive. They were higher, more powerful than her Highlands and she sensed she would have a fight on her hands resisting their allure.

Cat's eyes were wide with wonder as she linked the horses she had seen on the prairies with this landscape of foothills and mountains – a land with so much beauty and adventure, to be explored from the back of the horse Uncle Gordon had promised her. She couldn't wait.

With every mile their excitement and interest in what lay ahead gripped them tighter. A little relief came when the train began to slow and a steward entered their carriage to announce, 'Denver in ten minutes.' He helped them with their luggage and had it assembled by the time the train finally stopped at the platform. Gordon was first off the train once the steward had opened the door, and, at his signal, a cowboy hurried over to him.

'Welcome back, sir. I hope you had a good journey and all went according to plan.'

'It did, Mark, thanks,' Gordon said. 'Meet my relations. Mrs Glenda McKinley, my sister-in-law, and her two daughters Rosalind and Caitlin, better known as Ros and Cat.'

'Pleased to meet you all. Ma'am.' Mark touched the brim of his Stetson to Glenda. 'I hope you have had a good journey and it has not been too tiring for anyone.'

'It has been most pleasant. We have been well looked after all the way, thanks to my brother-in-law's splendid planning,' replied Glenda.

'Mark is my manager so you will likely see a great deal of him,' explained Gordon, slapping his hand on the cowboy's shoulder. 'He has been with me ever since I moved into the cattle trade. He helped enormously to make the Circle C what it is today. I wanted him as a partner but he preferred to remain an employee.'

'That way there would be no reason for us to fall out,' Mark explained. 'Gordon's the boss and the final decision on any policy regarding the ranch is his.'

Glenda liked the openness she could sense in the relationship between these two men, even in this short exchange. She guessed their friendship would have been almost instant, born out of immediate respect for one another.

She judged Mark to be about fifty years old, the same age as Gordon; six foot tall, well built, but, through the nature of his work, always retaining his leanness and strength. It was his grey eyes that caught her attention more than anything – they were alive, alert, with the power to command attention. Yet she also saw gentleness and consideration there. Here was a man of many parts but one who had earned the respect he was given.

Her own thoughts startled her and Glenda drew back into herself momentarily. It was unusual for her to consider any man in this way apart from her own beloved husband.

Then she saw Gordon helping Rosalind and Caitlin into a horse-drawn vehicle and Mark was standing beside her.

'Can I help you in, Ma'am?'

'Thank you,' she said, taking his hand.

127

He steadied her on the iron step that hung from the door level and only let go when she had sat down, facing forward, beside Caitlin.

'Comfortable, Ma'am?'

'Yes, very, thank you. This is not what I expected.'

Mark gave a little smile. 'Everyone who takes a first ride in this says the same. It was specially built to my specifications – thought them out one day when I had used the stagecoach into Denver from Cheyenne. It wasn't a very comfortable ride. But you'll be all right in this one.' He glanced over his shoulder on hearing footsteps. 'Ah, here's Boss-man,' he added jokingly on seeing Gordon.

He opened the door and Gordon stepped into the coach and sat down beside Rosalind.

'Everyone settled?' he asked. There were no dissension so he added, 'All right, shotgun, let's away.'

Mark closed the door and climbed up the outside steps to get to his seat beside the driver.

'Don't worry about that term,' said Gordon with amusement as he saw their questioning faces. 'We still have these so called "shotguns" on out-of-the-way trails, but attacks are now infrequent. Our Indian troubles are close to being solved and almost all outlaws have been accounted for. But there is still an outside chance of flare-ups and criminal activity. If the times are volatile then it is wise to have someone ride shotgun. I don't think we'll have any trouble today, so enjoy the view.'

The three women sat back, lost in wonder at the scenery as the trail swung through the foothills of the Rockies while making a steady climb. Every twist and turn brought a fresh breathtaking aspect or gave them a different angle on the landscape they had already passed through. The climb became steeper; the two horses strained in the harness to keep the coach moving. So far they had needed no cajoling. It was as if they knew the terrain and what was expected of them.

When Rosalind commented on this fact, Gordon gave them all something to think about. 'They are a good pair,' he said, 'but they always pull with extra strength in this section of the climb. I reckon they know they are near-ing home where food will be waiting for them, but I also believe they know they are nearing the top of the ascent and the strain will soon be over. They always automatically stop there for a rest. Not one of my four drivers, like Lance who has the reins now, objects unless there is an emer-gency. The driver will then use a different tone of voice to order them on.'

Some time later the passengers felt the coach slowing and finally come to rest.

'Everyone out!' called Gordon.

Mark, who had dropped from his seat before the coach was truly stationary, was already opening the door and was by the steps to help the passengers to the ground.

Gordon, wanting to help, slipped smoothly out of the coach the moment it had stopped. He was eager to watch the expressions of the women as they saw his ranch for the first time. He nodded to Mark and held out his hand to assist Glenda.

As her feet touched the ground she said, 'Thank you, that was a most comfortable . . .' The word trailed away as amazement at the view silenced her.

'Welcome home,' said Gordon, with a genuine feeling of

pleasure, 'and welcome to John. I know he is here with us in spirit.' He turned to come face to face with Glenda. 'My dream has finally been fulfilled,' he added.

A lump came to Glenda's throat; she could not stop the tear that trickled down her cheeks.

Mark had been helping Rosalind. 'Welcome to the Circle C,' he said quietly. She made no reply but her eyes expressed astonishment, which pleased him. Next he helped Cat out of the coach. Her eyes widened and her pulse raced at the sight of all the horses. 'So many,' she gasped as she watched them for a moment, moving around in their corrals.

'And one will be yours, I believe,' said Mark. 'I think I know someone who will help you make a good choice.'

Cat glanced at him with curiosity. 'Who?'

He gave a little laugh. 'You will have to wait and see. Your uncle is wanting to say something.'

Gordon looked at his relations. 'You have already seen much of the land and the cattle and horses that form the Circle C ranch. The mile-wide valley that stretches before you is its heart. This is some of the best land, as you can no doubt judge from the luscious grass before you. The fences you see are to keep cattle and horses off the best growth, from which we derive excellent hay to be used when needed. The barns built away from the other buildings are there for storage purposes. A little further round from them are the stables in which we can house fifty horses. We can quickly erect more stabling if necessary. We have wood already cut for that purpose. That has come from the woods and forests you can see along the mountainsides.' Gordon pointed further round. 'Close to the stables, you can see the blacksmith's forge. Two men are employed there, shoeing and making any metal parts we require on a working ranch. A hundred yards further round you see my house and a hundred yards beyond that you see a replica that was built when I expected John and all of you to be coming a while ago. If you would rather not use it as it is we can change it.'

Glenda looked at him. 'What did you just say? Did I hear you right?'

Gordon repeated what he had said, emphasising this extra house had been built just for them but could be altered. 'No, no,' she replied resolutely. 'It looks too good to think of any changes. But, Gordon, you have gone to so much trouble . . . just for us. I can hardly believe it.'

He smiled, ignored her remark and added, 'If you do want any adjustments made after you have lived in it, we can do them. I'll take you into mine in a moment then you can see what it is like living in a wooden ranch house. The other buildings I haven't yet mentioned are Mark's house, very similar to my own, and the two long buildings beyond the forge are the bunkhouse for our cowboys and their dining area with its own kitchen.'

'Almost like a little town,' commented Rosalind.

'Yes,' replied Gordon. 'But Mark and I insist that whoever works for us must keep the whole area tidy so the view across the valley is unmarred.'

As they had been looking at all Gordon was pointing out, Glenda had been astonished to see an encampment of about twenty Indian dwellings. 'What about the tepees?' she queried.

'The same ruling on neatness, cleanliness, et cetera

applies to anyone working on the Circle C. They know from the start they have to abide by our rules. If they do they are treated like our other employees.'

'You have Indians working for you? Don't the cowboys object to them?'

'No, they recognise the contribution the Indians make to the ranch. They and their families have all been handpicked. They are from a very noble race, the Arapaho, who are the dominant tribe in this area. As you can see from the rows of fruit trees, we have an orchard that needs care. The Indian women enjoy this part of our enterprise and have become expert in the care of trees, but we use the men for all other work, especially where the horses are concerned. They are fine riders as you will see and are essential to us at round-up and branding times.'

Glenda felt uneasy. Gordon had written to John regarding the terrible fighting between the Indians and the white settlers . . . but her thoughts were interrupted by her daughter's observation.

'I think the decoration on their homes adds colour to their area of the ranch,' said Cat.

'Be sure and tell them that,' said Gordon. 'They'll be pleased.'

'How can I tell them when I can't speak their language?'

'Most of them speak some English, but not so many of the older ones. They pick it up from the cowboys, so you do get some strange words and phrases. I know some of the younger ones will like practising their English on you and they'll attempt to teach you their language.'

'I'd like to try it,' said Cat, 'wouldn't you, Ros?'

'It could be interesting but I'll see,' she said with less

enthusiasm, as she tried to take everything in. It would take a long time to adjust to life here, she felt.

Gordon made no comment but said instead, 'Should we move on and I'll show you my house?'

Everyone returned to their places on the coach and Lance started off at a gentle pace down the track. On reaching the bottom they swept round a small rise and came up before the houses, to stop at the one belonging to Gordon, who was quickly out of the coach. He opened the door for Glenda and, when everyone else was on the ground, started up the path towards his own front door. As they neared it the door opened and out stepped a straight-backed young lady with jet black hair tied in a neat roll at the back of her neck. Glenda was enchanted by her beautiful smile as she said, 'Welcome home.'

Her pronunciation gave Glenda a surprise; the faint Scottish twang in its tone told Glenda that Gordon had taught this young woman to speak English. If she needed any proof of that, the truth of it was confirmed when he said, 'Glenda, Ros, Cat, meet my wife!'

16

Dear Fiona,

A short while ago I received a terrible shock. We finally arrived at Gordon's ranch where we were introduced to his wife: an Indian, not much older than Ros! I did not know what to do. It was not so long ago that we heard these people were killing settlers in the most brutal of ways.

I almost left, there and then, but I had nowhere to go. I realised I was dependent on Gordon who, I must say, has been kindness itself since he met us in New York. Here at the ranch he has built a replica of his own house for us; both are made of wood, and he has furnished ours for us and promised to alter it in any way we want. I really could not throw such kindness back at him, so I am faced with adapting to present circumstances, at least until the girls and I decide what else to do. I know they were as shocked as I was, but we need time to consider our future.

However, since the first surprising impression I

received of Zalinda, I have found her to be a charming young woman; she speaks English and is friendly towards us. Her tanned skin is smooth, hair almost black and her eyes dark brown, but it is her smile that is her most winning feature. She is the daughter of Chief Ouray, leader of the branch of the tribe to which Gordon has given some of his land. I just find the situation very unexpected and am sorry that my brother-in-law didn't prepare us better for it.

I cannot write more now but will do so soon.

How is Scotland?

Love,

Glenda

When that letter was sent to be posted in Denver the next day, it was accompanied by another addressed to Clive in Rosalind's handwriting.

'A letter for Clive Martins!' The shout came across the heather-clad terrain that tumbled into a shallow dip where Clive, who was planting some recently purchased fir trees, also enjoyed the warmth of the morning sun. Recognising the voice of the man with the post, he straightened quickly, dropped the spade he was using and ran towards the postie's Highland pony.

'Good day, Mr Macaulay,' panted Clive, rubbing soil from his hands.

'Couldn't get here fast enough, I see. One for you from America.' The postman held it out to Clive, but just as he was about to take it, Macaulay held on to it teasingly. 'Or maybe I should deliver it on my return?'

135

'Nothing of the sort, Mr Macaulay,' rapped Clive. 'I'll take it here and now!'

Macaulay steadied his horse, restless to be on its way. 'Wait, wait, Hughie. This young man wants his letter.' The postman flicked the letter over and glanced at it. 'Says on the back "Rosalind for Clive". Seems like it must be meant for ye.'

'Aye, it does,' snapped Clive. 'Now hand it over.'

Macaulay gave a shrug of his shoulders. 'I suppose I should, though it seems likely ye'll not tell me what she says?'

'Don't be nosy,' said Clive, grabbing the letter. He was away back down the hill without another word.

As Macaulay rode off he looked back at Clive, smiled to himself and wished he were young again.

Clive had only a few moments to wait until the postman was out of sight and then he raced to the building that had been special to him and Ros. As he dropped on to the hay so many memories came racing back but they did not stop him from ripping the envelope open and extracting a sheet of paper. New words in Rosalind's handwriting banished his memories.

My dear Clive,

The news I write here will surprise you: Uncle Gordon is married to a Red Indian. He had never breathed a word about it until we arrived at his ranch and he introduced us. Not one word until this young woman, maybe only a year or two older than me, stepped out of the house to greet and welcome us.

At that moment you could sense the shock we all felt. There were a few seconds in which no one spoke; possibly we were all wondering what to do. Then,

136

Mother trying to hide her surprise, stepped forward and held out her hand to Zalinda (that's her Christian name). I could see relief on her face as she warmly took hold of Mother's hand in return. We were invited inside and Zalinda clapped her hands to summon three nearby Indian girls, each around the age of eighteen; they came in to take our outdoor clothes and escort us to a room where we could refresh ourselves and get rid of our travel dust. Then, in the main room, we found tea and cake served in the British manner, to make us feel at home. It did the trick up to a point; the atmosphere began to grow more easy.

There is much more to tell you, much to decide after we get used to the situation here. No doubt we will consider in due course which way of life, here or in Scotland, will work best for us, but there is one thing I do know: I love you and *will* return, and nothing will change that.

Love,

Rosalind

Fiona finished reading the letter from her sister then sat and absorbed the news. Gordon and his Indian bride ... Fiona tried to put herself in Glenda's shoes but soon knew that she couldn't and could only speculate as to how she might have reacted to the way in which he had broken the fact of his marriage. Surely it would have been kinder to mention it before their arrival? And why had he chosen a Red Indian ... Love? Personal gain? Even as she considered these points Fiona knew she would have an irritating wait before she received more details.

Her thoughts were interrupted by the sound of a galloping horse. Someone in a hurry! She crossed to the window and recognised the rider immediately – Clive Martins. She swung round, hurried to the landing and ran down the stairs. She was on the stone veranda just as Clive brought his horse to a gravel-churning stop. He swung from the saddle and flung his reins over the wooden post. He took the steps to the veranda quickly and was breathing hard when he faced Fiona.

'Sorry, Miss Copeland,' he gasped.

'Come, sit down.' She grasped his arm and led him to a nearby chair. 'I think there's only one reason why you would ride to me at such a pace. News from America!'

He nodded. 'Have you heard?'

'Yes.'

That one word from Fiona sent relief surging through him – he wouldn't have to break the news that Mrs McKinley's brother-in-law had married an American Indian!

'My letter from Rosalind gave me no details,' said Clive.

'Nor did mine from my sister except to say that Mr Gordon's wife is the young daughter of an Indian chief. What it will mean for my sister and her girls, I can't even guess. You and I will have to wait patiently until they have sorted themselves out. Nobody locally knew what the McKinleys wanted from this visit to America but it certainly wasn't this! The next letter might tell us more. All we can do is wait.'

'Will you be answering your letter soon? I'm not sure if I should give any opinion on the matter to Ros; it is hardly my place.'

'Yes, I will answer it. I will be non-committal but will

show interest in what they are doing on the ranch and talk of life here. I suggest you use the same tactic until we learn a little more.'

In the time these letters had taken to reach Scotland, life in Colorado had settled down somewhat.

Zalinda had ordered that the visitors should be allowed to unpack, settle in and recuperate from their days of travelling. Although eager to explore the Circle C, they appreciated the thoughtfulness and the quiet time she had allowed them, even though they knew that she too must be curious about Gordon's relations.

A few minutes after she had woken on their third morning at the Circle C, Glenda heard a tap on her door. In answer to her, 'Come in,' the Indian girl who had been appointed her personal maid entered the room.

Not used to British ways, the girl spoke first. 'Good morning, Mrs McKinley. It is a beautiful morning.' She drew back the curtains and warm sunshine flooded in.

Glenda realised things were going to be very different here. 'Thank you, Namia. Are my daughters awake?'

'I heard talking coming from both rooms but that has stopped. I think they must have gone down to breakfast.'

'Then maybe I'd better hurry.'

With her toilette completed, Glenda chose a closer-fitting yellow cotton blouse and a light grey skirt that fell neatly from the tight waist to the tops of her buttoned black leather ankle boots. She knotted a silk tartan scarf at her throat, examined herself in the mirror, gave her hair a final pat, thanked Namia for her help and left the room to face their third day at the Circle C.

As she walked down the stairs she admired the construction of the building and thought how thrilled John would have been by it. She looked forward to seeing the other buildings. That amused her because she couldn't remember ever having felt that way before. By the time she had reached the bottom of the stairs she thought it must be because she had never lived before in a completely new construction; Pinmuir House had been built in the eighteenth century, and the castle long before. Reaching the hall, she paused and looked back up the sweeping staircase. Gordon had certainly put a lot of thought into this building, but then he had believed they were coming to live here permanently while John was alive.

Chatter and laughter coming from the dining room reminded her of the decisions she would have to make. She stepped quickly to the dining-room door and walked in to find her two daughters seated with Zalinda and Gordon at the long oak table. Glenda remembered then that when they had dined next door for yesterday's evening meal, she had invited her brother-in-law and his wife over for breakfast.

'Good morning,' she said. 'My apologies for being late.'

'No, no, you are not late,' said Zalinda, her tone banishing any guilt Glenda had felt. 'Gordon has always said breakfast is an open meal – have it when it is convenient.'

'But don't be too long, Mama!' urged Caitlin. 'Uncle Gordon's going to let us choose our horses.'

Glenda smiled at her younger daughter's enthusiasm. 'You shouldn't spoil us so,' she said, glancing at her brother-in-law.

'I told you there would be a horse for each of you. You

need one when you live here. They help you to see all that this place has to offer.'

'Please don't refuse,' put in Zalinda, and added, with a touch of amusement as she glanced at her husband, 'When the chief makes such a gesture it would be bad medicine to say no.'

Glenda replied, 'All right, I won't make bad medicine. Thank you very, very much, Gordon.'

'Then eat up. Your daughters are eager to make their choice.' He pushed himself up from the table. 'If you'll excuse me, I'll get my two fastest horsemen to cut out the best animals and drive them into an empty corral where you can take your pick.' He looked hard at Cat and Ros whom he could see were restless to be looking the horses over. 'And you, young ladies, don't rush your mother, let her enjoy her breakfast. Come with me. I'll show you where to wait on the veranda so you can see my cowboys driving the horses into the corral.'

The two young women rose eagerly to their feet to follow him.

When they had gone Zalinda offered more coffee, which Glenda accepted. 'I presume there are riding clothes in the luggage you sent ahead?' the young woman queried.

'Yes. We have brought split skirts.'

'Good. As you are obviously aware, they will be much more convenient for ranch life and will give you the opportunity to do more riding. Anticipating that you would have brought little else for riding, I have provided each of you with a leather waistcoat, slicker and Stetson, which is what the cowboys wear.'

'Zalinda, thank you, but this is far more than being

141

hospitable. We will ever be in your debt.' Glenda was beginning to wonder how she could pay her way. It now seemed a long time since New York when she was suggesting she could repay him by looking after Gordon's house. She felt slightly irritated by the recollection until she heard Zalinda speaking.

'Don't thank me, just be happy with us and for us. Gordon's hopes are fulfilled now that you are here. Of course he always had high hopes that his brother would join him, but he would never have pressured him to do so. Then fate stepped in. He thought all his plans for the future were in vain. I can tell you truly that your decision to visit us with your two daughters has given my husband great joy and healed a wound that was eating at him.'

'Was he really hit so hard by the loss of John?' asked Glenda.

'Oh, yes. You see, marriage was a big step for both of us. When Gordon allowed my father and some of his people to live on his land, my father, as the chief, arranged for the marriage to take place in order to seal the contract between our two peoples. Gordon believed that the presence of his brother and his family would help to quell any antagonism there might be to our marriage. I'm sure your presence here will do much to ease those attitudes.'

'I hope it does. I believe John would not have raised any objection to his brother's marriage to you.'

'I thank you for your support. There were at first strong objections from within my tribe. But even though I am much younger than Gordon, we now have a relationship built on love and the Arapaho and the Circle C employees understand that peace between them is possible. Hopefully that will continue when my brother takes over as chief. I will take you to meet my family sometime in the future, if you are agreeable?'

'Of course. I look forward to it, and no doubt Rosalind and Caitlin will do too. Though it had better be after we have chosen the horses!' Glenda drained her cup and rose from the table.

As they reached the door she stopped and gave Zalinda a warm smile. 'Thank you so much for all you are doing for us. As you will know from my letters to Gordon, Caitlin was badly affected by her father's death and I was advised to take her into a new environment.'

'Gordon told me everything. I hope the spirits of my world can help her. I believe they will, particularly if you believe it too.'

'I will trust that your spirits will unite with my God, and that their union will be enough to help my child make a full recovery.'

17

On hearing footsteps coming on to the veranda from the house, Caitlin and Ros spun round.

'Mama, how are you going to choose from all these horses?' asked Caitlin.

'Your uncle has certainly set us a problem but no doubt we'll hear some good advice,' Glenda replied.

'You will, and maybe even from me,' laughed Zalinda. 'I was hardly ever off a horse until I met Gordon. Even then we rode often together and, because I know this country, I was a great help to him. Well, I like to think I was.'

'Looking around, I'm sure you were. I didn't expect the Circle C to be as large as it is nor to find it so well organised.'

'It has to be if you run as many cattle as we do, as you will see in the fall when many of them will set out for the eastern states. It's a stirring sight, hundreds and hundreds of steers under the eyes of as many as sixty cowboys. Today some of those men will be eyeing the horses for the purpose of that cattle drive and may select some from those mustered in the big corral for you and your daughters to choose from. Would you like to look them over now?'

Glenda nodded. 'This is going to be so interesting and so different from home. Our ponies are bred for hardiness rather than speed.'

'Don't worry, when it comes to horse-talk the men here are not shy in coming forward with advice, particularly when they are offering it to such pretty listeners! But, whoever you listen to, make sure to let the final choice be yours. After all, you are going to be the horse's rider.'

As they watched the horses Ros commented, 'They look a wonderful herd, I wish Clive could have seen them.'

'Is that your man?' Zalinda asked her casually.

'Yes,' replied Rosalind, smiling at the Indian's turn of phrase.

'You'll have to bring him here one day.'

'I'd love to do that,' she answered wistfully.

'We must bear it in mind,' promised Zalinda. 'What is his work?'

'He's employed on our estate. At present he and his father are looking after it for us.'

'You must tell me about that sometime. I have only heard about it from Gordon so far and it must have changed since he left Scotland.'

Before any further exchanges could be made, Caitlin interrupted them. 'Look we have to go. Uncle is waving to us from the corral.'

'He must be satisfied with the horses Spike and Joe have assembled for you.'

Glenda and her daughters matched their pace to that of Zalinda as they hurried to the corral in high spirits.

'How many horses do you think they have in there?' asked Ros. 'I've been trying to count them.'

'Impossible when they're on the move.' Zalinda considered then said, 'But I reckon close on thirty-four.'

Gordon was waiting for them at the corral gate. 'All ready?' he asked. They nodded while eagerly eyeing the horses. 'Good, here's what we do. The adjoining corral is the one in which Spike and Joe will assemble your choices as you make them. After you have done so they will see that the others are returned to the herd. Take your time, there's no rush, make sure you have the one you really want.'

'What if we both pick the same horse?' asked Ros.

'I don't think that is likely but, if it does happen, Spike or Joe will remove it and replace it with another.'

'So neither of us will get our first choice?'

'Doing it my way saves any dispute. You accept that?'

'Yes,' the three of them chorused.

'Very well, let's get on with it. Look them over.'

Cat climbed up the pole rungs of the fence to the top one, on which she settled for a better view of the horses. She knew for her this was going to be a difficult task.

Circle C cowboys began to drift towards the corral when they realised what was taking place.

'Do ya reckon they'll know what they're about?' asked one cowboy. His face, battered by the wind and browned by the sun, betrayed time spent in Colorado's hills and mountains.

'They've dressed as if they do, but I reckon some of those horses will think different.'

'Who are they?'

'I had time off like you. I was in Denver but heard tell of

them when I got back. The Boss's sister-in-law and her two daughters are here for an indefinite period.'

'Husbands?'

'She's a widow; her daughters are single.'

'Mm, fancy-looking pieces, all of them.'

'Get that out of your mind. *Don't* fall foul of the Boss or you'll be spitting blood somewhere out on the prairie. He'll not pull his punches if you step out of line. And remember, I don't want any backlash, which there'll be if you cause trouble – I recommended you to the Boss because you're a damned good cattleman, but that will count for nothing for both of us if you try anything on. Keep your nose out of the Boss's family life.'

'All right. Quit worrying. I ain't goin' to upset this outfit. And we might be in for a show now.' The man nodded in the direction of the corral where Glenda was making her choice of horse.

She was glad John had taught her what to look for in their ponies and horses even though they did not keep many back in Scotland. After looking at one or two and comparing their points, she noticed a beautiful grey that reminded her of John's horse when she'd first known him. First she checked the animal's teeth; next she gently ran her hand over its forelegs indicating that she meant it no harm, yet with a touch firm enough to judge the animal's strength. The grey's hide was healthy and its skin revealed continuous care. Glenda stood back from it and took in aspects of its stance and the way it held itself. She particularly liked its lithe yet strong body. She voiced this to Gordon, who had been standing close by without expressing any opinion.

147

'You are right,' he replied. 'She is one of my best six mares. This breed was Spanish in origin and mixed with good racehorse stock.'

'And what was the outcome?'

'They had the strength and staying power of our general working horses, but from the imported stock gained speed and agility. They can outrun stampeding cattle and are agile enough to get in the most awkward places, to stop the animals from straying when we are driving them to cattle towns. You couldn't imagine the work they get through. The cowboy spends long hours in the saddle; his horse is so much a part of his life that it is held in great affection. We call them quarter horses because in some parts they were raced over a quarter of a mile.'

Glenda nodded with interest and was truly satisfied with her choice. Then she noticed her eldest daughter. 'I think Ros is near to making a decision too. She's in serous discussion with your manager.'

Gordon nodded. 'She's in good hands. Mark taught me a lot when I came into ranching. My niece will find no one better to give her advice about the horse she has chosen.'

Rosalind had taken the horse's bridle, Mark beside her, and they were approaching Gordon and Glenda.

'Miss McKinley has made her choice,' said Mark. Ros was pleased with the admiration heaped on her horse, a lean, shapely animal that seemed to be enjoying hearing its praises sung. Ros also showed delight at what was being said, for it confirmed that she was a good judge of horses even though her experience had been on a smaller scale in Scotland. She wondered what Clive would think, seeing so

148

many horses, one of which was a beautiful dun colour and would, in a few minutes, be hers.

'Ready, young lady?' The query from Gordon startled her, cutting into her dream world. 'Is this the one you've chosen?'

'Yes, Uncle. And thank you, not only for the horse, which I will call Brandy to toast this wonderful day, but also because you have widened my eyes to the variety within this world. It has been fascinating and I already love my new mount.'

Gordon called to the limping cowboy who had taken over the charge of Glenda's choice. 'Another one for your stable, Buck. Reckon you can manage these two, Suzie and Brandy, for some lovely ladies?'

'Just try me. They both have an eye for outstanding horseflesh. It will be my pleasure to look after their mounts.' Buck touched the brim of his Stetson as he inclined his head to each woman in turn.

'Right, that's settled,' said Gordon. 'Now for Caitlin,' he added, looking around for his younger niece.

'As a matter of fact, she seems to be talking about a horse now,' said Rosalind.

Glenda and Gordon glanced across the corral to the group that had gathered when Caitlin left her perch.

'Maybe I'd better go to her,' said Glenda.

'It strikes me she is holding her own with Sid, who is an expert on the type of horse she looks to be interested in. Leave her to put her own questions. Zalinda is with them but she'll see Caitlin makes the right decision, without appearing to intrude.'

Glenda's lip tightened. Gordon had no right to interfere

149

in what was a matter for mother and daughter. Then another thought struck her – was that what John would have said? She bit her lip, feeling a pang of jealousy at the way Zalinda appeared to be usurping a role she herself should be taking.

'What do you think, Cat?' Zalinda asked the girl.

'I certainly like the look of her. Her brown and white coat is so different and those eyes are so appealing, as if she's pleading to be mine. But is she on the small side?'

'That doesn't hinder her capabilities, as you will see.' Gordon called to the young Indian brave who was standing with the horse. 'Ahote, ride Gila for Miss McKinley to see how she performs.'

'Yes, Boss,' Ahote replied with enthusiasm. He tapped the horse as he turned and sprang in one quick movement on to its back. The horse took his weight without flinching and waited for another command. The Indian whispered something and Gila started walking. Ahote guided the horse with care through the throng of people, and then with the open space before him put the animal into a trot, holding that pace until they reached the end of the corral. There he turned the horse and brought it to a stop. The Indian surveyed the area before him. As if the audience had read his mind they cleared a space for horse and rider. No one could hear what was said then but whatever it was brought an instant reaction from Gila. In a flash she was into a gallop. The earth flew beneath her hooves, faster and faster, until people said she covered the ground without touching it.

About two hundred yards from the end of the corral, Ahote whispered an order. Gila almost simultaneously came to a halt. After a moment the Indian gave another

150

order. The horse turned on the spot; another order and it stepped sideways. It kept moving that way until ordered into another manoeuvre. The demonstration of the horse's capabilities went on until Gordon called a halt.

'There you are, Caitlin. A horse that has been trained to move and herd cattle, and one that has picked up, on her own, how to negotiate all manner of obstacles in the landscape in all weathers. You might never need that, but on the other hand one day your life could hang on it. Better to be prepared. What do you think? Is she the horse for you?'

Gordon had barely finished speaking before Caitlin was saying, 'Oh, yes, please, Uncle Gordon. Yes, please!'

'Very well, she's yours. But there is one condition.'

'Anything, Uncle Gordon, anything!'

'I see great disappointment on the face of that young Indian who has an attachment to Gila. I don't want any ill feeling to be caused by my giving her to you, so I am making Ahote responsible for looking after Gila for you. The skewbald is also known as the Indian's horse in these parts and Ahote has trained her well.'

The concern Ahote had felt disappeared in a flash. There was relief and joy in his dark eyes.

After most people had dispersed, Glenda waited for Caitlin. She did not like her being alone with a man who came from people who had, until fairly recently, waged war against the white man. She watched closely as Caitlin turned to Ahote and said, 'I admire the way you rode like that without a saddle. I will keep her name as Gila, and I thank you for training her so well. You must let me know what commands you use for her.'

She looked thoughtful as she gazed at a horse she had

18

Fiona was surprised to see a dejected-looking Clive leaning on the open gate leading to Pinmuir. He should have been working outside on the estate, taking his chance while the fine weather was still with them. He must have heard her horse approach and would normally have been instantly alert to find out who was coming. But not today. The hunched shoulders, his body slumped against the gate, told a different story.

Since the family had left, Fiona had become a more regular visitor here and did not show the airs and graces she might once have done. 'What's wrong with you?' she called as she brought her horse to a stop. There was no reply. She swung from the saddle and dropped to the ground. 'There should be no time for displays of misery on such a fine day as this. Whatever is biting you wants dealing with. Come on, tell me.' As he turned to lean his back against the gate, she saw his miserable expression and made a guess as to the reason. 'Bad news from America?'

'Not really, Miss Fiona, although I haven't had a letter

from Ros for a long while and that isn't like her. Maybe she's getting to like America too much. However, my immediate trouble is, I've no horse. Bonnie died four days ago.'

'One day's mourning then get on with life. We can't stand still because an animal has died.'

'That's harsh. Bonnie has been with me a long time, my constant companion. Besides, animals are kinder than humans and serve us without complaint,' answered Clive.

'There are plenty of other horses. We'll find you one. We have to or you'll be stuck here and won't be able to give the McKinley Estate the attention it deserves. Apart from that, I need you to have one.'

'Please don't start talking in riddles, Miss Fiona, I'm in no mood for them.'

'Nor am I. And I've told you before, forget the Miss – in a funny way it reminds me that I'm missing out on life. Now, young man, first we must deal with the horse problem.' There was no doubt Fiona was taking charge. 'Let us go to the house. Perhaps you could ask Mrs Lynch or your mother to make us a cup of tea, which we can enjoy outside while I make you a proposition.'

Once the tea had been organised and Fiona and Clive were settled outside she took up her story again.

'I was coming to tell you that my niece, who has just arrived back from touring Europe with family friends, is intending to stay with me for some time while her father's away and I hoped you would entertain her and remind her of our countryside. She is a little younger than you, a nice-looking girl but is a bit of a snob. She has no real reason to be. Gets that from Roger. It wants stamping out of her if she is to ...'

'And you expect me to do that?' Clive interrupted, showing incredulity at the request. 'I have plenty of work to do here.'

'Don't be too obvious about it. Anyway, it won't be every day; only on days I won't be around and the weather is fine. I think knowing you and being with you will do the trick . . . put her down a peg or two. Now, don't look so doubtful. A fine young man like you should have no difficulty in entertaining my niece and I dare say you might even enjoy it. I'll finance any expenses you incur. I expect co-operation and help from you. You need a horse, don't you?' The tone with which she put the question and gave him an encouraging smile left him in no doubt as to her inference.

'You're putting me in a corner – the offer of a new horse in exchange for my help?'

Fiona said nothing but gave a little nod.

'How do I explain it to my parents?'

'What is the point in trying to keep it a secret? Tell them the truth, a friend is helping a friend.'

'I suppose there's no harm in it, when you put it that way.'

'Then we have a deal?'

'Yes, but there is a condition.'

'What is that?'

'No word of this must reach Rosalind.'

'I wouldn't dream of writing to her about our arrangement.'

Clive hesitated for a moment then held out his hand to accept Fiona's, sealing the agreement.

'I'll return tomorrow morning at ten o'clock. Then we'll go and find you another horse.'

*

Fiona was as good as her word; she arrived at Pinmuir House just as the hands on the mantelpiece clock reached ten o'clock.

'Good morning, Mrs Martins.'

'Good morning, Miss Copeland, you have brought a fine day. Please come in and enjoy a cup of tea before you set off.'

'That is very kind,' returned Fiona.

Mrs Martins stepped to one side to allow her to enter the house. As Fiona did so she said, laughing, 'I'm going to follow my nose. There's such a wonderful smell of baking.'

Mrs Martins raised her eyebrow as Fiona headed for the kitchen. 'Mrs Lynch isn't very tidy. It's a mess in there,' she said, with a small note of protest in her voice.

'I don't mind, I don't expect tidiness in a kitchen,' called Fiona, continuing on her way.

In a few moments she was seated at the table, taking her first sip of tea.

'This is very kind of you, seeing about replacing poor old Bonnie. She had a long life,' said Mrs Martins.

'And I'm sure a good one,' commented Fiona.

'Clive thought the world of her. He was wondering what he was going to do without her. He could have borrowed Rosalind's Freya but she's too delicate for the kind of work he sometimes has to do. Your kind offer has eased his problem. The laddie needs a strong horse, and we had thought that he and his father could share, but that wouldn't have worked. You've stepped in at the right moment. My husband is sorry he isn't here to see you but he had work started at the northern limits of the estate that he hoped to complete today.'

156

The chat continued after Clive had joined them but having finished her tea Fiona was eager to be away.

Clive borrowed Freya and as they set off, Fiona said, 'I have four horse dealers in mind. Three of them combine their trade with farming, the other is a case of dabbling; if he sees a good horse, which he believes he can sell on at a good profit, he buys it. He knows good horseflesh is more expensive but you'll know you've bought good stock. We'll leave him until last.'

'I've always been pleased with the trader we've dealt with in the past,' said Clive, with slight annoyance in his voice. He intended to make sure he remained in charge.

So the hunt for a horse started, with Clive's mind set on obtaining a good-tempered mount, strong, capable of hard work in all weathers, and agile enough to meet with hazards of the Highland terrain.

They had visited two of the dealers but written one of them off as they were not impressed by the horses he had on offer. Fiona and Clive rode on to Glentorrent, the village five miles further on, and then she turned her horse towards some level ground behind the Trooper's Arms, a coaching inn.

'I hope you are as hungry as I am,' she said, drawing her horse to a halt.

'I hadn't thought of it,' Clive replied, following her, 'but now you've mentioned it, I wouldn't mind something.'

'Then let's away in. I have been here before and had an enjoyable meal. Let's see if we can say the same this time.'

Clive helped her from the saddle and looked a little embarrassed on following her into the inn.

'Where do I want to be?' he whispered.

'Right opposite me when we sit down.'

'But . . .'

'No buts about it,' she replied. 'Get used to it. One day you could be Laird of Pinmuir. Practise on my niece Adrianna. She wouldn't hold back but have the servants at such a place running around like scalded cats. You must teach her to do it in a more pleasant way.'

'Seems to me, Miss Fiona, you've all this worked out.'

'It's a good idea to keep one step ahead. I'm going to enjoy today's venison pie,' she said, indicating the board behind the bar. 'You relax and do the same.'

Clive's sharp mind helped him to observe closely and to keep what he'd learned in mind. He left the inn feeling more confident about the life that could await him when Rosalind returned from America.

Whether it was the result of the food or the relaxed atmosphere neither of them could decide but, whatever it was, at their next destination they quickly found a horse they both liked and thought would be ideal for work around the McKinley Estate. Clive felt sure his new acquisition would also become a favourite with Rosalind. He must start singing its praises to counteract the comments she was making about the horses on her uncle's ranch.

On their return Clive put all three horses in the stable, giving the name Merlin to his new mount.

'Did you succeed?' asked Jessie.

'Yes, we did,' replied Clive. 'Third place we visited. Struck a good bargain, didn't we, Miss Copeland? Well, you did.'

'Of course, always leave bargaining to the ladies.'

'Come in, Miss. Mrs Lynch saved some scones for your return but I can get you something else, if you wish.'

'No, thank you. We had a splendid lunch, but you do tempt me with your scones.'

They settled down to tell her about their day and to wait for the return of her husband. Time slipped away unnoticed until Jessie exclaimed, 'Oh, my goodness, it's dark. I wonder where Greg is?' She automatically left her chair and started closing the curtains. 'It's too dark for you to be venturing home, Miss Copeland. I've a bed made up if you'd like to wait until morning.'

'That is extremely kind, and I won't say no to you. I can't say I'm too fond of travelling in the dark.' After a slight pause she added, 'Please, my name is Fiona.'

'Did Father arrive after we had gone to bed?' asked Clive when he came into the kitchen the next morning.

Jessie gave a little shake of her head. 'No. I expect his work kept him too late to get back. He'll have stayed somewhere close to where he was working.'

That morning Clive chose to work near home and be there for his father's arrival. Fiona said she would check things were in order on the estate as she had promised to write to Glenda. She had expected to talk to Greg Martins concerning the book-keeping.

But that expectation weakened as the day wore on.

Fiona could wait no longer to return home and, as she was leaving the Martins, could see anxiety beginning to creep into Jessie's mind.

'As I am standing in for Glenda, please get word to me if

your husband doesn't arrive tonight,' said Fiona. 'It doesn't matter what time, day or night. I'll come over. One of the footmen can accompany me.' When Jessie hesitated, she added firmly, 'Promise, or Glenda will never forgive me.'

'I'll have Clive, but I promise I'll call you if necessary. I'm sure Greg will be back soon.'

But when darkness began to close across the Highlands, Jessie was not so certain.

19

'I'll have a quick breakfast then go and look for Father. I know where he was working.'

Clive's mother's usually bright and cheerful face was now cloudy by concern. Her face was drawn and pallor had overcome her familiar bloom.

'I'll tell Mrs Lynch to pack you some food.'

'Don't bother. I'll have my breakfast and if I need anything later I'll get something elsewhere.'

'Very well.'

Clive hurried his breakfast. He drained his cup of tea, grabbed his jacket and cap. 'I'll get Merlin ready,' he said, and hurried to the stable.

'Your first job for us is an errand of hope,' he said as he patted the horse's neck.

Five minutes later he hugged his mother, Merlin waiting patiently beside them.

'Find my Greg,' she whispered in Merlin's ear. The horse nodded its head as if it understood.

'Get word to Miss Copeland if you need her for anything at all,' said Clive.

His mother patted his arm and said, 'I will.' Then, with hope in her heart, she watched him ride away.

After riding three miles he voiced his praise for Merlin. 'Good boy. Already I can feel you are at home with us.' He was grateful to Miss Copeland for making a keen assessment of the animal and advising him to buy it. Clive had feared that when the McKinleys had left for America she would interfere in the running of the estate, but she had not; shown interest, yes, but did not attempt to alter the arrangements left in place by her sister. Clive showed keenness and ability but he and his father approached Fiona for advice if it was a decision of financial importance. Now he was pleased he had done so over the choice of the horse.

He rode at a steady pace on a trail that took him northwards towards the area he knew his father had been working in. Although he felt sure Greg would have a good reason for not returning home yesterday, something was telling him that all was not right. This was further than he would normally have gone and he was leaving Pinmuir land. Clive reached a tiny village he thought his father would have used as a base and decided to seek news of him there before venturing further.

He halted Merlin outside an inn that looked as if it had seen better days. Clive secured the bridle to a hook in the wall, gave Merlin a friendly pat, and went in to seek information. The taproom was gloomy but tidy. A well-built man was leaning on the counter talking with three men seated at a table on which stood tankards of ale. Clive did not recognise any of them. One of the men was wiping foam from

162

his lips. The conversation ceased as they all turned their attention to this stranger who had interrupted their drinking.

'Good day,' said Clive, a little tentatively, feeling eyes boring into him.

'Good day to you,' returned the landlord. He reached for an empty tankard in anticipation of an order as he looked enquiringly at Clive.

Though he wanted information and then to be on his way, Clive thought it best to acknowledge the landlord's gesture, so he nodded.

'Riding through?' queried the landlord as he prepared to pull a draught of ale.

'I'll be able to answer that if you can answer my question.' Clive made his request in a friendly tone and noted the suspicion in the landlord's eyes lift a little.

'What might you be wanting to know?' he asked.

Clive became aware that the three men at the table had stopped talking. His exchanges with the landlord must have caught their attention.

'I'm from the Pinmuir Estate and I'm looking for my father. I know he was working near the northern boundary; he had expected the job to take only a day and a half but he has not been home for nearly three days now. My mother was getting worried so, as I said, I've come to find him.'

Knowing that he had captured their attention, Clive turned so that all the men were in his field of vision. He caught reactions that made him believe these men knew something. He was about to tackle them when the landlord spoke up, 'Aye, I reckon we do. Angus here will tell you the story.'

The other man averted his eyes as he spoke.

163

'It isna a pleasant tale, mind ... We, that is Jock and I ... found him this morning. We were late leaving home so took a short cut. It is not a good idea unless you know the track. It's narrow and treacherous in parts, with some nasty drops. One false step can be fatal. Jock and I spotted a figure at the bottom of a precipice. It took us twenty minutes to get safely down to him. Before we drew near we could tell the accident had killed him. We got back here as soon as we could.'

Clive could barely take in what he was hearing. There had to be a mistake surely.

The landlord took up the story. 'We laid your father in one of the outhouses and reported it to the local constable. He took the matter in hand.'

'Has my father's body been removed?' asked Clive automatically, not knowing what the procedure would be.

'No, but we are expecting information about that very soon.'

'May I see him?'

'I would let you but the constable was very firm – no one to see him until I receive permission to release the body.'

Clive nodded, feeling numb with grief and shock.

The landlord drew another ale and put the tankard in front of him. 'Drink that and follow it with this.' He poured a whisky and put the glass in front of Clive. 'You look as though you could do with it.'

He was halfway through his ale when the door was opened and a burly man strode in.

'Constable said you have a body here that needs removing. Anybody know where to?' When there was no immediate response the man barked again, 'Come on,

164

somebody must know something. I have a coffin ready; it's outside. I want this job finished so I can get back to my home.'

Clive straightened. His eyes steely, he rejoined, 'I know about the body. It is my father's and you'll show him proper respect throughout.'

The other man was about to reply, but under the accusing gaze of the occupants of the bar, thought better of it. 'Where is he?' he grunted.

'Locked in one of my outhouses,' said the landlord.

The undertaker gave a little mocking laugh. 'Did you think he was going to run away?'

Clive scowled. 'What did I tell you? Respect the dead.'

The landlord led the way to the outhouse and within fifteen minutes the coffin was on a cart and underway. The so-called undertaker grumbled complaints about the time it was taking.

When they were in sight of Pinmuir Estate, Clive gave the man final directions to reach the McKinleys' house and then rode on to forewarn his mother.

Five days later, Greg Martins was laid to rest by the Reverend Kintail in the tiny cemetery at Gartonhag, with only Jessie, Fiona, Clive, the doctor and a few villagers in attendance.

That evening three letters were written at Pinmuir.

20

Glenda and her daughters settled into ranch life. Some of the cowboys had married quarters, which were central to the daily life of all. Glenda was welcomed in to their rooms by the wives and found they were meeting places for knitting, sewing and quilt-making groups, while other women shared their kitchens for banking and jam making. Glenda, however, soon discovered they were really places where friendships were built and laughter shared. Gordon had built a wooden schoolhouse where Mrs Bradley took charge of about thirty children for a few hours a day. She welcomed the input by Rosalind, whose stories of her own land with its green hillsides and frequent lochs filled the children with delight. Cat followed the daily chores of the ranch alongside the cowboys, riding Gila whenever she could.

Zalinda joined in the frequent activities when she could but today was a special day for her and the McKinleys.

'Uncle Gordon and Zalinda are arriving at eleven o'clock. We must see that our horses are ready and all of us prepared for the ride, which might take an hour at a good pace,' Glenda instructed. 'It would not be polite to arrive at the Arapaho encampment late; in fact, they would take it as an insult if we do. Your uncle would not want that after all the hard work he and Mark have put in, encouraging the chief to establish this settlement on friendly terms. Mark will be riding with us.' Glenda glanced at the wall clock. 'We have an hour and a half to get ready.' She rose from the table and left the room.

'This is the start of an exciting day,' said Caitlin. 'Are you looking forward to it, Ros?'

'Yes, I am. I didn't think I would be at first but I am curious as to how the Arapaho live, especially as they're our neighbours.'

'There's twenty miles or so between us,' Cat pointed out.

'I know, but no one else lives on that stretch of land. Hasn't Ahote offered to take you to their village?'

Making sure she was out of hearing of her mother, Caitlin answered, 'I asked him but he refused, telling me it would not be right until the chief had made his formal invitation and we had met the whole tribe.'

'So he sticks to tribal rules and Indian law?'

'Of course, but he also appreciates what Uncle Gordon has done in mending the tribe's relationships with the white man. He goes along with Uncle Gordon's philosophy of the best thing for his land being harmony, as does their chief now.'

'All very noble but will that ever be totally achieved?' said Ros doubtfully.

'Who knows?' said Caitlin. 'But it is up to everyone to try.'

'Yes, I agree,' said Ros. She made no further comment, but was struck by the thought that she had not until then realised that her sister had truly grown up or that this young Indian had made such an impression on her. Now she was looking forward to the coming visit with even more interest and ran to the stables, followed by Cat, to prepare Brandy and Gila.

With Gordon in charge, the party set out for the Arapaho encampment.

Although they had been aware of the magnificence of the distant Rockies, they were nevertheless struck by the spectacle as they rode out to an escarpment in the foothills. Though still thirty miles away, it was as if the mountains had suddenly risen from the ground to remind intruders of the power they held over them.

Glenda automatically halted her horse to look at the view. Gordon, alongside her, was quick to react. 'Ten-minute break!' he called.

They swung to the ground and walked the few yards to the point he had indicated would give them the best view.

When they reached the position Caitlin gasped, 'What a glorious sight!'

'Yes, quite wonderful, but no better than the views we've seen in our own Highlands,' commented Rosalind.

'Don't be stupid,' snapped Cat. 'You've never seen anything like this at home.'

'I'll grant you that. All I'm saying is that, in their own way, the Scottish Highlands can be just as impressive.'

'I think you've got a case of sour grapes because you aren't with Clive,' snapped Caitlin, feeling nervous at the prospect of this meeting with Ahote and his people.

'Rubbish! Say what you like, but I think you are becoming . . .' Rosalind's retort was cut short by her sister.

'There are no buts about it. You were obsessed with Clive before we left home and you are carrying him around in your mind even now.'

'No, I'm not,' said Rosalind, crossing her fingers behind her back at the lie.

'Oh, shut up and enjoy the scenery.'

Rosalind made no reply, nor comment, but silently agreed that from here the foothills made a wonderful introduction to the sweeping panorama of the mighty Rockies. The different shades of green, brown and yellow that dressed the lower slopes gave way to darker tones of brown, grey and black as the great mountain range soared above them, topped by splashes of snow that had found shelter from the sun.

Rosalind gave a silent sigh, wishing that Clive were standing beside her now, the beauty they witnessed drawing them closer and closer.

Their mother, who had caught some of the girls' conversation, allowed her lips to twitch in amusement.

Mark, standing close by, had also caught the sisters' exchange. As his lips curled into a little smile he saw Glenda too had been amused by her daughters' repartee. 'Does this often happen?' he asked.

She grinned. 'Reasonably often, but it never gets out of hand. They are the best of friends usually.'

'That's good,' he said.

'I'm thankful for it.'

Zalinda then came over to them and said, 'Gordon says we must be on our way again.'

At that they heard his voice shout, 'Mount up!'

Gordon's call had shattered Rosalind's dreams of Clive's arms around her.

'Boss is eager to be on,' commented Mark. As he walked with Glenda to her horse, he said, 'I've noticed you've been handling your horse very well. It's not always easy with a new mount but you have a natural gift, as do your daughters, most notably Caitlin.' He helped Glenda mount, which prompted him to say, 'Are you comfortable with our American saddle, Ma'am?'

She waited until he was on his own horse and Gordon had shouted 'Let's ride' before she answered.

'Yes. It was a little strange at first but after a few attempts I felt at home. I can understand why you cowboys need the design you use.'

Mark smiled. 'Today you may witness how the Indians ride, without any saddle, just as Ahote did the day Cat chose Gila. She and that horse hit it off straight away. It was good to see,' he said 'and it hasn't taken you long either to get used to our way of life.'

'Yes, I do enjoy watching you cattlemen working with the steers.' She left a fraction of a pause then said, 'If I am to call you Mark, which I prefer, then if you have no objection you should forget Ma'am and call me Glenda or Glen, I don't mind which.'

Mark touched the brim of his Stetson with two fingers and said, 'As you command, Glen.'

She saw relief in his smile and the atmosphere eased.

'By the way, Glen, that young man Ahote ... I noticed you were a little worried about the attention he has been giving Caitlin and how she responds. Don't let it cause you any alarm. He is an honourable young fellow. You can see that from his attitude when your daughter chose the horse he had trained and adored. I rather think Ahote had hoped he would one day have done enough to keep Gila for himself. That was why, when Cat chose her, Gordon put him in charge of the horse, so that there would be no cause for jealousy. You need have no worries about him, Glen.'

She smiled at him warmly. 'Thanks for the reassurance, Mark.'

They rode on without speaking, each sensing that they could enjoy silence together.

After ten miles riding through the foothills Gordon led the way from the escarpment into a grassy valley. In four miles it widened and the trail became more marked. When it turned, to be close to the flowing waters of a wide stream, they were met by the sight of twenty tepees spaced around and close to a rising mound that gave them shelter from the prevailing west wind. The tepees, with their colourful decorations, showed no sign of life.

Zalinda slowed the visitors to a walking pace as they approached the middle tepee. After a few moments the covered entrance in the side was drawn back. Zalinda and Gordon brought the party to a halt. At that moment an Indian stepped out. He was wearing a fringed and patterned buckskin tunic. On his head were two or three feathers and around his neck were beads of bright colours. He drew himself up proudly, feet set slightly apart, perfectly balanced. His dark eyes shone with pleasure at seeing his daughter again.

He stepped forward and held out his arms to Zalinda, who rested her head against his chest, as she had while a child. He moved her aside and held out his hand in welcome to Gordon's party.

'I am Chief Ouray.' Then, sweeping his arms to indicate the members of his tribe, who had appeared outside their tepees, he said, 'I and my people welcome you to our humble homes. Mr Gordon's relations are our friends. I hope your stay in our country is without care. I will meet each of you now and then we will feast.'

He made a gesture to indicate they should go inside his large tepee. In the centre was a hearth where meat was cooking. Smoke rose up to escape from a central hole. The chief signalled for the party to sit themselves down on the buffalo hides spread out on the ground before them. Young women brought in a variety of food. The wild turkey and deer meat were supplemented with herbs, prairie turnips and potatoes. At this sight Glenda realised how hungry she was.

When all was ready, six sharp beats on a drum signalled the time to eat but also brought silence from the few Indians and cowboys who had gathered together. Chief Ouray spoke a few words in his own language.

Cat glanced at Ahote, who had joined her. 'Thanks to Manitou, the Great Spirit, for this food and for our friends,' he translated in a whisper.

Heads were still bowed and Gordon also gave thanks; then they ate. Rosalind, Cat and their mother exchanged looks as they picked up their food with their fingers.

'What a wonderful gathering and greeting,' said Cat to Ahote. 'Don't you think so, Mama?' she added, turning to her mother.

'Yes, I do,' she replied, then curtly acknowledged Ahote without any real warmth.

'Mr Gordon is good to us,' said Ahote. 'He handed over land for us to live on when other people of our tribe were being sent to reservations. Although we used to be a nomadic people, Mrs McKinley, your brother-in-law helped us by teaching our men to do ranch work. Now Indians and cowboys work alongside each other with the cattle and horses. Mr Gordon has a huge area of prairie and wonderful grassland that spreads into the foothills of the mountains. You must let me show you some time.' As if to emphasise that, he added, 'You know how to choose a good horse, Mrs McKinley.'

'Thank you, Ahote. I noted your pleasure in the one my daughter chose; you too have an eye for a good horse.'

'They have been and always will be my life.'

'I would like to meet your mother and father, are they here?' asked Rosalind.

Ahote shook his head as sadness came to his eyes. 'Alas, no, they were killed by another tribe who raided for gain. I was only a baby then. An Arapaho found me wrapped in a blanket and hidden under a tree trunk. My mother must have quickly put me there out of sight. I am ever grateful to her for doing that and to the Arapaho chief of that time for adopting me.'

'So you are not related to Zalinda?' asked Rosalind.

'No. She is Chief Ouray's daughter,' he replied.

After the meal a display of Indian skills on horseback held them enthralled. Glenda was so absorbed by them that she had been unaware of Mark joining her. She started when he said, 'Did you enjoy that?'

'It was breathtaking. They are such wonderful riders, you'd believe they were born in the saddle.'

He smiled as he said, 'Without a saddle!'

She laughed. 'Yes, you're right, of course.'

'Chief Ouray is sorry he has to leave you now to talk with Gordon before we return to the Circle C, but gave permission for me to show you and your daughters around their encampment. They will welcome you, especially if you are with me.'

'You are close to them?'

'I like to think so. They are good people.'

Glenda sensed a deeper understanding developing between her and Mark, but it was to be interrupted by the arrival of two letters the following week.

21

Dear Mrs McKinley,

I am sorry to be burdening you with bad news at this time. My beloved Greg has died as the result of a fall while working in a remote region at the northern end of the estate. He was working alone and not found for three days. Clive went in search of him and was able to return with his father's body.

The funeral has taken place in Gartonhag. Reverend Kintail conducted the service and spoke well of Greg. The attendance was small but we expected no more from the remote area in which we live.

With your permission, if this loss will mean changes for you, Clive and I will carry on until we hear from you.

In sadness, my regards,
Jessie Martins

Dear Glenda,

You will no doubt have received a letter informing you of the terrible tragedy that has befallen Mrs Martins and Clive. From what was gleaned when Clive went to look for him, it appears his father took what he believed to be a short cut, but unsure of the changing terrain, fell down a precipice resulting in his death.

Mrs Martins and Clive are bearing up very well. I have assured them that you would wish for them to carry on while you consider the situation. I hope I did right?

I have our niece Adrianna coming to stay with me for a few weeks whilst her father has to be away. She has recently returned from abroad and it seems she is growing up too fast for Roger's liking. He wants me to take over the role of mother to her! What does he expect me, a maiden aunt, to do with her? She is a high-spirited girl . . . or should I say young woman? Ah, well, life can bring unwanted tasks! We have to cope with them and hopefully gain something from them. My competence will be severely tested, no doubt.

I do hope life in Colorado is proving interesting.

My love to you, to my two nieces and to Gordon.

Your sister,

Fiona

Glenda's immediate reaction on reading her letters was, 'I should be there. I must go. Oh, why am I so far away when I'm needed?' Irritated, she stamped her foot. But this was no way for her to be acting. Nothing positive could be achieved here. That could only be done by going to Scotland. There would be much to decide and act upon. It was no good expecting problems to solve themselves. Plans must be made. She called out to one of the Indian servants, who appeared as if from nowhere.

'Namia, please find my daughter Rosalind and tell her I want to see her as quickly as possible.'

Namia sped from the house. She had seen Rosalind heading for the stables. In a few minutes the message had been delivered and the girl was hurrying to the house.

'You wanted me, Mama?'

'Yes. Bad news, I am sorry to say.'

'What's wrong, Mama?'

Without considering the contents Glenda held out the letters from Mrs Martins and Aunt Fiona. 'Read these.'

Rosalind took the letters and read the one from Jessie first. She paled at the tragic news. Then she read the letter from her aunt. She saw confirmation of the news about Greg and her aunt's description of Adrianna. A lively young lady in the vicinity? Was she the reason Clive had not corresponded with Ros lately, not even to report his father's death? Had he already met Adrianna and become mesmerised by her? As hard as Rosalind tried to dismiss this idea the more it persisted, taking precedence over what her mother was saying.

'Ros, I fear I must return to Scotland immediately. Changes will have to be made at Pinmuir. Do we wish to return there permanently or to move here? I had not expected to have to face such a choice until we had given life here a full test. Nor did I wish to do so until I was certain that Cat was completely cured of her nightmares.

177

Though she is sleeping better there are still times when I hear her having uneasy nights. She has been doing well, but this news of Mr Martins might just tip the balance again. I don't like leaving her but I feel I must attend to Pinmuir's future in person.'

'Oh, Mama, please may I go too? I am sure Caitlin will be safe here. Besides, you will need a travelling companion. Please, please.'

Her daughter's plea was difficult to refuse, but Glenda answered by taking Ros's hands in hers and saying, 'Oh, my dear, dear girl, I know you want to go back. You love Scotland so much, and besides I know you will want to support Clive, but I need you here. Yes, Cat's nightmares are a part of it but I worry also about her getting too close to Ahote. I am not happy about her forming a loving relationship with an Indian. There is too much that could stand between them.

'I'm sorry, Ros, but if you stay it will take a weight off my mind. I could ask Uncle Gordon and Zalinda but they are not familiar enough with Cat's problem to cope with it alone.'

Rosalind looked crestfallen. She so badly wanted to see Clive again, to hold him and for him to remember what he had been missing. She needed to detach him from this cousin of hers as quickly as possible. Tears of frustration filled her eyes. Cat was a grown woman, let her get on with her own life, thought Ros, but then remembered how her sister had needed her in the past. There was a long pause while she composed her thoughts then she said 'Think no more about it, Mama. I will be here for her. All I ask is that you take a letter from me to Clive.'

'Of course I will. You get it written. I'll find Uncle Gordon and Zalinda and explain what has happened, seek their advice about travelling, but first I must explain to Caitlin.'

Glenda guessed rightly that she would find her daughter at the stables. Caitlin and Ahote were grooming Gila when her mother walked in.

'Good day, Mrs McKinley.' Ahote smiled at her.

Glenda nodded. 'Hello, Ahote,' she replied. 'I need to talk with Caitlin for a few minutes.' She looked at Cat who laid down her brush. 'Should we walk?'

'Very well, Mama.' She glanced back at Ahote and left the stable with her mother.

Caitlin, though shocked by the news of Mr Martins's death, met it with a calmness her mother had not expected.

'I will be returning to Scotland,' Glenda informed her, and went on to explain why she needed to go and what arrangements she intended making for the time she would be away. Then she added, 'I know Ahote is a good friend, Caitlin, but that's all it can be – friendship. It is still early days in the peace between the Indians and the ranchers and we don't understand all the Indian ways. Please don't do anything foolish in my absence. Remember, I trust you to keep your father's good name.'

Cat looked her mother in the eyes and decided it was better to make no objection to this.

As Glenda went on to see Gordon and Zalinda she thought of Caitlin's meek reaction. Her daughter was quickly absorbing the Colorado way of life so perhaps this was truly the solution to her troubled mind.

When Gordon and his wife received Glenda's news they

expressed their sorrow for Mrs Martins and Clive, but also concern about Glenda travelling alone.

'You really should have an escort at least until you have found a passage to Britain,' said Gordon. 'Let me take you, I can always mix it with business.'

'I will be perfectly all right,' Glenda insisted, but Gordon would not hear of it.

Zalinda, not happy to be seeing her husband leaving her again, came up with what she hoped would be the solution. 'I believe Mark is due a break even though he hardly ever seeks one. It would do him good to get away for a while, and what better way than to make him feel useful? He hates time off unless he has a purpose in mind.'

'Splendid idea,' Gordon agreed. 'I'll send someone to find him right away.'

A quarter of an hour later they heard the sound of a horse approaching at a gallop. Gordon got to his feet and went outside on to the veranda. Mark, with a query on his face, greeted him from the saddle.

'Here I am, Boss, what have I to take on board?'

'Get out of that saddle and come inside, I have something to ask you.'

'Something troubling you? You rarely call me in from the range. A good job I hadn't ridden further away.'

Mark took off his Stetson, slapped dust off it and then gave his shirt a brush down and unfastened his chaps.

'Forget all that,' Gordon told him. 'We aren't house proud, I've told you that before.'

'Yes, Boss.'

'And I've told you, I'm not your boss.'

'Yes, Boss.'

'Aw, get inside. There's a job for you. If I'm your boss, I'm ordering you to do it. If I'm not your boss, you have a choice – do it or don't do it. So decide what I am.'

'After I've heard what the job is.'

'You're a real cuss.'

Gordon opened the door and Mark followed him inside. He dropped his Stetson on an oak chest and was only a step behind when they entered the large room furnished with two settees, a round table and six accompanying tall-backed chairs. He hid his surprise at seeing the two ladies and acknowledged them with a friendly, 'Good day.'

'Sit down,' said Gordon. When he had settled Gordon continued, 'We are seeking your help, Mark.'

This raised his curiosity, especially as Glenda was there and therefore the request must include her.

'Mrs McKinley has received news from her native Scotland that requires her immediate return. She wishes her daughters to remain here, which presents no problem. The trouble is that, although she insists she will be safe travelling alone, Zalinda and I do not think it a good idea.'

'So you are going to ...' Mark stopped talking. He looked askance at Gordon, and said thoughtfully with a little nod, 'Boss or not Boss?'

'Your decision,' said Gordon.

Mark had made up his mind but hesitated deliberately, in order to annoy Gordon. Mark glanced at the two ladies who looked puzzled, not knowing what this banter was about.

'Not Boss,' said Mark, a note of defeat in his voice.

'The full sentence, please,' said Gordon.

Mark pulled a face at him. 'You are not my boss!' he said firmly.

Gordon slapped his thigh in delight. 'Ladies, you witnessed that statement. "You are not my boss." He looked hard at Mark. 'Remember that in future. We are now partners, signed and sealed by your words in front of witnesses. That's far more binding in my mind than any piece of paper lodged in a Denver safe. This deserves a toast!'

Once the glasses were filled and the toast was drunk, Zalindar said, 'Now that is settled I think, Gordon, you had better relieve Glenda of her problem and convince Mark he wasn't brought here merely for you to trick him into making that admission.'

Gordon chuckled. 'I think we had better do that, but first I believe Mark wants to make an offer.'

'Mrs McKinley, I would be honoured to escort you to New York and see you safely on board a ship to take you home.'

'I am grateful to you, Mark, and it will be a pleasure for me to have you as my escort.' Glenda inclined her head gracefully with her eyes meeting his, expressing thanks and pleasure.

She sought out Rosalind and Caitlin, and received their approval of Mark as her escort.

'Have you anything in mind about the estate?' asked Rosalind.

'I'm not sure. I really need to assess the situation when I get there. I have no doubt that Clive will have learned much from his father, but whether he is capable of running Pinmuir should I decide to settle permanently in Colorado, I will have to see. I think he will be eventually; if he had had more time with his father, I'd be certain of it. What do you think, Ros?'

'He was always interested in the estate and talked a lot about future developments; he seemed keen enough and I think he spoke to Caitlin about it too, but things change and that may just have been pie-in-the-sky. The whole situation has been altered by his father's death. I'll go along with whatever you decide, Mama.'

'So will I, Mama, but I do love it here,' said Caitlin.

Glenda wondered why Ros had been so lukewarm in her opinion but thought it best to let the matter rest. Glenda looked ahead: she would have plenty of time on the journey to think over the future, though she could not of course ignore the handsome cowboy who would be escorting her to New York. Not that she had any desire to do that.

22

'Thank you, Mark, for all your help. It has not only been reassuring to have you with me, it has also been a pleasure.'

Mark took Glenda's hand in his. 'It has been a delight for me too. You have been wonderful company. Perhaps we could spend more time together after your return?'

She smiled and looked deep into his eyes, nodding and answering, 'That could be a possibility.' Glenda was not going to allow herself to appear too keen. Who knew what lay ahead?

'When you know the date of your return to New York, let me know and I'll arrange to meet you here.' Mark gave a little smile. 'And the boss won't be able to say no. After all, I'm officially his partner now.'

Glenda laughed. 'So you are.' She gave him a light kiss on the cheek, turned and hurried up the gangway on to the ship. She found a place against the rail among the other passengers calling goodbyes to friends and relations on shore. Glenda saw Mark smiling at her as he touched his cheek where she had kissed him.

The ship left the dock on time, but Glenda and Mark stayed where they were until both were lost to view.

Glenda heaved a thoughtful sigh. Mark was recalling where life had taken him since Glenda and her daughters had arrived at the Circle C. He would carry in his mind a picture of the lady on board that ship for a long time to come. Would she return or would the power of Scotland prevail?

The next day, as Glenda's ship met the Atlantic waves, Caitlin searched for Ros and found her with Zalinda in the house. 'Ros, please may I have a word?' They walked on to the veranda.

'Ahote has asked me to go riding with him and I thought I would let you know.'

Ros remembered her promise to their mother. 'Where are you going? How long will you be away?'

'He hasn't told me.'

'Cat, I know you have a strong friendship with Ahote, but be careful. Don't get too attached. You've never experienced love with a man before and we may, after all, be returning to Pinmuir soon.'

'But I could stay. What is there at home for me? You have Clive. If I go back, I'll end up an old spinster!' Cat's voice was angry now, which antagonised her sister.

'My relationship with Clive is none of your affair,' Ros shouted, releasing the anger generated by disappointment at having no letter from him recently.

Zalinda, hearing raised voices, came out and asked for an explanation after which she took hold of Ros's arm gently and said, 'Cat is only going for a ride with a friend. Ahote

185

will do nothing wrong; he is a good man. Don't get so worked up about it.'

Ros ignored Zalinda, looked to the ground and then at her sister and said, 'Cat, Mother asked me to keep an eye on you. I know you can take care of yourself, but she is worried. Remember, it was not long ago that these people were known as savages. No offence to you, Zalinda, that's just the way it was.'

Cat gasped. Zalinda looked sad, restrained her anger and said, 'Unfortunately that's true, Cat. Your sister is asking you to be careful, for the sake of your mother. Why don't you ask Ahote to speak with Ros before you go?'

Caitlin and Ahote turned their horses in the direction of the foothills and the Rockies beyond. They rode at a steady pace, at one with their mounts, ready to talk or prepared to share the silence.

'Where are you taking me, Ahote?' asked Cat after they had ridden some distance.

'To a beautiful secret place that I have locked in my heart, a place I have shared with no one else, but would like to share with you.'

'Where is it?'

'It wouldn't be a secret if I told you now.'

'Then let's get there quickly.' Caitlin laughed, happy that Ros had, in the end, agreed to this outing.

'No, no! The ride there is beautiful. We have plenty of time, and we will be back before dark as I promised your sister.'

'We'll think about the time later,' she said, a mischievous challenge in her eyes.

'As much as I might like what your eyes are telling me, I made a promise and I will keep it. Besides I want a good report about us waiting for your mother when she returns.'

'She need never know what we do.'

'True, but we will do nothing we might be sorry for and that could result in me being cast out by family and tribe. I can't risk that. Besides it would tarnish this ride in our memories and we would lose our respect for each other.'

'You talk like a parent.'

'What is wrong with that? What they say and teach us is for our own good.'

'Nothing, I suppose,' Cat quietly agreed. She pulled her horse to a halt. Ahote drew up beside her.

'Get down,' she said.

He sensed determination in her voice so did as he was told.

She got to the ground and stepped quickly over to him. Before he could do anything, she pulled him into her arms and kissed him on the mouth, holding her kiss beyond the moment when she felt him relax and respond to her.

'Ahote, I love you. I have done since I first saw you riding Gila.'

'Love is too strong a word, Cat. We haven't spent enough time together for that. But when I recognised your riding ability, I realised you were a special woman, and more so when I witnessed your love for Gila, which meant a lot to me. My heart sank when you chose her, but then watching you I recognised your love for her, and from that came respect and a real liking for you.'

Cat was disappointed by his measured response but knew time had to be on her side. She looked into his eyes and smiled.

187

'This is a memorable day,' she said. 'Now take me to this beautiful secret place you want to share with me.'

'And with you only.' Ahote smiled at her, his dark eyes deep and warm.

They rode on, content in each other's company.

Ahote guided them carefully on a track that grew narrower and narrower, never widening more than the width of a horse and rider. The huge wall of rock, seeming determined to block their way, rose higher and higher and began to weigh on Cat's feelings. She swayed in the saddle, starting to feel short of breath. The walls of rock began to spin. She tried to call out but no sound came. Ahote, in front, glanced round. The sight of a deathly white face drew him out of his saddle. In three paces he was reaching up to Caitlin, grasping her before she could collapse and taking her full weight, steadying her then lowering her to the ground. Alarm surged through him. He cradled her in his arms.

'Caitlin! Caitlin!' Over and over her name came from his lips as he gently rocked her. 'Speak to me. Speak to me! Cat! Cat!' He felt strongly about this young woman, more than he had indicated to her. He pulled her against his chest, gently supporting her.

How long they remained that way they never knew. Ahote felt her stir against his arms. He straightened up and looked down into eyes that were flickering open.

'Cat, speak to me.'

Looking bewildered, she asked, 'Where am I?'

'Safe with Ahote,' he said gently.

'But where am I?'

'In Colorado, America.'

188

She looked beyond him and then shrank back against him. 'What is that towering over us?'

Ahote was puzzled but realised it was no good trying to deceive her. 'A mountain in the Rockies.'

She nodded. 'Now I remember. You brought me here to show me something.'

'My secret place.'

'Yes.' She looked hard at him. 'Please take me there.'

'Wouldn't you rather go back and see your sister?'

'I will in due course, but first show me your secret place.'

As they had been speaking she was scrutinising his face. He sensed that whatever seemed to have been troubling her was slowly receding. He waited until she felt ready to stand.

'Come then, I will take you there.' She took his outstretched hand and felt kindness and safety in his touch.

He held her hand as he led her through a gap in the wall of rock. Ahote thanked the Great Spirit that Cat did not have another reaction to the towering walls. Whatever had sparked that darkness had been vanquished!

Ten yards further on the gap widened enough for them to step out on to a rocky shelf that gave them a perfect view across a tranquil deep blue lake into which, on the opposite side, a narrow waterfall ran, light catching its downpour in a series of dancing rainbows.

Ahote felt in Cat's touch that the magic of the place was affecting her just as it had done to him the first time he had seen this hidden masterpiece of nature. He had sworn then never to reveal its presence to anyone, but now he no longer held the secret!

He realised she must have read his thoughts when she stooped down and scooped some water from the lake into her left hand. She dipped her right fingers into it and made a blessing on his forehead, saying, 'Your secret will also be mine until the end of time.'

He pulled her towards him and kissed her brow.

23

The sound of horses approaching drew Rosalind's attention away from the book she was reading. She looked up from the veranda where she had been sitting in its shade. A sense of relief sped through her. Caitlin was back. Then her eyes were drawn to her sister. Something was different about her. She seemed to be more assured, relaxed and totally at ease in this land. Ros felt a lightening of her spirits. The promise to her mother was still binding but it looked as though Cat was managing life here perfectly well already.

Something had happened on this ride, something Ros was eager to know about. Even before she halted her horse, Cat called out, 'Ros, we have had a wonderful ride! Somehow I've come back lighter of heart.'

She was out of the saddle almost before her horse had halted. Ros was out of her chair. They met at the top of the veranda steps and Caitlin locked arms with her sister.

'I've been in such a wonderful place. I had a terrible fright getting there, but that disappeared when we arrived.

I feel my bad memories of Father's death have finally left me.'

Ros saw tears welling in her sister's eyes. What had happened to her? It must have been while she was with Ahote but he had ridden away to the stables as if he did not wish to become involved. Anger and suspicion rose within Ros. Their mother had told Cat she did not wish her to develop a relationship with him yet their day together seemed to have brought them closer. Ros thought of the trouble that lay ahead when her mother returned and felt annoyed with Cat for putting her in this awkward situation. She held back the words that were forming on her lips, words that would wound. She was all too aware that Caitlin's emotions were fragile still.

'I think we had better go inside,' said Ros.

The coldness in her tone needled Cat. 'What do you think I've done?' she demanded.

'You tell me,' rapped Ros and stepped past her sister.

Cat followed her, slamming the door shut. 'You think the worst because I've been out with an Indian!'

'Yes, I think the worst because you are disobeying Mama's instructions not to get involved with Ahote. You dare to do that in spite of my reminder to you. You are placing me in an invidious position when Mama returns. I don't suppose you ever gave that a thought. You were only thinking of yourself.'

'I was not! I was not!'

'Then you were letting Ahote take advantage of . . .'

'No! You are wrong . . . terribly wrong. Why are you condemning me without hearing my side of the story?' Tears started to stream down Cat's cheeks.

Angry with herself Ros snapped, 'Well, tell me what really did happen!'

A downcast Cat said nothing.

'What is this all about?' Ros said in a more patient tone. 'Begin from the moment you rode out from the Circle C today.'

Cat steadied herself. At least her sister sounded calmer and was now trying to be helpful. Cat described her ride with Ahote and the visit to the hidden lake.

'Is that all?' asked Ros. 'You're sure you've told me everything? You say Ahote held you in his arms ... did anything else happen?'

'No,' replied Cat ingenuously.

Ros let the silence stretch and then said, 'I will send for Ahote.'

'No, please don't,' Cat requested.

'I must.'

Cat started to plead but nothing could prevent Ros from pursuing this matter and she believed she must speak to Ahote.

On his arrival, Ros plunged straight in. 'My sister tells me that you were with her when, for some reason, she fainted.'

'That is true, Miss.'

'What happened then?'

'Nothing happened except that I held her in my arms and prayed to the Great Spirit for her recovery.'

Cat quickly continued. 'When I came round I realised I'd fainted because, in my nightmares, I sometimes relive what Father must have gone through ... walking over rocks while feeling the castle walls tumble around him. As you know, my bad dreams have nearly disappeared but now I feel Ahote has finally helped me put the terror behind me. I felt light at heart again.'

Ros looked hard at her sister and then at Ahote. She recognised in them the feelings she had shared with Clive before she'd left him to come West. She was happy for her sister then but felt the contrast with her own situation. Ros went to her and embraced her, saying, 'I am glad you seem well again, Cat.' She glanced towards Ahote. 'Thank you for helping my sister.' He nodded in acceptance of her words and said, 'I must get back to my work.'

As the door closed behind Ahote, Cat said, 'I wish Mother had been here.'

'She will get a surprise when she returns,' commented Ros wistfully.

'It's too difficult to explain by letter,' said Cat. 'Besides I want to be quite sure the nightmares have gone. Let's surprise her with my happiness with Ahote.'

'Are we sure she will come back? She will have much to see to in Scotland during which time I think she will have to consider her plans for the future. Maybe she will choose to stay there,' said Ros.

'What will you do then, Ros?' asked Cat

'I don't know,' she replied. 'There have been times recently when I have thought Clive's feelings for me are not what they once were, though he has never said so. He has not written as often as I'd hoped, but then I haven't communicated with him as much as I used to. Maybe we have both let other things crowd our lives. Everything here has been so new to me, and Clive must take on many extra responsibilities since his father's death.'

194

'Clive still loves you, I'm sure of it. You were always the one who was so adamant that you would return to Pinmuir,' Cat pointed out.

'True, but life has a habit of changing our outlook. Who ever would have thought you would fall for a Red Indian and do it in defiance of Mother?'

Cat smiled at her. Ros was changing her attitude a little; their mother's return though would prove more testing.

24

Glenda hired a coach in Fort William to complete her journey to Pinmuir. The horses swung round a bend to break away from the encroaching mountains and embrace the widening panorama of the view along Loch Pinmuir and beyond. She was home! The world had spun round and brought her back. White clouds parted to allow the sun to shine on her. She sighed contentedly but it was laced with regret that Ros and Cat were not sharing this homecoming with her.

Then at a glimpse of the ruined castle sadness choked her throat. If only John had not decided to pay it a final visit before they left for America.

A tear slid down her cheek and she forced herself to rein in her emotions. There was a future to be grasped here and choices to be made.

The driver manoeuvred the horses and carriage through the gateway, which she automatically noted had been widened since she'd last passed this way. She had no time to consider anything else; the coach was coming to a halt close to the front door.

Jessie Martins, ever alert for unexpected sounds, came to see who was calling at Pinmuir House. When she opened the front door she stopped as if she had hit a stone wall. Her eyes widened in disbelief.

'Mrs McKinley!' she gasped.

Glenda smiled. 'Yes, it is me, Mrs Martins. I am so sorry for your loss.' She noticed a thinner woman than she remembered, the traces of her recent grief showing in Jessie's face.

'Thank you for your letter. You have arrived sooner than expected but it is so good to see you again and be able to say "Welcome Home".'

'I'm sorry I could not give you an exact date. It's good to see you too. How about a cup of tea for both of us? I'll see to my luggage and pay the coachman and then I want all the news of Pinmuir.'

Mrs Martins bustled back inside and a moment later a maid appeared to help her mistress.

Within a quarter of an hour something nearing normality was restored; the coach had gone and the baggage had been deposited in Glenda's room. When she had refreshed herself, she walked downstairs into the small sitting room where Mrs Martins immediately started to pour the tea.

'Ah, scones! I must thank Mrs Lynch. I have not encountered any to match them on my travels. It feels as if I am truly home.'

'That sounds reassuring, Ma'am.'

Glenda gave a weak smile. 'Not so fast, Jessie. Presently I am here to assess what will happen to this estate. My daughters are still in America and their opinions and suggestions are important to me. After all, they are the ones who will inherit Pinmuir. Apart from that, I expect there will be the accounts to see to and payments to be made. And we must discuss plans for the future, for everyone's sake including yours and Clive's. How is he?'

'Losing his father has thrown a lot more responsibility on him but he has managed quite well. He was upset for a while when Bonnie died but Miss Fiona helped when she bought him Merlin, a strong working horse.'

'Has he taken on anyone else to take care of the maintenance work Greg was doing on the estate?'

'For two months Clive went out on his own but found the work too difficult to get through. He tried hard to find someone and then he heard the McBains were selling up and moving on. You'll remember them, they lived at the end of the loch?'

'Yes, of course I do. They helped in finding John. A good family.'

'Well, their son Tim wanted to stay in the area. When Clive heard this he jumped at the chance to employ a friend. Tim was pleased by the offer and they seem to be working very well together.' Jessie hesitated momentarily then said, with a touch of regret in her voice, 'I'm sorry to say, though, that Clive's work has suffered recently.'

'Well, if Tim is the cause he had better go,' said Glenda crisply.

'Oh, no, it's not that. Clive is managing much better now that he has Tim to help.'

'So what is it? What does he want? I thought Clive would spend the rest of his life here?'

'That is what I have always thought and hoped too.' Jessie tightened her lips and shook her head. 'No, Ma'am, it's because of that Miss Adrianna, your niece who is staying with Miss Copeland. Your sister requested that Clive should accompany her niece on her rides round the area and now she's turning his head. It's a pity that young miss ever came on the scene. I've talked to him, pointing out the pitfalls if he gets involved with someone who thinks she can have everything her way and tries to make us all jump to her bidding. Oh, dear, you don't want to listen to a fussy mother. But I don't want him getting in over his head with Miss Adrianna, nor do I want Miss Rosalind to be hurt. Has she heard anything about your niece from Clive?'

'I don't know. If she has, she has not mentioned it to me. She was very upset when I insisted she must stay with Cat instead of coming here with me, but I do have a letter from her for Clive.'

'He sleeps back at our cottage but will be here for his evening meal, so you could give it to him then,' replied Jessie. 'I'm afraid this evening it will only be a potato and onion pie.'

'Excellent, Jessie. Potato and onion pie was always a favourite with John and me. In America it seems to be nothing but beef. It will be good to have a change.'

Feeling weary, Glenda added, 'I think I am now ready for a rest after my long journey.'

Jessie smiled and said, 'I prepared your room as soon as I received your letter, Ma'am. Now I suggest you have a good sleep. The maid will already have unpacked your things.'

'Thanks, what would I . . . '

'No need to say another word, Mrs McKinley. It's good to have you back. No matter how long it's for, it will be a pleasure to have you here again.'

When Glenda opened her bedroom door, the comforting feeling of being back home swept over her and she could not resist opening the window.

The colourful hills with their mountainous backcloth seemed to fill her mind and draw her thoughts away from America. She breathed in deeply, the clean air tinged with moisture reminding her of harsh dry days when the prairies gasped for water. As she settled under the eiderdown she gave a little smile. In the forthcoming days there was much to decide: the Highlands or the Rockies, the prairies or the gentle valleys, and would she find love again? Could Mark fill the void left by John? How did her daughters wish to spend their futures and would she ever be free from worrying about them?

Glenda decided there was nothing for it but to sleep, and later this evening she would assess whatever trouble Adrianna had brought in her wake.

25

Jessie had informed Clive that Mrs McKinley was returning to Pinmuir for a while but he had not expected it would be almost immediately. As he sat down for his meal with them Glenda greeted him warmly and was pleased that he immediately enquired after Ros.

'She is well and wanted to come back home with me but I insisted she stay to look after Cat. Ros was very upset. I know she wanted to see you very much, Clive ... oh, but I nearly forgot, she has sent you a letter.' Glenda pulled it from her skirt pocket and watched him put it in his jacket, hopefully to read later.

This he did in the stables that held so many happy memories.

Dear Clive,

It was with shock and a heavy heart that I learned of your father's death after your mother and Aunt Fiona wrote to us. I was surprised that you did not write to me yourself rather than letting me hear about it from others, even though I know I haven't written so frequently lately. Maybe you had perfectly good reasons but I was hurt by the omission. I know it will have been a trying time for you although it does not take long to send a brief word. I felt you left me out and ignored the saying, 'a trouble shared is a trouble halved'.

Did you not think I would have sympathised with all my heart? Or have you found consolation with someone else? I miss you and wish I could be there to help.

Rosalind

He clutched the letter to his chest then slowly screwed it up.

Clive's lips tightened. He did not like being scolded. Did Ros expect him to be always at her beck and call? He did not care for her insinuation that he might have found someone else. Was that just probing or had she heard about his meetings with Adrianna?

His mind flew back to the last moments he had shared with Fiona's niece. He had wanted to know all about her and she told him about her days in Europe and especially Paris, where politics, art and literature were discussed in every street café, frequented by people of all ages. He was fascinated by these glimpses of, what seemed, another civilisation . . . and she had been sharing it with him. Adrianna had slid her fingers between his. He had not pulled away; in fact her boldness made him wonder what might happen between them next time they met. He knew she was tempting him, but . . . why not? Adrianna was here now; Ros was far away and might never come back. Was she looking for a reason to sever their relationship, or was her final sentence really how she felt?

202

Why did Ros have to go? He stood up and went over to Freya, put his head against the horse's neck and whispered, 'You're all I have of her now.'

The following day Glenda felt she needed to clear her mind so that she could concentrate on the books that would reveal the condition of the estate's finances. She informed Mrs Martins she would go for a walk; it seemed a long time since she had roamed these hills and glens and today's sky held the promise of a good day. She put on her ankle boots and wool jacket and went in search of solace.

Glenda kept to a leisurely pace and enjoyed her surroundings. After a quarter of an hour the path climbed a small hummock that hid the creek from view. Reaching the top, she stopped to regain her breath and admire the vista that held so many memories for her. John and she had done their courting in these surroundings. Nostalgia swept in with such a force that Glenda had to stop it overwhelming her. She realised she was not alone. A figure she did not recognise had appeared in the far reaches of the wood. What was a stranger doing on her land? Glenda stepped back so as to be hidden. She felt guilty about her action but really did not want to meet anybody now and hoped whoever it was would quickly leave her in peace.

She saw a young lady walking with a purposeful stride. Glenda began to suspect who this was. She glanced around her and, seeing an outcrop of boulders, stepped into a more secure hiding place from which she could keep an eye on the stranger's movements.

She could see that the young lady's clothes were of good quality and fitted so well that Glenda immediately assessed they had been tailor-made for the wearer. She was around eighteen, with beautiful chestnut hair. Her face was gentle with a smile that seemed to be recalling a private secret. She was slim and straight-backed and radiated a beauty that Glenda reckoned could play havoc with any young man's feelings.

This must be Adrianna.

No wonder Clive's mother was worried.

Now Glenda was alarmed too. Ros was so far away. It was always said that absence made the heart grow stronger, but being apart could work the other way too. Had it done so in Clive's relationship with Rosalind? Glenda wondered if she should interfere. Maybe not directly. But how?

She tried to remember the landscape of this area. She needed to recall the quickest path to where she had last seen Clive working. Adrianna seemed confident of the route she was taking but appeared to be in no hurry. Maybe the rendezvous was some time away. Glenda made another survey of the landscape. Then she started off.

She was soon breathing heavily and cursing herself for not doing more walking in America. After nearly half an hour she wondered if she had strayed from the path she had chosen. Espying a rise in the ground a short distance ahead to her right, she took a detour to it. She breathed a sigh of relief when it gave her a wider view and she recognised where she was. A quick survey revealed no evidence of Adrianna, but that did nothing to calm her mind. She resumed her walk at a rapid pace.

Soon Glenda saw two figures working side by side in a small plantation of firs. There was no one else nearby. Though she was relieved Glenda did not slacken her pace.

She saw Clive straighten and look in her direction, surprise on his face. He spoke to Tim beside him and he also pulled himself up, his face too expressing surprise. She saw them exchange a brief word and then Clive started towards her.

'Mrs McKinley! It is a pleasure to see you up here. Is there anything wrong?'

'I just came for a walk to prepare myself for all the paperwork I have to do while I am here. John and I walked here sometimes and I thought it would bring me peace to see it again.'

'Then Tim and I will leave you. We both have other things to attend to elsewhere.'

Glenda saw her opportunity. 'Please would Tim go back to Pinmuir House and tell your mother I may be late for lunch before he starts work elsewhere?'

Clive looked at him and nodded. Tim gathered his tools with a promise to look at some trees they had previously spoken about.

Clive watched him go and said, 'I hope you enjoy your walk, Mrs McKinley. And thank you for Ros's letter. I will send one back for her with you when you return to America, if I may?'

Glenda nodded and stood a while as she watched him walk away in the direction from which Adrianna was approaching. Had they a secret hideaway?

Once Clive had almost disappeared from view she followed him, keeping her distance. It was not long before he turned north to the outer reaches of the estate. Glenda hid behind a tree and watched him leap down into what she remembered as a small hollow. She crept after him quietly.

'Well, if it isn't the Laird of Pinmuir!' Adrianna teased as she held out her hands to grasp Clive's.

He thought how beautiful she looked and in a low voice said, 'We'll have to be careful in future. Mrs McKinley's back and she likes walking this way. I've just spoken to her where Tim and I were working.'

'She's back from America?'

'Yes, but I don't think it will be for long.'

Glenda was seething inside. Hadn't Ros's letter meant anything to him? And what was that about the Laird of Pinmuir? Was Clive getting above his station or was it just Adrianna's wishful thinking? Should she interrupt them? But the couple moved closer and Adrianna put her fingers to his cheek. 'Kiss me, Clive. I hardly slept last night for thinking of you.'

Clive's eyes met hers. Recalling the way Ros had chastised him in her letter, he pulled Adrianna roughly to him and kissed her passionately. Glenda turned and ran down the low hillock, tears for her daughter starting to fill her eyes. Ros did not deserve this.

26

Over lunch Glenda was quieter than usual. When should she approach Clive, if at all? The problems seemed insurmountable. They had just finished their meal when they heard the sound of a horse approaching.

'Miss Fiona, no doubt,' commented Mrs Martins. She glanced at her son. 'You be careful what you say.'

Clive made no reply to this but went to open the front door ready to greet their visitor. His mother proved to be right. Fiona was slowing her horse. He went out to help her from the saddle.

'Good day, Fiona,' he greeted her amiably.

She gave him a nod and asked, 'Is my sister inside?'

'Yes.'

'Please tell her I am here.'

'Certainly.'

He turned away, but before he could reach the front door, Glenda appeared.

'Hello, Glen,' Fiona greeted her. 'Thank you for your letter. If I had known the exact day of your arrival, I could have arranged to meet you. And why didn't you let me know you were back?'

'Because I've only just returned,' laughed Glenda, 'and wasn't sure of my plans. There's a lot to see to here, as I'm sure you can imagine.'

'Well, no matter. I was hoping to bring Adrianna to meet you today but she had other arrangements. No doubt you will meet her soon.'

Glenda, relieved not to have to face her niece, answered, 'Don't worry, I am sure she has a lot to do now she's home again from Europe. Besides, her father disowned me so she has no reason to seek my acquaintance now.'

Fiona quickly changed the subject. 'It's good to see you looking so well. American life must suit you. You must tell me all about it. And perhaps you might invite me to experience it for myself sometime.'

Glenda gave a short smile. 'I'm not sure you would fit into their way of life! It's hard, dusty work, and we all pull together for the good of the rest.'

'I won't know until I try it.'

'Knowing you, you will probably jump in without thinking, but don't do any jumping yet. I'm not sure I will be remaining there.'

'Are you serious? Will you be here some time, or perhaps permanently?'

'That remains to be seen. There's more than one life to be considered.'

'I expect there is,' Fiona agreed.

'Cup of tea, ladies?' Mrs Martins called from the doorway.

'If it's accompanied by one of Mrs Lynch's scones,' said Fiona with an anticipatory smile.

'Already warming in the oven.'

The sisters settled to enjoy their time together, and once they had grown accustomed to each other again, Glenda decided this might be a good time to bring up the subject that had been preying on her mind.

'Fiona, Mrs Martins mentioned you had asked Clive to partner Adrianna on her rides. Why was that?'

'So that she would rid herself of this high-and-mighty way of behaving she has. It isn't attractive and she will soon be in the market for a husband. She'll never get anywhere with men, acting like that.'

'You never contemplated that something might develop between her and Clive?'

'No ... Never.' Fiona looked surprised but from her sister's expression realised something must have happened. 'Surely not? It can't be ...'

Glenda raised her eyebrows. 'I happened to come across them together while I was out on a walk. I don't know how serious their relationship has become but it has certainly passed beyond being good friends.'

Fiona looked truly shocked. She buried her head in her hands for a moment. 'Oh, Glenda, I am so sorry to hear this and will try and stop it immediately. I'll have words with Adrianna when I return.'

'That might just make her more rebellious. She has that same impulsive streak I had at her age. I was hoping the letter from Ros I brought for Clive might have helped, but I fear not.'

'Glenda, I'm sure Clive really loves Ros.' But while she spoke Fiona recalled the times Adrianna had talked of the handsome young estate manager. How could she have been so blind?

209

Glenda went on, 'I think Ros will return to Pinmuir sometime in the future. She does not share Caitlin's enthusiasm for America. I will tell you all shortly but I realise now that I need to consult a solicitor about the future of the estate and to make sure the girls are taken care of no matter where we decide to make our home.'

'So it looks as if my offer to buy Pinmuir is blown away.'

'More than likely, but who knows what tomorrow may bring?'

'Remember you promised me first refusal, if selling becomes a possibility.'

'I will remember.'

'Now tell me all about America.'

Jessie Martins could hear the chatter and laughter coming from the sitting room. It was good to have the house come alive again. She hoped Glenda would decide to make a permanent move back here within the year.

27

Anxious to see her future settled, Glenda set about putting things into place.

Wanting the girls' inheritances settled, she consulted her solicitor. He agreed with her suggestions for making the legacies of Rosalind and Caitlin watertight provided she did not leave herself destitute in doing so.

'I'm sure my daughters would see that did not happen, Mr Fielding,' Glenda countered his cautious approach.

'From what I know of them, I'm sure you are right, Mrs McKinley,' the solicitor hastened to reassure her, but he added, 'New ways of life change people. I'd advise you to be cautious in your disposition of your assets. First and foremost you need to provide for yourself and think in the long term. You are still a young woman. From what I hear your estate seems to be thriving now and you are comfortably off; you have cash and land to provide an income for you in the years to come. Think carefully about all this and come and see me again.'

'I will, Mr Fielding, and I will make it soon because I don't want to delay too long before I return to America.'

'Very well, Mrs McKinley, I know what you are trying to do. I will have the necessary documents drawn up for your approval, shall we say three weeks from today?'

'That would be splendid. Thank you. I look forward to seeing you again then.'

On reaching home Glenda asked for a fresh horse to be ready for her when she had finished a light lunch. She had decided that with the weather holding fine, she would look over the estate and see the progress Clive and Tim had achieved during the time they had been working together. As her ride progressed, she became increasingly impressed by what they had achieved.

New plantations had been established in places where she would not have seen the potential. The sheep seemed to be thriving and there was a stone fold behind one of new stands of trees, providing shelter for the flock. Rocks had been dragged from the riverbed and a small waterfall now made a picturesque approach to the front of Pinmuir House. She halted her horse and sat drinking in the view, marvelling at what the two young men had achieved already.

Glenda let her thoughts drift. Though her immediate future was mapped by the return to Colorado – what then? Return to what she was looking at, to what she still thought of as home? Or was there something new that was tugging at her – a new beginning in a new land, perhaps with another person's encouragement. How much did she love the handsome, kindly American cattleman? Would she ever feel for him as she had for John?

'Hello, Mrs McKinley.'

She started on hearing a man's voice and turned quickly, 'Oh, hello, Tim.'

He smiled. 'You were far gone, Mrs McKinley.'

Glenda laughed. 'I was, wasn't I?'

'Somewhere nice, I hope,' he said politely.

'It might be . . . I don't know. Do you know where Clive is?'

'He should be the other side of this hill, on the flatter ground. Would you like me to ride with you, to see if he's still there?'

'That would be kind. I've been on my own since early afternoon.' Glenda wondered if she would find Clive working or maybe with Adrianna.

As they rode together Glenda took the opportunity to ask Tim, 'Do you like working at Pinmuir?'

'Oh, yes, I do, Mrs McKinley. It was a godsend to me that Clive was looking for help when my parents decided to move nearer Edinburgh. I didn't want to go. I love this part of the Highlands. Anywhere else would have been a foreign land to me.'

'So you are settled here?'

'For as long as you wish to employ me, Ma'am.'

'I'm pleased to hear that, Tim. I am busy making plans for the future.'

He looked startled and concerned. 'You aren't thinking of selling, are you?'

'I'm not fully decided yet but I think the answer will be no.'

She could not mistake the relief that came into his face then.

They had topped the rise. 'There he is, Ma'am,' said Tim, pointing ahead to his right.

'Seen him,' Glenda answered, relieved that Clive was on his own.

'Would you like me to leave you, Ma'am? Do you wish to speak to Clive alone?'

'No,' she replied. 'Stay.'

'Yes, Ma'am.'

In a few minutes greetings were being exchanged with Clive.

'I've been riding round the estate,' said Glenda, 'and I met Tim. When I asked where you were, he offered to escort me. There's a big flat-topped stone over there. Let's sit down and talk.'

Clive swung from his saddle, wondering what was coming.

When they were at ease, Glenda said, 'I am very pleased with what I have seen today. Your work and ideas are splendid. Far better than I could have directed you to do.'

The young men murmured their thanks, but inwardly they were feeling delighted by the praise.

'Have you further plans?' she asked.

'At the moment we tend to act on short-term improvements,' said Clive.

'Not a bad idea but you must not forget the bigger picture,' Glenda pointed out. 'With the progress you have made I think you could start looking into increasing income from the estate.'

'Tim and I have discussed that.'

'We have two small plantations of pines we believe are ready for felling,' said Tim enthusiastically. 'Clive has been sounding out a local timber dealer.'

'And he has promised he will have a look and give us his opinion within the next week.'

'Well done! It is good to see all the enthusiasm you have put into looking after the estate. You have enhanced its beauty, but also viewed it as a paying enterprise. Keep on this way and you will not go unrewarded.'

As she left them Glenda felt more convinced about her decision to keep the estate. Now she would consult Mrs Martins about the accounts, visit the solicitor with the books and then her work would be done.

'I may be able to return to America sooner than I thought,' she told Jessie later.

'I see. Does that please you, Ma'am?'

Glenda screwed up her face doubtfully. 'I don't know. I don't seem to be able to make up my mind.'

'Something will happen to make everything slip into place exactly as you want it,' Jessie told her encouragingly.

Glenda sighed.

'You have great faith, Jessie. I hope you are right.'

28

The next morning Glenda rose early and after breakfast wrote to the shipping company, reserving the best cabin available on the first liner sailing from Liverpool to New York the following month.

She went over the accounts closely with Jessie and went to see the solicitor, who seemed impressed with what he saw. 'The villagers thought that once your husband had gone and the family and you left for America, the estate would die. You have two good workers there by the look of it,' he said and Glenda was gratified to hear it. If only Adrianna were not around, causing complications.

The reply from the shipping company came a week later informing Glenda that she was booked first-class on the *North Star* leaving Liverpool for New York on the fifth of August. Her ticket and sailing documents could be picked up there.

She immediately penned a letter:

Dear Mark,

I write to tell you that I would like to avail myself of your kind offer to meet me in New York on my return to America. I have taken passage on the *North Star*. I leave from Liverpool for New York on the fifth of August. All being well I should arrive in New York a week later, I hope this is suitable for you. If not, please say so.

I look forward to seeing you again and hope all is well at the Circle C.

With my thoughts and good wishes,
Glenda

She then wrote to both Rosalind and Caitlin informing them of her plans for returning to the Circle C, ending the letter:

... It will be good to see you both. I have much to tell you. Everything has gone smoothly here so I am able to return earlier than expected. I hope all is well with you and that life at the ranch is still enjoyable.

Love,
Mama

Even though she was busy with her preparations to leave Scotland, Glenda found time to be with Fiona. Adrianna was not mentioned and Glenda did not press the matter, wanting Rosalind to settle everything herself. Glenda's last days before leaving were spent absorbing the changing spirit of Pinmuir. One day her attention was drawn to two figures, hand-in-hand, climbing a distant slope. Clive and Adrianna! What had Ros's letter said to Clive that had driven him into another girl's arms? Glenda waited until they had passed from her sight then she hurried home. She was due to leave Scotland in a couple of days. Clive had told her to tell Ros that he was only halfway through the letter he was writing her and would post it shortly. Glenda would more than likely reach Colorado before it arrived. She dreaded what it would say.

When Fiona came to bid her sister goodbye and a safe crossing of the Atlantic, Glenda could not restrain herself. 'Did you mention Clive to Adrianna?' she asked.

'Yes, I did, and she said there was nothing serious in it.'

'But they seemed very close when I saw them together two days ago.'

'Adrianna assured me it was just simple companionship on both sides. She has few acquaintances here since she's been abroad so long. Let her live a little, as we did at that age, Glenda. Remember, you had just met John when you were Adrianna's age.'

'But . . .'

'Oh, don't worry so! Clive *does* love Ros,' Fiona told her impatiently, then changed the subject. 'Are you being met in New York?'

'Yes.'

'By Gordon's partner at the Circle C, the man you mentioned escorting you on your way over?'

'Yes. He's called Mark. You'd like him.'

'Seems to me he's made for you,' commented Fiona, with a sidelong look.

Glenda smiled.

'We'll see.'

'Whatever you say, but take notice of your sister's advice: follow your heart.'

That advice was still ringing in Glenda's mind when all she could see was the ocean stretching around her.

She'd hoped the Atlantic crossing would give her an opportunity to resolve her problems but it did not. The week on the liner passed quickly and she enjoyed meeting new people. What would she tell Ros when she saw her, though? And how would she feel about Mark after her time back at Pinmuir. Glenda felt herself becoming despondent as the ship drew nearer and nearer to the quay.

She scanned the crowded dockside for a sight of him. Her eyes searched the crowd again. Her heart missed a beat. But two people were waving frantically as if trying to capture someone's attention. It couldn't be ... It was! It truly was! Her heart brimmed over with joy – Ros and Cat were here. But how? Why? Their faces were wreathed in joy as they made their way nearer the ship's gangway. Then they were battling against the tide of passengers pouring on to the dockside. In a few minutes Ros and Cat had their arms locked round their mother, and the three of them wept with happiness.

Then the questions. How did you get here? Why aren't you at the ranch? Did you have a good voyage? Is everything all right at Pinmuir?

Then Glenda heard: 'Welcome back.'

The deep drawl brought her spinning round. 'Mark! This was your doing?'

'I thought it was what you would want.'

'It is, it is!' There was no denying the pleasure he had brought her. 'This is such a wonderful surprise.'

219

'Well, I'm delighted you approve. I'll escort you all to the hotel. We have a compartment booked on the train for Denver the day after tomorrow.'

'How thoughtful. It's so good of you to take all this trouble.'

'My pleasure,' replied Mark, with a little bow of his head. 'But let me say, here and now, that Gordon insisted on paying for the hotel and train travel. I protested but he won. He usually does.' Mark cut short the topic by waving to Sam, who drew up in his cab.

'Good day, ladies. I'm happy to see you once more,' said the driver as he climbed down to help with the luggage.

'Sam!' gasped Glenda. 'We meet again. Another splendid surprise.'

'Kind of you to say so, Ma'am.'

Mark rode outside with the driver as they left the docks, allowing the women some privacy.

As soon as they were seated, Glenda said to her daughters, 'You both look well. Colorado life must be suiting you.'

Neither of them took up this observation, merely replied, 'We'll tell you all about it at the hotel.' Glenda realised she would have to take her chance then of telling Ros the distressing news about Clive. So far she had passed over it by telling her of the letter that would soon be arriving and of all the work he had done on the estate.

At the hotel Mark left them to settle in. Glenda's daughters, as prearranged, came to her room to exchange news.

'What have you to tell me?' she asked when they were sitting comfortably.

Both of them talked animatedly about life at the Circle C.

'Yes, but how have *you* been?'

Ros and Cat looked at each other.

'Mama, you asked me to take responsibility for Cat's welfare, and to watch out for any signs of her illness recurring. Well, I must report there have been no nightmares,' Ros told her. 'However, she fainted while she was out riding . . .' Ros hesitated for a moment.

'Go on,' Glenda prompted her.

Ros continued without expanding on all the circumstances. 'That's it,' she said, when she had finished. A momentary silence filled the room.

'You are telling me that Cat fainted because she was in a narrow space?'

'Yes, Mama. I believe it was a form of claustrophobia that caused me to faint,' Cat confirmed.

'Did you fall . . . hurt yourself? Where were you, Ros? What did you do?'

There was a short silence. Caitlin decided there was no use trying to cover up the incident. 'No, Mama. I slid out of the saddle rather than fell. Ahote had seen me fainting. He caught me and stayed with me until I felt well enough to return to the Circle C. By the time we reached it I was feeling perfectly well. Much, much better than I have done since the tragedy at Pinmuir. It seems like a miracle.'

Glenda hid her surprise at Caitlin's open recollection of the tragedy in Scotland and its outcome. 'And that was it?' she asked.

'Yes.'

Glenda approached her elder daughter and looked at her closely. 'I'll ask you again: where were you, Rosalind?' she asked, rather accusingly.

'Back at the ranch, Mama.' Ros hung her head momentarily.

221

'What?' Glenda exploded. 'I told you to look after Cat while I was away. It seems you took no notice.'

'I *was* looking after her,' countered Ros quickly. 'I judged Cat to be strong enough for the ride and believed the fresh air would do her good.'

'But out alone with an Indian . . . you can never tell what might happen. You seem to have forgotten, it's not long since they were killing General Custer and his men.'

'Mother! That was during a war! We are at peace now.'

'And look at the Indians on Uncle Gordon's land,' put in Caitlin. 'They are peaceful and friendly enough. Besides, if Ahote hadn't been with me I might have lain there until I died from the heat. It wasn't a place other people go.'

'So why had he taken you there?'

'To show me a beautiful secret place.'

'Secret? *His* secret, Cat, so anything could have happened and nobody would have found you.'

An angry tone came into Cat's voice. 'I am disgusted if that is what you think of him and of your own daughter. Ahote is an honourable young man and would never allow any harm to come to me. I suggest you forget your anger with Ros and with me, and realise that there is good in everyone – even those who aren't white.'

Cat stormed from the room followed by Ros, who looked back over her shoulder, calling out, 'You've only yourself to blame, Mother,' before slamming the door behind her.

Their words shocked Glenda. She sat quite still for a few minutes, expecting the girls to come back. They did not. This was not the reunion she had expected. If only John were here. He would have handled this far better than she had done. Glenda sank on to her bed and wept.

29

A restless night did not solve Glenda's problems. She woke after a short shallow sleep wishing she was still back at Pinmuir. She realised it was up to her to make peace with her daughters and there was still the conversation about Clive that she must have with Ros.

She realised she must re-examine her attitude towards Ahote. Had she properly examined her feelings towards him? She had observed what was happening between the Indians and the white men on the Circle C. Efforts were being made to forge an alliance. Now, when she really considered the situation, she realised how deep her intolerance was, and how it was all she had ever known; people of different races weren't really understood in the Highlands. She knew she must put a stop to this way of thinking if she wanted to repair the damage she had caused between herself and her daughters.

There was a new day to face.

When she walked into the dining room she found Ros and Cat already at the table with Mark.

'Good morning to the three of you,' said Glenda brightly.

'Good morning, Mama,' replied Ros and Caitlin politely but she could hear the underlying ice in their tone.

'Good morning, Glenda,' Mark replied with a smile.

She wondered if her daughters had mentioned anything to him about the disagreement, but she guessed they would not have done.

Breakfast was a slightly stilted occasion. Mark noticed that something was amiss, though he was gentleman enough to make no observation. Instead he tried to take the conversation along a different tack and was immediately successful.

'First thing we do this morning is go shopping. I am going to buy three dresses or three riding outfits for three people, not far away. It has been my pleasure to escort them so far and I hope it will continue to be so all the way to the Circle C.'

He was pleased to see his offer had brought the bright light back into Rosalind's and Caitlin's eyes.

'You are being far too generous. You shouldn't spoil us,' Glenda protested.

'My pleasure,' he replied. 'Now which is it to be?'

'Riding clothes, please,' Rosalind and Caitlin replied without hesitation.

'That was a quick decision,' commented Mark. 'What about you, Glenda?' Seeing her hesitate, he quickly added, 'I won't take a refusal. You must make my pleasure complete by accepting my offer.'

'Then I agree. What I would really like is a good outdoor coat ready for winter.'

'It shall be yours,' he replied, with undisguised pleasure in his eyes.

So began two days of enjoyable shopping and fine dining at some of the best restaurants in the city. A joyous spirit enveloped them and Glenda hoped their disagreements had been exorcised by their time spent together in New York. It seemed to be that way on their train journey west. There was plenty to keep them occupied and more than enough for them to see. All three women had much to consider as they sensed their arrival in Colorado would lead to a watershed in their lives.

Gordon and Zalinda welcomed them all back with an invitation to dinner. There was much conversation about Circle C, New York, Pinmuir, the horses and cattle . . . topics ranged far and wide. But between Glenda and her daughters there was still a slight air of restraint.

The next morning Rosalind and Caitlin left the breakfast table to see their horses and used the time together to talk over their future.

'Do you think Mama has got over her prejudice against Indians and especially Ahote?' asked Caitlin, hoping that her sister would not brush the question aside. Caitlin desperately wanted Ros's advice. She felt relief surge through her when her sister answered.

'I knew you would eventually ask me that. It's a question we both have to face and better two minds than one.'

'I don't want to hurt Mama but her attitude towards him is just blatant prejudice.'

'We have to try and put ourselves in her shoes,' said Ros. 'It must be a shock to her on many counts. Remember, none of us faced the question of race before coming here, and we are young and open to new challenges. She cannot understand your growing friendship with Ahote. She also believes that I disobeyed her instructions to look after you while she was away.'

'But can't she see it from another point of view? Can't she see the example of Uncle Gordon and Zalinda?'

'But remember how shocked we all were on our arrival, when we first realised they were man and wife. I suppose the difference is that they were already married and we just had to accept that. It would have been worse for Mother than it was for us as Uncle Gordon had not made any attempt to tell her and they are old friends. She must have felt betrayed. Also, Zalinda is no common Indian, but what we might term royalty within her tribe. I suppose Mama sees Ahote as merely an Indian brave who is taking her daughter away from her.'

'So what can I do?'

'Be patient. Let her see there is no harm in your friendship with him.'

'Do you think that will work?'

'You and Mama must try and see things from one another's point of view.'

'Ros! Can I talk to you about something?' called her mother, coming out on to the veranda.

Both girls turned to her.

Catlin nodded thoughtfully to Ros. 'You'd better go. We don't want to upset her further.'

'Can you get Brandy ready for me?' Ros asked.

Caitlin gave her sister a quick hug. 'Of course! Thanks, sis. You are a Godsend.'

Ros approached Glenda.

'What is it, Mother?'

226

'Ros, sit down. Have you received a letter yet from Clive? Gordon and Zalinda went into Denver yesterday and I wondered if they had collected one for you?'

'No, Mama, but you did say he was busy.'

'I have something I need to tell you. I am only sorry I have not been able to confide in you before now. I know it will upset you and while we were in New York I wanted us all to enjoy ourselves.'

They sat down. Glenda took Ros's hands in hers. She told her daughter what she had seen at Pinmuir: 'But your aunt seems to think it will soon blow over when Adrianna's father returns. She implied there was nothing serious between our niece and Clive, just a deep friendship.'

Ros sat in shocked silence. Glenda rose and rested her hand on her daughter's shoulder. 'Think hard about what you want to do. You can build a good life here for yourself and I'm sure you will fall in love again.'

Ros raised her head and looked her in the eyes. 'I didn't want to come here, Mother, but I did it for Cat. This is not the place I want to be. I long to breathe the Scottish air and scramble through the rocky glens again. I was happy there with Clive. I believed in him and he in me. Coming here, so far away, was bound to cause problems. I don't know what has happened with my cousin but I still believe he and I can have a future together.'

'But . . .'

'Yes, it means I must go home to Pinmuir.' Relief surged through Ros as she said those words. She rose from her seat decisively and added, 'Please don't oppose me. I will ask Uncle Gordon to arrange the travel side of things, but,

227

Mother, I want to go home as soon as possible. Don't let the Martins or Aunt Fiona know.'

Glenda paled at the thought of losing her eldest child. 'Ros,' she pleaded. 'You mustn't be so hasty. This is what you feel in the immediate aftermath of hearing about Clive. Think again, discuss it with Caitlin, and if your answer is still the same in a few days, ask me then about going back. I need to think about how it will affect Cat and me.'

Glenda was certain that Cat would want to stay in America. If Ros went back to Scotland, where did that leave her mother?

30

Later that night Ros told Caitlin of her plan. Her sister was upset but they had begun to realise their lives were taking individual paths. Although the parting would bring great sorrow, each would know the other was living as she chose. In one thing they were united: they would not allow their mother's prejudices to colour their own attitudes. Neither of them spoke to her about this but Glenda sensed the unease they'd felt since the argument in New York.

Eventually she broke the ice. 'I need to say something to you both now that you're setting out on the courses you will take. I would like to say that I am sorry I upset you both on my return. I should not have criticised you in the way that I did. I should have listened more to what you had to say. In my defence, and after due consideration, I believe my extreme attitude was probably caused by the way I was brought up and the problems I have had to face over the last four years. I will learn to adjust to life as it is now but it will take time. Please will you forgive me and let us start again?'

Ros glanced at Cat, who nodded at her to speak for them both. 'Of course we will, Mama. And we have something to discuss with you, so let us start with a clean slate.' They rose from their chairs and set a seal on the peace between them by exchanging kisses.

When they were settled once more, Glenda asked, 'Who wants to be first?'

'I think I had better be. I intend to return to Pinmuir.'

'Very well,' Glenda conceded. 'And I take it you still want to be reconciled with Clive.'

'Oh I do, so very, very much,' replied Ros fervently. 'I will brook no opposition from Adrianna, if she is still around.'

Glenda approved of her elder daughter's determination. 'Then we had better get organised, telling your uncle, packing your things for shipping, booking your passage – oh, so many things to see to! I'll come with you to New York. You'll be able to manage by yourself from then on, I'm sure.'

'And I'll come with you, Mama, then you'll have company for your return to the Circle C,' offered Cat.

'That's very thoughtful of you, dear. Thank you. It will be hard watching Ros leave but we'll make the best of it and try to enjoy another visit to New York.'

Glenda fixed her attention on Cat then. 'That's Ros settled as far as we can see. There'll be a lot left for you to do when you get back to Scotland, Ros, but I know you'll succeed. What about you, Cat?'

'I want to stay in Colorado.'

Glenda felt a pang of disappointment; she had hoped they would all stay together but it was evident now that this was not to be. She warned herself to be careful how she expressed her opinions this time. 'Very well, Cat. What do you intend to do here?'

'I'll sweetheart Uncle Gordon into allowing me some land to start a horse breeding business, particularly quarter horses. There'll always be a market for them as long as cattle-rearing thrives. I can see no reason for it not to succeed.'

'You are serious in this?' queried Glenda.

'Oh, yes! You know my love of horses. But I'll seek Uncle Gordon's advice and guidance.'

'I'm sure he will help. I think Mark will be interested too. One thing I would ask of you: don't just rely on their charity. I would ...'

'I would never do that, Mama. If they see the possibilities, I would wish everything to be placed on a business footing, drawn up legally so there can be no argument about anything in the future.'

'Sensible young lady,' commented her mother. 'Now, I've got to ask this and please don't think I am trying to derail your plan ... I just want to be clear about everything so you won't be upset if anything goes wrong with your scheme.'

'Nothing will go wrong, Mama. I'll make sure it doesn't. But what do you want to ask me?'

'Where does Ahote stand in your plans?'

Caitlin did not make an immediate answer but after a moment's silence she said, carefully and deliberately, 'Mama, this idea was not a sudden whim of mine. I worked carefully on it before I confided in you. Knowing Ahote's love of horses too, and the special affinity he has with them,

231

I told him what I intended, making him promise to tell no one else. I know he has kept to his vow as I would always trust him to do.

'There is something else you should know. Contrary to what you imagine, nothing happened between Ahote and myself while you were away. I say again, it did not. Neither of us would have allowed it to. If we had it would have destroyed the special relationship we have. These are the terms on which I desire to stay in Colorado.'

Silence reigned for a few moments before Glenda spoke up. 'Cat, you have been very forthright with me and I thank you for that. I most humbly apologise for thinking ill of you and Ahote. Please forgive me.'

Cat jumped up and rushed to her mother, to hug her and say, 'Of course I do, Mama.'

'Ros, you will find when you get home that there is a great deal of legal work to be studied and documents to be signed. I went into it all when I was last there. I had also to consider Caitlin's rights in the estate. That has all been settled with the necessary documents. I hope you will agree that the provisions I made are fair to you both, and will not impinge on any future developments in your lives. Should you and Clive decide to marry, your future at Pinmuir is assured.

'Now all I can say is: remember I am here and will help you both in any way I can, even though that might be difficult at times when there are thousands of miles between us.'

'We'll manage somehow,' said Rosalind.

'Yes, we will,' Glenda agreed. 'But your situation is the one that requires immediate attention. We'll concentrate on that for now. Start packing whatever you will need with you.

Everything else can be consigned for shipment to Pinmuir. Cat, for now please help your sister. I know you will want to see your business started as soon as possible but it must not be rushed.' She looked thoughtful for a moment and then announced, 'I think we will arrange to have a family meal in a few days' time and celebrate your plans for the future. So there will be we three, Uncle Gordon, Zalinda . . .'

'And Mark,' cut in Cat. 'He'll be needed for escort duties, Mama, when we go to see Ros set sail for Pinmuir.'

'I'll have you for company,' Glenda objected.

'But you'd like him along too. If you aren't going to ask him, I will.'

Glenda capitulated with very little protest. She then said, 'If Ahote is going to be involved in your project, Cat, he had better dine with us too.'

Cat's eyes dampened as she silently mouthed, 'Thank you.'

31

Zalinda, impeccably dressed in a close-fitting housecoat that matched the colour of her hair, hurried into the room when the maid informed her that they had visitors. Her broad smile and open arms expressed a warm welcome as she hugged each one of them in turn. 'This is a lovely surprise,' she said. 'And so early in the morning.'

'I hope we are not intruding?' said Glenda.

'Of course you aren't. You know you are most welcome any time.'

Gordon walked in dressed for the outdoors, carrying his Stetson and wearing the heeled calf-length boots that showed some part of his morning would be spent in the saddle.

'Great to see you all,' he said, smiling. 'Stay and have some coffee?'

'Thank you, but we have just had breakfast. If you can spare the time, we have something to ask you,' said Glenda.

'Anything for my dear sister-in-law.'

'I must tell you that Ros and Cat have made some

decisions about what they want to do with their lives. I'll let them tell you. First Rosalind.'

At a nod from her mother Rosalind announced, 'I am returning to Pinmuir.'

'For good?' queried Gordon.

'Yes. Although hopefully I'll have the option of visiting you in the future.'

'And is the young man I've heard talk about still in the picture?'

'He'd better be or else I'll want a very good reason why not.'

'Be wise about it, Ros,' said Zalinda in her quiet way. 'Don't rush in too quickly. You have a long future before you; choose your man carefully.'

Ros nodded her acceptance of this advice.

'Now you, Cat,' Glenda prompted.

Cat swallowed, a little embarrassed now to reveal the scope of her ambitions.

'I want to stay in Colorado.'

Nobody spoke. Zalinda glanced at her husband, who for a moment looked a little bemused by this bald statement.

Cat then broke into a torrent of words as she outlined her scheme. When she paused for breath, her uncle said, 'If I understand you rightly, Cat, you want to spend your life here, in Colorado, raising horses?'

'Yes, Uncle Gordon. But I'll need your help.'

'I understood that,' he said with a wisp of a smile. 'What does your mother think to this idea?'

'When we decided to take up your offer and visit you, that is all we had in mind – just a visit, but I did say if it led to any of us wanting to stay permanently I would support

235

that choice. Now you've just heard the decisions of my daughters and I will stick to what I agreed with them.'

'And you ... what have you decided to do, Glenda?' asked Zalinda.

Glenda gave a little shake of her head. 'I don't know. I'm torn between the two options. Ros must go as soon as possible. I have been to Scotland recently; all is in order there regarding the estate, so she can easily move in without my being there. For the moment I will see how Cat fares and whether she still wants to settle here once she has tried horse-rearing.'

Gordon nodded his approval. Turning to Ros, he said, 'First, all of us on the ranch will miss you, Mrs Bradley and the school children especially so. Zalinda and I are sorry you will be leaving and wish you every happiness in the future. Pinmuir is clearly the place for you and in that you are more like your father than you realise. I think he might have done the same thing after visiting us a while.'

Zalinda added, 'Please don't ever forget us, Ros. May the Good Spirit be with you for ever, and may you always walk in happy shoes.'

Ros's eyes were damp as she hugged her aunt and uncle.

'Now, Cat, have you thought your idea through?' Gordon asked her. 'You do realise you still have much to learn? Rearing horses can be physically draining even for the cowboys, and there's a lot of mental strain too. Above all you must understand quarter horses: their way of working, their physical make-up, character, and what makes them different from other breeds plus, of course, gaining an affinity with them. That can mean spending long days in the saddle, no matter if the weather is searing hot, blowing a gale or thick with snow. You'll also have a business to run and accounts to keep. But the work can bring you much joy in the friendship and love you gain from horses.'

'I will take notice of everything you have said and make sure I don't let any of you down.' Cat looked to her mother who gave her a nod of approval.

'If I could say a word?' said Glenda. 'No one else knows of our plans so may I ask you not to breathe a word of them for the moment? I would like to give Rosalind a farewell supper at which Cat can announce her plans to all those who will be included in them. Shall we say six o'clock in three days' time?'

A murmur of agreement was given.

'If you need any help, I'll make myself available,' Zalinda offered. 'And I am happy to accompany you on the journey to and from New York.'

'Thank you. That would be most helpful,' said Glenda. 'And our further thanks to you and Gordon for making our time with you so enjoyable and now fruitful.'

'Your family is our family,' replied Zalinda, 'and always will be no matter where we are.'

32

It was a busy three days for Glenda and her daughters and they were grateful for Zalinda's help in organising the preparations for the celebration meal. This resulted in a splendid array of choices for each course, which brought praise from every guest there including the senior cowboys, their wives and Ahote as well as the McKinley family.

When they had all been served coffee, Glenda rose from her chair. Silence settled in over the room.

'I want to thank you all for being here to bid farewell to Rosalind. She is returning to Scotland to see to the running of the McKinley Estate. She has my full support and blessing for the life she will lead in the country she loves. I'm sure we all wish her well in the course she has chosen.'

Clapping broke out and good wishes were called out across the room.

As the sound faded, Glenda resumed: 'You now know what Rosalind is doing but what about Caitlin?' Glenda allowed her audience to consider this then she said, 'You need to hear from Cat first and then from her uncle.'

Cat stood up. 'I will come straight to the point. I wish to remain in Colorado to work with horses, eventually to breed them.' She paused for a moment to allow a buzz of speculation between the guests to die down. 'I approached Uncle Gordon for advice. He pointed out the pitfalls but said that if this is what I really wish to do then he will support me. For that encouragement I thank him.' Cat sat down amidst clapping and good wishes.

As it died down Gordon stood up. 'Tonight is Ros's chance to say farewell to all those who have helped her over the past few years. Let us raise our glasses and wish her God speed.' Everyone raised a glass and said, 'To Ros.'

She nodded her thanks and added, 'I have loved the time I have spent here and I am sure I will visit again in the future. So thank you from the bottom of my heart.'

During the celebrations that followed Gordon sought the chance to tell Glenda, Mark, Ros, Cat and Ahote to stay behind when the others were leaving. With that accomplished, once they were all settled comfortably with more coffee available, he said, 'I asked you to stay behind because I had more to say to you, which the others need not hear.

'Since the moment Cat first sought my advice, I have given her idea much thought. I believe it could be a viable consideration but it will need your help in various ways. The land needn't concern you; that will be for me to deal with. I will put Cat under the care and instruction of the most-skilled person I know at getting the best out of any horse – Mark.'

Congratulations and cries of approval rang out across the room.

Mark nodded his acceptance. 'From what I have seen of Cat's dealings with Circle C horses, I am sure she will succeed in what she dearly wants to do. I look forward to teaching her all I know.'

'Mark, in this venture Ahote will be your assistant. He has a natural affinity with horses. I have rarely seen such a special gift among white men so perhaps we will all learn something too.'

Murmurs of approval rang out again, and Ahote's expression revealed how he felt about his appointment. Amidst the excitement, he and Cat managed to exchange glances.

Gordon added, 'I had hoped that one day I would share all this with my brother. Sadly I can't, so helping his family is the next best thing.'

As hard as everyone tried to ignore the coming departure they found it impossible to do so. Zalinda insisted on accompanying the party travelling to New York. But once bookings for the sea passage had been made and they had reserved their rail travel and accommodation in New York, they were able to concentrate on their final days together in Colorado. They were thankful for the fine dry weather, which enabled them to enjoy riding in the mountains and store away memories of sharing the wide prairies together. Cat noticed how her mother and Mark seemed to be growing closer and thought their three futures at the Circle C were assured.

There were times when Mark, accompanying them, took the opportunity to study Caitlin's riding and handling of her horse, though he never made these outings into serious lessons. That would begin once Rosalind had left for Scotland.

Although eager to be on her way to Pinmuir, Ros had to curb her desire until all the necessary formalities were completed. She held back from writing to Clive to tell him she was coming home. She wanted nothing to prepare him for her arrival. She sensed she would know at their first meeting if Adrianna had taken her place. If she had done, what would Ros do: accept it or fight for him? Then she remembered what she had told her mother and that stiffened her determination to vanquish her rival. But, of course, it was Clive who would make the final decision.

33

Although everyone tried to enjoy the train journey to New York it was overshadowed by the thought of Ros's departure. Having observed Glenda sinking deeper and deeper into silence as the train ate up the miles, Zalinda took the opportunity to have a chat with her.

'Need company?' she asked.

Glenda nodded and smiled weakly. There was a part of her that would have liked to travel the return journey with Mark alone, but Ros had wanted her 'aunt' there, thinking it would make the parting from her mother easier to bear, especially when going back to the Circle C without her.

Zalinda sat by Glenda's side and said, 'It is not easy to make light of parting with a loved one, no matter what the circumstances,' Zalinda sympathised. 'You are sure to miss Ros, even though you'll still have Cat.'

'I know,' Glenda agreed. 'This will be the first time we have been truly parted. I sometimes wonder if we did right coming to Colorado.'

'You must look at that with a positive attitude and count

242

the blessings it has brought you all. You still have your children, no matter what the distance between you and no matter where they are. I have sensed a strong bond between you all that will last throughout your lives. They are two wonderful young women.' Zalinda added with sadness in her voice, 'I envy you.'

Those three words startled Glenda. She eyed Zalinda as she tentatively asked, 'You mean ... ?'

She nodded. 'Twice. We lost them both at birth.'

Glenda took her hand. 'Oh, I am so sorry. I did not know.'

'There was no need for you to have our sadness thrust on you. You were far, far away. As it had been a secret for so long we saw no reason to disclose it later.'

'And you have both had to observe my relationship with my daughters. It must have tugged at your hearts?'

'It did, but we thrust that aside. The past is the past and we must dwell in the land of the living. As well as my own joy in having Ros and Cat with us, I know that Gordon has derived much pleasure from having them here. He thinks the world of them and, having no one else to help in the same way, wishes to do all he can for them.'

Glenda gripped Zalinda's hand. 'Thank you both again. I won't breathe a word of what you have told me, but I am glad you did.' The look of sympathy in her eyes changed to one of query. 'Zalinda, do you mind if I ask you about someone? If you would rather I didn't, do say so. I will understand and won't mention it again.'

Zalinda gave a small smile of anticipation. 'Mark, you mean?'

With a slightly embarrassed note in her voice, Glenda said, 'Yes.'

'I thought there might be something blossoming there. And why not? You are both free agents. Mark has never been married. He's a good man, considerate towards people he takes to, hard-working, shrewd, but doesn't enjoy fuss ... well, you saw that when Gordon tricked him into admitting he is his own boss.

'They met while they were young, when Gordon was new to America. They were friends from the start, both wanting to make their fortunes, so decided to do it together. Mark is a naturally loyal and generous man. You need fear nothing from him and he will always respect you. Remember, when he abandons his role as a hard-working cowboy, he is a quiet man. There may be times when you have to do the roping.'

Glenda smiled at this. 'Thank you, Zalinda, I am grateful to you for speaking so openly.'

'Do you believe you might have a future with him here in Colorado?'

'It's a possibility. It depends ...'

The following day dawned dull. Grey cloud persisted but the folk from Colorado did their best to try to make light of Ros's departure. Hugs, kisses, tears, good wishes, last-minute advice, were all exchanged before the watery distance between solid land and the unsteady ship widened, leaving no alternative but for them all to accept the parting.

34

An hour before the ship was due to dock in Liverpool Rosalind sought the help of a ship's officer to arrange a coach for Scotland. He gave her message to a driver and his young assistant, who welcomed the thought of a long journey and were happy to see a pleasant young lady safely to her destination.

An overnight stop was taken at a country inn north of Glasgow where Rosalind was thankful to be free from the movement of ship and coach. A sound sleep saw her ready to welcome and be welcomed by her beloved Highlands. The good weather helped her to relax as she watched the countryside go by. With the flat land left behind, the steepening hills painted in autumnal yellows, browns and greens seemed to be welcoming Rosalind back to the land where she belonged. The sense of coming home intensified as they approached her final destination among the mountains. But Rosalind held back from the decisive moment. Instead of taking her directly to her home, she ordered the coach driver to deposit her at the Trooper's Arms, a coaching inn she knew of but had never visited.

The rumbling of a vehicle stopping brought the landlord James McLaren to a window. 'Maggie!' he shouted, sending his voice echoing around the stone building huddled at the foot of a rocky hill.

'Coming!' The acknowledgement came quickly; Maggie had recognised the tone in her husband's voice that indicated a female customer was arriving, and a lady too since she was in a carriage. Maggie wiped her hands on her apron, unfastened it, threw it into the kitchen, patted her hair and hurried to the front door where her husband was already stepping outside to assist the newcomer.

'Good day . . .'

Maggie cut in quickly with '. . . Miss' to complete his greeting, having noted that the young lady wore no wedding ring. Maggie was curious – a young lady travelling alone in this remote area? Who was she? And why pay the driver as if she had no further need of the coach? 'The young lady's bags, Mac,' Maggie prompted her husband.

He nodded, took them and bustled inside.

Ros exchanged a few words with the driver and his assistant and then turned to Maggie, hovering nearby and wondering what would happen next.

Ros gave her a pleasant smile and, concealing her local knowledge, said casually, 'This is beautiful countryside. Have you a room for tonight?'

'How long would you want it for, Miss?' asked Maggie, as if letting the room depended on that answer.

'I'm not sure at the moment but let us say three nights. It could be more.'

246

'Very good, Miss. I'll give you one at the front, the one with the bow window, it will give you a better view of the mountains.'

'Splendid,' said Ros, not saying it would also give her a clear view of anyone coming to the inn.

'Will you be wanting to take your meals here?' asked Maggie.

'Certainly.' Ros smiled as she added, 'I don't want to starve, and walking makes me hungry.'

'You are here for your health then, Miss?' Maggie queried.

'No,' replied Ros. 'I enjoy walking and it does me good. I love this part of the world.'

'You've been here before?'

'Not here, but nearer the coast.'

'I am sure you will enjoy our countryside just as much.'

'I hope I shall.' Ros decided she had said enough. 'The room, please,' she said pleasantly.

'Of course, Miss. Follow me.'

Maggie led the way up the stairs to the landing, which was flooded with light from two sash widows. She opened the first door on the left and stood back for Ros to enter. She found herself in a square room of generous proportions.

'You have an attractive establishment. I hope it is well patronised?' said Ros.

She was pleased when her fishing for information made the catch she'd hoped for.

'Locally, no. We draw more local trade from Glentorrent, which is only five miles away. Some of the younger ones like the walk and enjoy using the time to do their courting.'

Ros gave a little smile of satisfaction. This inn was certainly convenient for Pinmuir, yet sufficiently far away to allow her privacy from prying eyes.

'Thank you. I look forward to my time here,' she said.

When Maggie McLaren left her, Ros took another look out of the bow window, summing up the lie of the track along which she hoped she might soon espy Clive and have her first glimpse of Adrianna.

35

For four days Rosalind kept vigil, either from her window while reading *Agnes Grey* or else discreetly when she went out walking. She remained alert for any movement in the landscape but her disappointment mounted when the sightings were of nothing more than deer or birds. She'd wanted to see Clive and Adrianna together but was also relieved she did not, even though the wait prolonged her anguish. Ros tried to tell herself that whatever romantic involvement they might have had must now be over.

Then on the fourth day, while striding up an unfamiliar hillside, she realised she was about to break the skyline. She stopped for a few moments to catch her breath. Hearing a slight rustling of leaves she moved cautiously, copying the way the Indians stalked deer on the hillsides of Colorado.

She lay flat on the ground, listening. Nothing. Using her elbows, she propelled her way forward. After a few yards she stopped. She strained her ears to catch any new sound. She could hear whispering. She edged forward, easing herself up until she could see over the rim of the hill. The ground in front of her dropped away gently and into her view came two figures, their arms around each other, lips touching.

Clive and ...? This could only be Adrianna! Ros's lips tightened in anger. It took all the strength of mind she could muster to keep her presence unknown. She didn't want to be accused of spying. If that happened the whole situation could rebound unfavourably for her. Was this situation of Adrianna's making and Clive too weak to resist or had he seen his chance to take advantage of a young lady? Either way Clive must be shown that he was in the wrong. Ros shrank into the hillside and moved quietly backwards until she knew she would not be seen. She paused to calm herself. That would only alienate Clive in a way that might thrust him back into Adrianna's arms. If she shouted at them now, lost her temper, she would risk all. She had come all the way from Colorado to claim the man she loved. Adrianna must be erased from his mind. If she wanted Clive's future and her own to be as one, together here in the Highlands where they had shared so much, she had to be dignified even though she did not feel like it. She felt numb and hurried in controlled temper back to the Trooper's Arms where she would await their arrival, certain that this would be their destination. Ros went straight to her room, changed into more suitable clothes, tidied herself and sat in the window to wait.

The minutes ticking by felt like hours. Then doubt began to creep in. Maybe they weren't coming to the inn ... Then two figures came into view. Ros stiffened. The lovers were walking hand in hand, laughter on their lips and in their eyes. Automatically she inched back so she would not be seen but they were so intent on each other they would never have noticed the unexpected. Ros guessed Clive would take Adrianna to the small room they called the snug.

She let them settle in then stood up, brushing down her green skirt, a colour Clive had always liked to see her in. She took a deep breath, instructing herself to be dignified at all times, then she negotiated the stairs and the short passage leading to the snug. She took hold of the door handle and strode abruptly into the room.

Startled by the unexpected intrusion into their privacy, Clive turned towards her and Adrianna started to protest. Clive looked at Ros in disbelief, his elbow catching his tankard hard sending ale swilling across the table to drain like a small waterfall into Adrianna's lap. This could not be happening he thought; Ros should not be here.

'Clive! I'm soaked. Whatever . . .' Adrianna stopped protesting, noticing his pallor and the look of shock on his face.

'Ros! What . . . ? I don't understand,' Clive exclaimed.

Ros gave a little smile, pleased by the turmoil she had created. 'Don't look so shocked, Clive. This truly is Rosalind standing in front of you, all the way from Colorado in the heart of America.'

'But . . . why?' Slowly he began to gather his scattered thoughts.

Adrianna stared at her cousin and rival.

'I am back for good,' replied Ros firmly, believing she would hold the initiative by coming straight to the point.

'What!' Clive's face blanched. He rose from the table.

'I am back for good,' Ros repeated emphatically. 'I have come home. So there are some things that you and I had better sort out and one of them is this young lady. She appears quite dumbstruck by learning who I am. I think the first thing for us to do is to take this fly-by-night safely home to our Aunt Fiona.'

'Now hold on!' put in Adrianna, realising she should strike back. She glared at Ros. 'Don't you start trying to throw your weight around! You disappeared from Clive's life. You can't just come barging in again, thinking he has held a torch for you. You ran out on him!'

'I did not! It was always my intention to come back.'

'You never made that clear,' blustered Clive, adding, 'your letters were mainly about your new life and the people around you. Your interest in Pinmuir seemed to vanish. What was I to think?'

'I did tell you I would return to you, repeatedly, but obviously this hussy here intervened and you ceased to pay attention.'

'Don't you dare use that term about me,' snapped Adrianna. 'You left Clive. I'd been away for years and when I returned he offered to show me round the area. We became friends and I wasn't going to pass up on a chance like that.'

'So you admit you set your cap at him?' Ros challenged her.

'Of course. An eligible young man – how could I resist?'

Ros glared at Clive. 'So she replaced me, did she, even though you were still writing me love letters?' She gave herself a moment to calm down, regain her dignity, and let the idea of the 'love letters' register with Adrianna. Her anger hung on the air for a few seconds and then she shouted, 'Well, Clive, which of us do you want? You had better make up your mind about the future. Do you want to spend it with me or with her? I need to know. I have to start working on my plans for Pinmuir. I want you there with me but I need love and loyalty. You'd better say where your feelings lie.'

'And I want the same,' rapped Adrianna. Her sharp tone left him in no doubt where she expected his choice to lie.

'She's right!' put in Ros, much to his surprise. 'It is your decision.'

Clive's eyes narrowed as he stared at the two young women, momentarily lost for words. He straightened his back and walked over to the door.

'Very well then. Tomorrow. Eleven o'clock. I will have reached my decision by then.'

He made his retreat speedily, not wanting to be around when the two young women decided to voice their opinion of each other.

36

Thousands of miles away, two friends rode slowly beneath the Colorado sun.

'I don't like it, Boss.' Mark looked up from the ground he had been grubbing with his hand. He held up his fist so Gordon could see what happened when he opened his fingers. The earth he had held sifted through Mark's fingers to be caught by the hot breeze that sprinkled it across the parched grassland.

'Nor do I,' agreed Gordon with a worried frown. He looked over the countless cattle, listless in the heat that shimmered across the prairie. 'They need water and so does the grass. It's far too dry, been that way too long. We need rain or there'll be no food for the animals.'

'Even the storage tanks we put in are nearly dry.'

'It's gotta rain, it must!' Gordon stared into the sky. 'Rain! Rain!' he yelled at the heavens as if he could command clouds to appear and pour life-giving water over the parched land.

'In all my time in the West, I've never seen a November

start as dry as this,' said Mark, tipping his Stetson towards the back of his head so he could wipe the sweat from his forehead. That done he added, 'Let's get home and out of this damned sun.'

When they reached the ranch their first thoughts were for their horses. They rode them into the stable. Gordon and Mark slid thankfully from their saddles and immediately started to relieve the animals of their harness.

Two cowboys ran into the stable. 'We'll take over, Boss!' they called.

'Thanks.' Gordon and Mark waved their appreciation. 'When's this damned weather going to change?'

A week later the question was answered.

The wind that had helped to dry out the prairie began to exert a different influence right across the grassland. Clouds gathered and thickened, massing around the foothills of the Rockies. The sky darkened.

'Rain!' yelled Gordon, as if he could command a deluge, but all that happened was a drop in the temperature that, with the help of the wind, singed the land completely dry.

The weather remained like that for four days, never fulfilling its promise to revive the land, never allowing the clouds to release the water they carried. Passing by seemed to be the game they were playing, to irritate everyone and leave them wanting and restlessly waiting. Glenda and Cat found it difficult to breathe and recalled the cool of Scotland with longing.

Midway through the fifth day of this, one of the cowboys who had been checking cattle on the prairies reported to Gordon and Mark that the Indians had left.

'Gone?' Their surprise was evident.

'Yes,' came the reply. 'Everything's gone, with barely a sign they were ever there.'

'I don't like this,' said Mark. 'It's a bad omen when they move everything so quickly, and at night too. Another sign of urgency.'

'Does anybody know where they go to?' asked the cowboy uneasily.

'No,' replied Gordon. 'It will be the foothills of the Rockies or even into the mountains themselves. Their trails are secret. They'll know if you try to follow them and they'll lose you. They don't use the same route every time, that's part of the mystery, but it's no secret that within three days of their moving, bad weather sets in and remains with us until spring. Sometimes longer. So let's get back and organise animal feed.'

The three men turned their horses round and put them into a gallop. The urgency of their arrival at the Circle C alerted the cowboys; even the women came out of their houses to listen to what was being said and contingency plans were immediately put into action to ease the trouble they all knew was coming.

A rolling rumble disturbed Glenda's sleep. For a few moments she could not identify it. The low sound came again. This time Glenda identified it as thunder bouncing off mountains and rolling along valleys. She had heard similar sounds in the Highlands near Loch Pinmuir only this was much deeper, as if determined to make itself known. Another crack from the heavens shook the timbers of the house. Now wide awake she swung out of bed just as a shout came from Cat, a frightened scream. Glenda's thoughts raced. She ran to her daughter's bedroom and reached Cat as another clap of thunder broke over the house. But Glenda had her daughter tight in her arms and was saying in a quiet voice, 'It's only thunder, Cat. Don't let it frighten you. It won't harm you. You're safe with me.'

Cat nodded. They waited together, warm and comfortable until the rumbles became distant as if at last acknowledging defeat. Cat sighed and sank deeper into her mother's arms. In a moment she was fast asleep. Glenda breathed a sigh of relief and laid her daughter on the bed before she went quietly back to her own room.

The thunder slowly faded away.

Glenda lay comfortably on her pillows looking out of the window. Moonlight brightened the sky but the cloud thickened and began to sprinkle the countryside, prairie, mountains and valleys, first with a delicate film of white until it gave way to torrents of snowflakes, large and unyielding, forming ever-deepening drifts.

In the Scottish Highlands Ros had risen early. She had struggled to sleep, recalling the look on Clive's face as he first saw her. It was one of disbelief and horror rather than the love and excitement she had expected. Ros was no longer feeling as confident as she had been. Would she, as Mistress of Pinmuir, be able to throw Clive off the estate if he chose Adrianna? Mrs Martins would most likely go with him, so would Ros have to return to Colorado? Aunt Fiona would then buy the estate and Adrianna would have a claim on it ... No, Ros had to stay at all costs. Clive *had* to choose her.

When she had arrived at her aunt's the previous evening, Adrianna had asked her aunt to reason with Clive on her behalf but Fiona refused, saying the girl had to stand on her own two feet. Now Adrianna had another plan.

That dull November morning each young woman prepared to outshine the other.

The time was approaching when Clive would normally have been leaving to work with Tim on the fencing surrounding the outskirts of a maturing stand of Scotch pines. It was a job that needed completing before winter settled in. He had dressed accordingly; no fancy clothes to try to impress; the young women would have to take him as he was – dressed for work. Not wanting his mother to influence his decision, he had not even told her that Rosalind was back at Pinmuir.

'I'm off, Ma,' he called as he picked up the box of sandwiches she had prepared for him. He went to the stable, collected Merlin and wished women were as uncomplicated as horses. He sighed as he mounted and was thankful it was a fine morning with a warming sun. Clive fished his pocket-watch out of his waistcoat. He was early. Twenty minutes to wait. He entered the inn and a few minutes later, carrying a tankard of ale, returned outside. He took a swig to bolster his confidence then sat down to try to relax, but there was no chance of that; his mind was awhirl as he tried for the umpteenth time to convince himself that his choice was the right one.

Then his thoughts were frozen by the sound of horses' hooves. He stared at the rider as she came into sight. Adrianna, smart in her green split skirt, blouse, checked jacket and small but attention-grabbing hat, cut a figure that made Clive's heart miss a beat. By her side she led a horse that reminded him somewhat of his Bonnie. A lump came into his throat.

'Good morning, Clive,' Adrianna called as she dismounted and turned a radiant smile on him.

'Good morning,' he returned, then let his eyes slide towards the horse she had brought with her.

'A present for you,' she said.

'No, no,' he protested. 'I cannot accept.'

'Yes, you can. It is my gift to you, hopefully to seal a future between us. But, if not, Erelin can be a reminder to you of what we once shared.'

He was about to object again but was suddenly aware of movement elsewhere. He turned and saw Rosalind appear on the slope behind the inn. He noted how she paused on first seeing them. She must have summed up the situation quickly. Her stride became more purposeful.

'You must be short of confidence,' Ros taunted her cousin, 'resorting to a bribe.'

'You're wrong there,' countered Adrianna. 'Clive knows I love him and Erelin is my gift to him, no matter what the outcome this morning.'

'Love? You know nothing of love. Would you have waited as long as I have?'

'*You* may have!' Adrianna jeered. 'What do you think *we* were doing while you were in America?'

For a moment Ros froze. Her inner certainty failed her. She must cover it up quickly. But Adrianna had already sensed the doubt she had stirred up in Ros. 'Did you expect Clive to be a monk while you were thousands of miles away? Let me tell you, he was far from that.'

Clive stepped in between them, arms and hands outstretched to stop them trading any more insults. 'You two had words last night. Don't say anything else you might regret. Besides, I really don't like what I see in either of you right now. I think it's time we finished this.' He bit his lip as his eyes switched from one girl to the other. 'I don't want to hurt either of you but it seems I can do no other. I respect you both and hope, in return, you will respect my decision.'

37

Two impatient young women forced themselves to stay silent. Search as they might they could learn nothing from the inscrutable expression on Clive's face. He began to speak.

'Adrianna, your aunt asked me to reacquaint you with our country again and I have enjoyed our days together far more than I ever thought I would. You are beautiful, fun, and one day some other man will take you to his heart and deserve you far more than I do. You are not right for me, and I think you have always known as much deep in your heart.'

She took a step towards him. 'No, Adrianna,' he said, holding out his arm to fend her off, 'it is Ros I choose. I know now that I might have used you to take my thoughts off Ros, and for that I am ashamed. I am sorry. Believe me, you will always have a special place in my thoughts.'

Tears streamed down her face. Earlier that morning she'd thought she would return to her aunt with her future settled. Yes, Clive was below her in status, but he hadn't bored her like the men she had met abroad. She turned to go and saw him step towards Rosalind. Adrianna envied her deeply at that moment. Ros stood in front of Clive and looked deep into his eyes. 'I missed you, Clive, and I trusted you. I could have had the pick of men in America, but I kept true to you. Can I ever trust you again?'

Clive hung his head in shame and shook it from side to side. 'I wouldn't blame you if you walked away right now, Ros, but I love you and always will.'

Ros took his head in her hands and kissed him passionately on the lips. The years she had been away disappeared in an instant and a bright future beckoned.

Clive heard the horses move, separated himself from Ros with difficulty and ran to Adrianna, helping her into the saddle. 'Take Erelin back,' he said. 'I know he was a favourite of your aunt's but she would never tell you that. Thank you, though. Now go gently and forget about me.' His eyes were sad as let her go, knowing of the hurt that was in her heart whilst he held such happiness in his.

He turned back to Ros. 'I never was her lover. You may not believe that right now, but it is true. When I saw you in front of me again yesterday, I immediately knew it was you; always you for me.' He stroked her cheek. 'Come, let's away from this inn,' he said to Ros, 'it is no place for us right now.' They led their horses to the special place that had remained only theirs and Ros knew she had come home for ever as they sealed their love. Afterwards all thoughts of Adrianna were gone; they were reunited and their time apart forgotten.

'I wonder if we will see my cousin again?' said Ros.

'Probably not,' said Clive, 'I think her father is returning soon anyway. Let's surprise my mother with our news,' he urged. 'She doesn't even know you are in this country.'

With joy surging through them they hurried hand in hand to Pinmuir House, where they found Clive's mother seated at a table in the study sorting through some accounts.

'Hello, you two,' she greeted them absently and then looked up from the notebook in her hand. Disbelief filled her face. 'Ros! Are you real?' she gasped.

Jessie Martins was on her feet, arms held out; then she stepped back keeping hold of Rosalind's arms and saying, 'Let me look at you.' She eyed Ros for a moment, nodded her head and said, 'Yes, America hasn't marred your bloom, but I think you've fined down a little. Mrs Lynch will soon put that right. How long are you here for?'

'Forever, I hope,' replied Ros.

For a moment Jessie didn't pick up on her statement. 'Forever?'

'Yes. I've come home for good.'

'Oh! Then I must see that your old room is got ready for you!' She took a step towards the door. 'I'll get you moved back into your rightful home while I return to the cottage with Clive.'

'You can't do everything at once, Jessie. I will keep my room at the Trooper's Arms for tonight, so you'll have plenty of time.' Ros saw Jessie was going to protest so stopped her by saying, 'Mrs Lynch will be spared cooking for us this evening. You and she must eat with Clive and me at the inn in celebration of my return to Pinmuir. Then I can fill you in on all that has been happening back in Colorado.'

38

Cat twisted and turned in her bed, wondering at the strong light streaming into her room. Her eyes flickered open. She sat up, threw off her blankets and slipped out of bed, shuddering as the cold air touched her skin. She grabbed a shawl and swung it round her shoulders. Moving quickly to the window, she pushed back the curtains. Fully awake in an instant, she gasped at the wonderland she had revealed.

Snow sparkled as the sun shone brightly in a clear blue sky. The frosty air brought a sharpness to the scene that tantalised the eye. Circle C waited to be noticed.

The door of Caitlin's bedroom opened and her mother walked in, elegant and comfortable in the dressing gown she had had sent from New York via Denver.

'Something wake you?' Glenda asked brightly.

'The bright light,' replied Cat. 'The snow has turned every-thing into a beautiful winter picture. I must go outside ... I really must.'

'I'll come too,' agreed Glenda. 'We'll go for a walk together.'

'Maybe a ride?' suggested Cat.

'Depends how deep the snow is. Wrap up well. Breakfast in a quarter of an hour.'

Eager to be outside they both took a light breakfast. With help from their maids they donned their outdoor boots and warm clothes, adjusted earmuffs to their liking and were finally helped into their overcoats.

Cat was first to the door. She gripped the knob. 'Ready, Mama?'

Glenda nodded. Cat opened the door.

An icy blast surged at them causing them to catch their breath. Glenda cast a look at her daughter and then raised her eyes heavenwards as much as to say, 'We are stupid to be going out in this cold.'

Wondering where Ahote was and how he and the tribe were coping with this cutting wind, Cat said, 'You'll soon be used to it, Mama. The Indians manage.' The young woman laughed at her mother's antics as she tried to stay warm and upright. Cat sped away in front, taking no notice of the snow and icy patches.

Glenda, envious of her daughter's confidence, watched her go.

'Come on, Mama,' urged Cat. 'You've never been bothered like this before.'

'I'm certain you haven't,' said a quiet voice behind her.

Startled, Glenda almost lost her footing. She felt strong hands grasp her. She looked up and saw the amused expression in Mark's blue eyes.

'It's all right for you – you have more experience of Colorado weather,' she protested.

'I thought you would know deep snowfalls from Scotland?' he said innocently.

Glenda's lips tightened with annoyance at herself for overreacting. 'Sorry,' she said, through gritted teeth.

'Take my arm,' he offered. 'You'll be safe with that to hold on to. Besides I won't let you fall.' His eyes were fixed on hers.

'Thank you,' she replied, and Mark was instantly overwhelmed with happiness. He almost let go of her arm as the shock of it hit him. He had never felt this way before about a woman.

'Doesn't your daughter mind the snow and ice?' he asked, for something to say.

'She's young, doesn't see the danger in falling.'

'Exactly. You should start thinking the same way.'

'It never used to bother me.'

'Then think the same way now. Come on, let's walk together. Don't think about falling, and when we get going let your hold on me gradually diminish, until you aren't holding me at all.'

She saw he was right, and, knowing that, could not reject his offer.

Glenda found herself soon adopting the way she had dealt with the snow and ice of the Highlands. There she had had John's help and now it was that of a cowboy she figured was about the same age. She pulled her thoughts up sharply. She should let their relationship mature rather than push it. She felt certain Mark would prefer it that way too.

Any further talk between them, which both were enjoying, was interrupted by Caitlin's return. The happiness she was feeling shone in her eyes and was reflected in the way the frosty air had brought a bright glow to her cheeks.

'Will we be able to ride tomorrow, Mark?' she asked.

'This sun is just warm enough to be giving us a slight thaw. If that continues and we have no more snow during the night, I think there is every possibility of a ride tomorrow. We will have to judge then.'

'If we can, will you come with us?' Cat asked. 'You'll know the best trails in the snow.'

'Wouldn't miss it,' he replied.

Cat was out of bed early the next day. Her heart raced with excitement when she drew back the curtains and saw there had been no snow during the night. The clear sky offered a chance to fulfil her desire to ride in the snow.

She and her mother were just finishing their breakfast when the maid, who had answered the knock on the front door, announced, 'Mr Mark is here, Ma'am.'

'Show him in.'

Mark came in breezily. 'You two ready?' he asked.

'Soon will be,' replied Cat. 'Would you like some coffee?'

'Please. I've just been seeing to the saddling of the horses. I thought you'd be keen to ride when you saw we had the ideal day. The others weren't too pleased with me as in this weather there's a lot to do but I argued that some of the horses needed exercising anyway.'

'It's a glorious morning,' commented Glenda.

Settled with his coffee, Mark issued a warning. 'It does appear so but we did have a fall of snow during the night ... not much but it could have made one or two places a little tricky. The main thing is, be sure to stick to the trails. I will be taking you on those used mostly by our cowboys so there should be little difficulty, but you're sure to meet something that isn't straightforward.'

'Cat, don't get too far in front,' warned Glenda as they walked outside to the horses that had been brought to the front of the house by three cowboys, who helped them into their saddles and adjusted their stirrups.

They moved off at a walking pace, allowing their horses to get used to the conditions. The surface was slippery, with yielding softened earth beneath.

'The horses are coping well with changes along this track,' Glenda observed to Mark. 'Will it be like this wherever you take us?'

'No. When we get to the treeline the bad conditions will ease. The snow wasn't deep enough to penetrate the foliage. There we'll find the best riding. We will not venture any further up the mountain than there. Only expert riders trust themselves and their horses to venture higher.'

They rode on in silence, Glenda wondering what Mark had in store for them. She soon found out. Ten minutes later the treeline ceased, leaving them to gaze across an open expanse of black rocks. Beyond that the ground rose steadily for about half a mile into a huge peak, its pinnacle proudly thrusting skywards. Mark checked his horse. Glenda pulled to a halt on his right-hand side and Cat positioned herself to his left. She leaned forward and patted her horse's neck, saying softly, 'Well done, Gila, enjoy your rest.' She turned to Mark. 'This is truly magnificent. It really is.'

He looked at Glenda, who had said nothing. He waited, trying to interpret her expression. Then she said, as if to herself, 'Awesome ... overpowering ... frightening.' She drifted into silence. Mark let it stay that way. He glanced at Cat and saw that she was completely lost in admiration of the whole landscape, as if she was saying, You are mine. You'll never escape me. And I'll always be here. Mark looked back at Glenda. Her expression had relaxed into contentment, as if she was now accepting the life the gods had allotted for her.

She sighed aloud and Mark asked, 'Something wrong, Glen?'

She caught the worried frown that furrowed his brow. 'No, no. Nothing. It's just the wonder of all this and what it has given me. Thank you so very much for bringing me here.'

She offered no more but Mark reckoned it had been enough. He would let this relationship proceed at its own pace; he knew she still thought often of her husband, and the shock of her loss had not been completely obliterated, maybe never would be, but he sensed she was leaving the door ajar in case someone else wanted to step inside, with care and respect for her feelings.

'We'll ride a little further along this track around the lower slopes of the mountain,' he called. 'Don't get too far ahead, Cat. I'll be taking you on another trail back to the ranch that will give me a better chance to size up the weather.'

She acknowledged his instructions and rode on ahead.

'Your daily predictions have been right on the nail,' Glenda said. 'And I know Cat has appreciated being able to exercise Gila.'

'I'm glad she has enjoyed it and I hope you have too.'

'More than I can say.'

A few minutes' silence was broken when she asked, 'How many mustangs do you normally round up from the wild?'

'We have the *remuda*, which Gordon and I like to keep at about one hundred.'

'And those are the mustangs from the open range from which you replenish your stock?'

Mark smiled as he said, 'You're learning. We'll make a cowgirl of you yet.'

Glenda was beginning to worry about Cat whom she hadn't seen for a while but she did not voice that to Mark, who had not expressed any concern. She did not want to appear over-protective. Another quarter of a mile and the trail swept round a stand of firs. Glenda felt relieved to see Cat there, sitting quietly on her horse.

'Hello, you two,' she called out. 'I thought this might be the split in the trail you told us about so I'd better wait here.'

'Quite right,' Mark praised her.

'It's wonderful,' Cat enthused. 'I saw a small herd of buffalo back there, about a quarter of a mile away.'

'You were lucky. That was an unusual sighting for this part. Overall there are not many left. Hunters slaughtered the herds for their hides and left the carcasses to rot. The Indians traditionally used the hides for clothing but lost that supply as well as an important source of food. It led to trouble but that is settling down now and hopefully won't be the cause of further hostility.' He eased himself in his saddle, surveyed the land and then said, 'Right, let's head home for the Circle C. But this time, Cat, stay with us.'

'You think we might run into trouble?'

'Of a kind,' was all he said.

Cat was about to ask what it might be but caught her Mother's glance indicating that Cat should press him no further.

They rode on. No one spoke. Glenda noted that Mark was casting his gaze in a wider arc than he usually did. Something must be troubling him but she knew better than to query what it was. If he thought they were in danger he would make it known. He put his horse into a gentle trot and mother and daughter matched his steady pace.

Forty minutes later he drew to a halt against a board nailed to a post on which was roughly painted with the words, **You Are Now Trespassing on Circle C Land**. As Glenda and Cat stopped beside Mark, Cat observed, 'That notice is old and flaking. It needs painting.'

'Tell your Uncle Gordon, he might take notice of you.'

'I will!' promised Cat.

Another half hour's riding brought them within sight of the ranch buildings. Glenda slowed her horse and stopped. Wondering why her mother had done so, Cat did likewise. Mark turned his horse to stop beside her.

'Something wrong?' he asked.

'What's been the matter, Mark, you've hardly spoken since we headed for home?'

'Sorry. I was bothered about the weather.'

'It's been a beautiful day. Still is,' said Glenda.

'You're right, but haven't you noticed the wind is changing direction?'

'No, but I had no cause to.'

'True. I should have thought of that. It has started to veer to the north. Blowing from that direction, the temperature could drop drastically at this time of the year.'

271

'Are you saying it's likely to happen?'

'Yes, and along with other signs, it worries me.'

'Such as?'

'The cattle are getting restless. Horses are heading for the shelters provided for them. The sun is losing heat and cloud is thickening on the horizon, which is not a good sign, particularly if the wind direction doesn't change and I don't think it will. The birds and the rest of nature don't take easily to what is happening. I just have a feeling we're in for some very bad weather.'

As if in answer to his observation, the wind sharpened accompanied by a cold blast that penetrated their clothing, making them wish they had put on their thickest coats.

'Ride!' Mark yelled above the howl of the wind.

Glenda and Cat reacted instantly. Hoofs beat a tattoo on the land. With darkening clouds driving in from the north on the strengthening wind, the three riders urged their mounts on.

'Stables!' yelled Mark.

They raced towards them. Gordon and the Circle C hands were already shepherding horses out of the paddocks and into shelter. Gordon grabbed Cat by the arm as she dropped from the saddle. He pulled her round towards the house. 'Inside, now!' he yelled. 'And don't come out until you're told!' He pushed her towards the building and she ran, hunched into her coat.

Glenda swung out of the saddle. Her feet had hardly touched the ground when a voice called out and a hand gripped her arm. 'House!' She ran, fighting the wind that would have swept her away, thankful for the help that someone was giving her. A scarf was wrapped around her. She pushed it away from her eyes – Zalinda's. Glenda knew she would have been blown off her feet but for this help and the reassuring grip on her arm from someone who had left the safety of her home to come to her aid. They ran together, Zalinda in command, urging Glenda and Cat to her house. They were almost there when the door opened. The maids reached out to them and swiftly helped them out of their coats. Relieved, they drew warm air deep into their aching lungs. Soon hot coffee was ready; it soothed away thoughts of what could have happened if they had been caught for long in the ferocity of the wild wind.

Zalinda calmed such thoughts even though she was willing Gordon to walk through the door. She knew Glenda was feeling the same, and saw in Caitlin's restless pacing to and fro in front of the large window, worry for the horses. Some time later all anxiety fled when Gordon and Mark walked in, showing the after-effects of battling against the wind while keeping a weaker section of corral fencing in place to prevent horses escaping.

Coats were shed and the two men sat down to revive themselves with the food the servants brought. It was only then that Zalinda put the question that was on everyone's mind. 'Is this going to get worse?'

Gordon's expression was serious. 'I am not going to hold back on this one. I am afraid it is. I talked with Mark and he thinks the same.' He allowed Mark to take over.

'If it stays this way we are in for bad time. Experience tells me we'll have bitter winds and a lot of snow.'

'How bad?' Zalinda urged him.

'Difficult to say but we would be wise to lay in as much food as possible and anything that will keep us warm. We'll keep our eyes on the weather and, if there is any sort of lull, take the chance to stock up.'

'What about the men?' asked Glenda.

'They know what is required of them and have already started on that,' replied Gordon. 'I have also told them to slaughter several steers so we should be all right for meat. We must work together and stay indoors as much as possible. Inform someone if you have to go outside and report back when you return. I have delegated two men to keep the necessary paths usable.'

'Is one of those between our house and Glenda's?' queried Zalinda.

'Yes,' replied Gordon.

'Good,' said his wife. 'We should be able to overcome any difficulties that might arise.'

'You really are expecting a bad time?' asked Glenda.

'It is best to be prepared for the worst,' replied Mark. 'It could start any time.'

'But, listen, the wind has lost some of that disturbing howl.'

'Don't be deceived. We'll be lucky if this is the end of it. I seriously don't think it is.'

They could never have foreseen what was to come.

39

The weather eased. The wind still reminded them that it was there but it had relinquished a few degrees of cold. As if it was rejoicing the sun rose into a clear blue sky, tempting the people on the Circle C and those beyond to venture outside.

Zalinda, using the path that had been cleared between the two houses more than once, hurried to Glenda's. 'Gordon is sending two men with a wagon into town to obtain more supplies, if the road is still passable and if there is anything left there. Is there anything you desperately want?'

'More flour and butter, if possible. Oh, yes, and matches. I almost forgot.'

'Will that do for you?'

'It's only guesswork, on top of what we have and your advice on what we should stock.'

'I'll instruct them to do their best.' Zalinda looked out of the window. Glenda came to stand beside her.

'It looks settled,' she said.

'It does but it could turn again. Anyway, I'd best get back with your list of requirements.' Zalinda hurried away.

Glenda and Cat watched from their window and saw her have a few words with the two wagon men before she went inside her house.

'Mama, I'm going to the stables to see if Gila is settled and warm,' said Cat.

'I was hoping you might help me with some baking.' Seeing disappointment in Cat's expression, Glenda added, 'All right, I'll get Namia to help me. Off you go. But if you see the weather changing, get back here quick.'

'I will.' Cat shrugged herself into her outdoor clothes, crammed a hat on her head and slid her fingers into gloves. She ignored the frosty snow that glistened in the sunlight and strode quickly in the direction of the stables. This is not much worse than I've experienced in Scotland, she thought.

With the large double doors to the stables closed, she used the small door cut out of the left-hand side. It squeaked and groaned as she pushed it open. She stepped inside and turned quickly to close the door again. A middle-aged cowboy stepped out of one of the stalls to see who had come to disturb him.

His smile on seeing Caitlin was broad and furrowed a face that was badly weathered from a life spent outdoors until the day he was injured in a fall. Now he was only fit for less strenuous work but still managed to help out among the horses he loved.

'Hello, Miss Caitlin,' he greeted her.

'Hello, Buck,' she replied with a smile. 'How are you today?'

'Better than the weather, Miss.'

'It's a lovely day, Buck, the sun is shining,' she contradicted him gently.

'Aye, it is, Miss, but the wind bites and that ain't a good sign. Heed my words, there's more bad weather coming.'

'I've heard this before so I'm going to change the subject to a better one,' she said with a smile. 'How's Gila today?'

His eyes lit up. He liked this young lady who had learned quickly and put into practice all the knowledge about horses he'd willingly planted in her mind. Because of her, he paid particular attention to her horse and she appreciated that.

Cat wandered off to Gila's stall, leaving Buck to get on with his routine work; she knew he didn't like being interrupted for too long. Grateful for Gordon's kindness to him after his injury, he liked to be on top of his work. Cat sang quietly to Gila as she gently rubbed her down. The horse nuzzled her fondly.

After half an hour Buck came to her. 'I'm going to stable two,' he said. 'Shan't be long.'

Cat settled herself on a heap of hay, content to be with Gila. She became lost to time until the stable door crashed open. Startled, she jumped up.

'Miss, Miss,' panted Buck. 'Sorry I've been a while. My opinion was wanted. Took longer than expected.'

'It's all right, Buck. Get your breath back.'

He leaned forward, hands on his thighs, taking his weight, as he drew air into his lungs. He gave a little shake of his head. 'It's not all right. It's beginning to snow ... big flakes. The wind is strengthening from the north. You'd better get back home.'

'I hadn't looked out, Buck. Thanks for the warning.'

'I'll see you safely home, Miss.'

Cat was at the door. She opened it wide enough to look out then shut it again quickly. 'I'll be all right, Buck. You

277

get off back to your cabin. By the look of things outside you shouldn't linger.' With that she was gone.

The sky was darkening. Snow whirled down thickly and the wind was strengthening by the second. Cat pulled the neck of her jacket tighter, and bent herself against the gale, thankful there were still traces of the track home visible. She stamped the snow off her boots on the porch and stepped inside, closing the door as quickly as possible. She took off her coat and sat down on a bench arranged against one wall. She was taking her snow-boots off when her mother bustled in.

'Thank goodness you're here,' she said, her expression full of concern.

'Did the wagon get back?' Cat asked

'Yes, but without the goods. The conditions got so bad they turned round.

'It's getting worse out there, the clouds look heavy with snow and look set to stay. Come and have a warming drink.'

But by the time Cat had had her coffee the weather was contradicting Glenda's observation. The falling snow had all but stopped and remained at bay throughout the rest of the afternoon and into the early evening, when it ceased completely. The contrary wind had finally made up its mind to stop playing with the window shutters that Glenda and the maids had closed before dark. Thankfully it had changed its yowl to a gentler note, as if it no longer wished to disturb the people living on the Circle C.

After checking they were not required the two maids retired, leaving mother and daughter quietly reading by the light from their oil lamp.

An hour later Glenda caught herself nodding off. Rousing herself, she said, 'I'm off to bed.'

'So am I,' said Cat. 'I was only waiting for you to wake up!'

'I wasn't asleep.'

'Yes, you were.'

'No, no, I was only resting my eyes.'

'Oh, so that's what you are calling it now,' laughed Cat.

Glenda stood up without replying. Instead she said, 'Are you coming to look out?'

'Of course.' It had become almost a ritual that on the way to bed they looked out of the window they left unshuttered so that they never felt completely cut off from the outside world. They went quietly to another bedroom and drew back the curtains, allowing light from a bright moon to flood the room. They both gasped with surprise. In marked contrast to the wild day, night and moonlight had brought a serene stillness to their world.

'Oh, Mama, that's just so wonderful,' said Cat quietly, not wanting to mar the peace surrounding them.

'I judged the weather wrongly,' Glenda admitted.

They stood for a while, lost in the wonder of the night, then a little reluctantly left the mesmerising vision and went to bed.

They slept the sleep of contentment.

'Mama! Mama!' Someone was shaking Glenda awake.

'What is it?' she asked, alarmed to find Cat standing beside the bed.

'Come and see.' The urgency in her voice caused Glenda to swing quickly from her bed, grab her gown and follow her daughter to the window.

'Where on earth did all that come from?' she gasped.

'Not the earth!' laughed Cat.

Snow was piled as high as the windowframes and they were on the side of the house most exposed to the wind, which they both realised was now beginning to strengthen and driving the fresh falling snow across the land like an engulfing shroud.

'It looks as though we will be prisoners in our own house for a while,' commented Glenda. 'We won't be able to go outside until it's safe to do so.'

'But I'll have to see Gila is all right,' Cat protested.

'Don't you dare think of that.'

'But . . .'

'No, Cat, there are no buts about it. I'm sure Gila will be all right. You said yourself that Buck was looking after her, along with other horses in his care.'

'But will he be able to get to the stable?'

'There'll be others to help him. They'll do all they can for the horses. Just settle down and don't worry. This weather can't go on forever.'

Two days later it appeared as if it would do so. The snow had not stopped and the howling wind curled itself around whatever was in its way; together they sought to destroy all before them. Marooned indoors the womenfolk watched the drifts getting higher and higher, except in places that were sheltered. The hope that the direction of the wind would not change was uppermost in everyone's minds. In even the slightest respite from the weather, the men of the Circle C battled with the snow to keep communications within the ranch as open as possible. They fought the elements to reach the stables and lavish care on the horses. They regretted they could not give the same attention to the cattle. On the open range the animals had to take their chances with whatever the weather threw at them.

Apart from her own concerns Glenda tried the best she could to keep Cat's thoughts away from Gila. Whenever he could get word to Cat, Buck informed her that her horse was coping well with the lack of exercise. Mark and Gordon tried to visit regularly and to be reassuring, though Glenda wondered how much of the true situation on the Circle C they were not revealing.

Zalinda also tried to visit Glenda whenever she could. Nor could she give a positive answer to Cat's query, 'There is never any news of the Indians that used to be on Circle C range; how will they be in this?'

'I'm sure they will be safe. They always find a way. Indians know all about the weather. That is why they will have moved earlier than usual.'

'Where do they go?'

'It is a different place every winter. Before I married I used to be with them, but once I became your uncle Gordon's wife, I was excluded from knowing where they would be going. They took the view that now I had your uncle to look after me. Don't you worry about them. I'm sure they will reappear after the winter passes.'

So the freeze went on and on, causing concern to all; the womenfolk found cooking tasty meals more difficult as their meat, vegetable and herb supplies began to diminish; tedium set in to home life and even the most experienced men were heard to say, 'Never known one like this.' 'This will leave terrible destruction in its wake.' 'It will break many ranchers.'

281

On hearing that last assessment, Cat was prompted to ask, 'Will it break you, Uncle Gordon?'

'It is impossible to answer that yet. We'll need to make an assessment once the situation improves.'

Another two weeks passed before the weather showed some reluctance to continue along the destructive path it had chosen. There was a glimmer of hope. But the conditions were still treacherous, particularly where ice was covered by snow.

Cat woke early. Her first thoughts were for her horse. She was tired of not being able to see Gila. She slipped out of bed and went to the window. The sun was just lighting an eastern sky free from cloud. It promised to be a nice day. This must be a turn for the better. Maybe the winter was being dismissed. Perhaps this was her chance to see Gila. She listened. No sound. The house was not yet stirring for the day. She dressed quickly, put on her outdoor clothes and silently left the house. The cold air still bit at her lungs but that was to be expected after being closed in for so long. She felt free.

Excited by the thought of seeing her beloved Gila again she headed for the stable, expecting to see Buck. She knew he was an early riser, but there was no sign of him outside. Maybe he was in the stable. She pulled up short at the horror of what had only just impinged on her mind. The corral gate and stable door stood open! Panic seized her. Where were the horses? She ran to the stable, only just managing to stay on her feet. She burst into the building. The horses? Gone! Gila? Gone!

'Help! Help!'

The call startled her. Buck!

She ran, glancing in each stall as she passed it. The fifth one brought her to a halt.

'Buck! What happened?' She was on her knees beside him, looking into a face that was bleeding from several cuts. Then the sight of his right leg, twisted badly beside him, gripped her attention. She was about to try to lift him when caution prevented her.

'Buck, I'll get help.' She rose to her feet.

'The horses, Miss. They . . .'

'Never mind them. I'll be back. Don't try to move.' She grabbed a slicker that hung in one of the stalls and laid it over him. Once again she commanded firmly, 'Don't attempt to move until I'm back.'

Buck winced.

'Don't move!' With that Cat was gone. She ran out of the stable. She slithered on some ice, crashed through some small snowdrifts, veered away from the large ones that would have stopped her in her tracks, but all the time she propelled herself in the direction of her uncle's house. She was breathing heavily with the air burning her lungs by the time she reached it. She supported herself against the wall as she hammered on the door while trying to call out, 'Uncle Gordon! Uncle Gordon! Aunt Zalinda! Aunt Zalinda!' Her voice strengthened. She heard movement in the house. Then the door swung open.

Her aunt and uncle, shocked by her distress, helped her over the threshold.

'Hot drink!' Zalinda called to one of her maids, who had been woken by the noise. The other was already bringing two blankets.

Zalinda asked, 'What's happened, Cat?'

Gordon was asking the same question.

'It's Buck. He's badly hurt in the stable. Come quickly!'

'What!' gasped Gordon.

Concern clouded Zalinda's eyes. Calling new instructions to the maids, she headed for the stairs followed by Gordon. In a few minutes, swathed in his outdoor clothes, he was leaving the house. Mark was called to attend to the injured man. After seeing to Buck, he called the men to assemble and told them what had happened.

'Buck came to the stable as usual and because the weather was more favourable, and showed signs of improving, he decided to let the horses have a run in the corral. They had been cooped up for so long that he rightly thought it would do them good. What he hadn't banked on was weakened fencing. Once the horses had found it they were able to break out. Buck only just managed to fling himself out of their way but he took some hefty blows.'

'Are we going after them, Boss?' someone asked.

'Sure, there's money roaming around somewhere out there. Thank goodness there was only the one corral affected. We'll start on that immediately in organised groups so we cover an area systematically. As we search for the horses we'll keep our eyes open for cattle. Goodness only knows where any survivors will have got to. A word of warning – don't take any risks. Watch out for wolves and grizzlies, they could be mighty hungry and hunting for food. Remember, it will be icy in patches so it will be dangerous riding. One other thing: take plenty of ammunition. Usual three shots if you've found something.'

As the men were dispersing, a distressed Caitlin confronted her uncle and Mark. 'My Gila's gone!'

40

Cat was almost inconsolable. When she expressed her desire to ride with the men searching for the missing horses, Glenda found herself agreeing but adding, 'And I will ride with you.'

A surprised hush descended on the men of the Circle C, busy gathering into search parties, when they saw the two women approaching on horseback, their intention obvious.

Gordon and Mark saw them at almost the same moment, looked at each other and immediately rode to meet them.

'What are you two doing?' demanded Gordon.

'Helping you find Gila,' replied Cat.

'No, no,' he answered. 'We want no more casualties.'

'We won't be any bother,' Cat shot back.

'We can't risk it. We'll be searching in some awkward places.'

'We can help without going into them.'

'You can't guarantee that. Situations develop and have to be dealt with there and then.'

'Uncle Gordon, please don't refuse me. I want to help find Gila.' A pleading note had come into Cat's voice.

Gordon looked to Glenda for assistance, but knowing how deeply her daughter wanted to be part of the search, Glenda gave him a neutral look and shrugged her shoulders helplessly. Gordon cursed under his breath but then decided if Cat was to learn more about horsemanship and conditions, he had to give way.

'All right,' he said reluctantly. 'Keep out of trouble and don't take any risks. Join the group Mark is assembling.'

Glenda saw his signal acknowledged but Mark's face looked like thunder; he was being made responsible for his friend's niece and sister-in-law in frightening conditions. Glenda knew then she should not have let Cat have her own way.

When the women reached him Mark informed them that his party of ten riders would search in an area that included a section of the foothills. The conditions had eased and visibility had improved. There was speculation that they might have had the worst of the weather but all hopes were dashed when the late afternoon brought a change that none of the searchers liked. The skies had darkened and sleet began to fall, stinging their faces and making visibility difficult again.

Mark called his party to gather around. 'I'm calling the search off. We have had a modicum of success, finding those ten horses in a coulee. They should be safely back at the Circle C now. I think it wisest to return to the ranch and hope this weather does not worsen.'

While he had been speaking Cat had brought her horse closer. 'No, Mark, no,' she protested. 'We can't give up. Gila must be . . .'

'Stop,' Mark cut in sharply. 'This weather is changing

286

for the worse and that could endanger the men. I can't and won't put them at risk. We return to the ranch, now!'

Glenda saw defiance in Cat's eyes and could sense her daughter was on the point of arguing with Mark, and even continuing to search for Gila on her own. 'Cat! Don't think about it. Mark is in charge. He knows what is best for us.'

'I want my horse,' she said defiantly.

'You won't find her today. Now do as I say, young lady,' rapped Mark. As if on cue a drop in the temperature changed the sharp sleet into a thickening white blanket of falling snow, with the winds starting to whip it into a frenzy. 'Home!' Mark shouted in a manner that told everyone he would stand against anyone who said otherwise. He added quickly, 'And stay close together so no one strays in the white-out that is coming.'

They had to match their pace to the depth of the snow that was becoming harder to overcome. Horses fought against the deepening drifts. The riders huddled in their saddles and battled against the biting wind. Snow turned them into ghostly figures. The riders relied on Mark's knowledge of the terrain to get them back to the Circle C. All were relieved when they became aware of shadowy shapes emerging through the falling snow. A few more yards and the outlines of Circle C buildings were visible. The riders vented their feelings in thanks to Mark. He raised his hands in acknowledgement as he guided his horse towards the corral where he expected to find the ten horses his men had found. His tension eased when he saw them safely inside the repaired fence. They looked bedraggled and miserable, seeking shelter in the stable attached. He started to turn his horse away but pulled it sharply to a halt.

'Cat! Caitlin! Glenda!'

The call came again and again.

'Did you hear that, Mama?' she queried.

'Yes. It was Mark.'

'What on earth can he want? He knows you and I are back safely.'

'Cat! Cat!'

'That call's coming from the corral we were using,' said Glenda. 'Better see what he wants.'

Thankful that the snow in this section was not too deep, they covered the ground quickly.

The corral and horses appeared out of the swirling snow. Mother and daughter saw a skewbald horse nuzzling Mark.

Excitement surged through Cat as she pulled her horse to a halt. She dropped from the saddle almost before the horse had stopped.

'Gila! Gila!' Cat hugged her. 'How did my Gila get back here?'

'I don't know,' said Mark. 'It's a mystery to me. It doesn't look as though Gordon is back yet so I must have counted wrongly when we found those horses in the coulee.'

'I counted them with you,' said Glenda. 'There were ten and I would swear Gila wasn't among them.'

'I agree but here she is,' said Mark. 'Perhaps she was separated from the herd and decided to come back on her own, but I doubt it in these conditions.'

'In that case she must have been brought here.' Glenda paused then added thoughtfully, 'There's only one answer – Ahote.'

'You think he found her?' queried Mark.

'It's possible,' said Cat. 'Gila would trust him. Ahote

288

would want to get her back here before he might be seen at the ranch and in case he was followed afterwards by someone wanting to discover the location of the Indian camp.'

'Well, we'll have to wait for better weather to find out if Ahote is the answer,' said Mark.

The other search parties were returning, only one more reporting success in finding and rescuing twelve horses.

'This has been a tiring but fruitful day,' commented Mark. 'We'd better get some rest. If the weather is suitable tomorrow we'll search for the other horses and see how the cattle are surviving in this cold.'

But the next morning despondency fell heavily on the whole of Circle C. Snow was billowing in the wind now, blowing with more ferocity. The intense chill attacked anyone who dared to venture outside. All the Circle C hands and their families were prepared for a bad winter but as the days dragged on and on, with little let up in the bad weather, despondency began to set in. Were they never going to be visited by the sun, a blue sky or a moon to brighten the night? Were they never again going to be able to walk or ride through the valleys, climb ridges, relax by water tumbling over stones? They relied on their belief that nature doesn't stand still.

But after nearly two months even the best of relationships were growing frayed. Tempers snapped, mild criticisms struck deep, and apologies were not easily made. Wives and husbands found faults they would never have noticed and children were more miserable and argumentative. Everyone longed for a change in the weather so that they could look forward to better days. They waited and waited. They bemoaned the fact that they were isolated, with more rain, frost, ice and snow, and the ever-blowing wind cutting deep into their minds, causing them to dub this the worst winter in living memory.

Then one morning Glenda woke to find the wind no longer howled. She looked out of her window and saw the shape and size of the drifts had not increased. The sky was no longer shedding snow. Clouds were parting to allow a glimpse of the sun. A new day, a new time, had been born.

Hope was revived. Shovels came out and were used with new enthusiasm to clear pathways and entrances to homes and buildings essential to the resurrection of the Circle C. Any item that could be set alight was burned to hasten the melting of drifts blocking movement around the land.

Gordon and Mark took stock of the essential tasks to be tackled first. They quickly drew up a rota of fences to restore, buildings to repair, anything and everything that would bring normality to the Circle C. They delegated men to work teams, drew in the women to see that food supplies were restored.

Satisfied with the organisation at the ranch, Gordon and Mark turned their attention to forming search parties to look for the missing horses and, more importantly, cattle. The future of the Circle C depended on it. The severe weather must have taken its toll on the cattle exposed to the elements but they were still hopeful of finding a surviving core from which the Circle C could expand again to its usual four thousand head.

41

The next day the air was full of tension. Eight men were chosen to search with Gordon and Mark. Some of those left behind assembled to see them off. All had a premonition that today would decide the Circle C's future.

Gordon called out to those who were to wait at the ranch: 'I can't say how long we will be away. You will realise from the food and spare clothing we are taking it may be some time.' He turned to his search party. 'Listen up! Until we are all back here, care is a priority. No one is to search by himself. Danger might lurk anywhere and a fall, if you're alone, could mean death by freezing. That is why I have instructed you to ride in pairs. We will use the usual system of three gunshots to raise the alarm if necessary. Take care, each one of you is more important than the cattle.'

Zalinda laid her hands on Gordon's shoulders and looked deep into his eyes. 'I love you. My spirit will ride with you and be by your side to keep you safe.' She kissed him and they held each other close for a few moments.

Mark swung down from his saddle. He threw his reins to

a twelve-year-old standing with his mother to see the riders leave on their mission. 'Keep him quiet, Jed.'

'Sure will.'

Jed liked to be around the cowboys and they appreciated a youngster who wanted to follow their trade.

Mark turned to Glenda. 'Good to see you looking so well and pretty in the nicest of ways.'

'I think your eyes are deceiving you. But thank you.'

'My pleasure,' he replied, eyes fixed on her as if he was trying to imprint a picture on his mind.

She laid her hand on his arm. 'Promise me you'll take care? Don't try anything foolish. The land will be treacherous.'

'I know it like the back of my hand.' He gave a little smile. 'And I have an incentive to return – you.' He kissed her gently on the cheek.

She eyed him with a directness that had something in it he had never seen before. 'I think we can do better than that.'

'I think we can,' he said. Pulling her close, he kissed her for a long time, only stopping to say, 'I'm lucky to have you.'

'Take care on this search. I need you to come back safe and sound.'

'I will. Nothing is more certain, knowing that you are here for me.'

She kissed him again. 'Now go, before I persuade you to stay.'

The searchers knew the cattle would head for shelter but after two days and no sight of even one steer, Gordon and Mark began to wonder what condition the animals would be in after having endured such harsh freezing conditions for so long.

'Don't worry, they'll be fine. It will be the weaker ones we'll have lost,' said Mark. Gordon gave a thoughtful nod. He had expected to hear some kind of signal from the others by now.

It was midday on the third day when Mark called out to Gordon, riding a parallel track a short distance away. Gordon's hopes rose. He rode as quickly as the patches of deeper snow would allow him. Then he saw Mark, a dejected figure, sitting in the saddle awaiting his arrival.

Gordon swore when he pulled his horse to a halt alongside Mark. This was precisely what he had feared. Steers had piled on top of each other in their attempts to force their way over a fence before succumbing to the inevitable. They lay, rigid in death, stark evidence of the ferocity of the storm that had swept from the north during the last few months.

'Some of them were set on by hungry wolves,' commented Mark, having read the evidence in the torn bodies.

'We can't do anything here, we'd best ride on,' said a dejected Gordon, 'but I don't hold on finding any change of fortune.'

Over the next four long days they found nothing to raise their hopes, and reports from other searchers were equally gloomy. They were all feeling drained and longed for decent home cooking. Suddenly a gunshot echoed through the snow-covered hills. Their horses raised their heads and both men looked at each other with hope in their eyes. Another shot echoed over the hills.

'There!' yelled Mark, pointing towards a rock face that had been to their left for the last mile.

They turned their mounts and quickened their pace as much as they dared. At one point the snow deepened but the horses showed no fear. The riders urged them on, anxious to see why there had been a signal. Another hundred yards and they rounded an outcrop of rock where one of the Circle C hands awaited them.

'There's cattle trapped in there.' He indicated a cleft in the rock face. 'Goodness knows how they got in.'

'They'd be desperate for shelter from the storm,' said Mark. 'Thought of food would come later. What matters now is, can we get them out?'

The two Circle C hands who had been riding together had already examined the site. They quickly passed an assessment to Gordon and Mark. 'The main problem is caused by a fall of rock, which must have happened after the cattle had squeezed in and injured some of them. They were trapped. We tried some of the rocks but two large boulders were too much for us. Three or four of us might be able to manage them.'

'Right,' said Gordon. 'Let's get on with it.'

The four men, having sized up the situation, worked with the shovels, picks and sledgehammers brought from the ranch. It was back-breaking work; sweat poured from them but, when enough groundwork was done, they pushed the boulders out of the way inches at a time. With the unfamiliar activity and their lack of food, the trapped cattle grew more and more unsettled. They were becoming a danger to their would-be rescuers.

As the work became harder the four men took breathers more regularly. During one of these Mark scrambled over some rocks to a higher position. From there he believed he would be of more help in directing the final clearance of the area where twenty steers were held prisoner.

Having weighed up the possibilities from his position he called out, 'Work to your right. You should be able to clear a passage wide enough for one steer at a time to pass through. Then we can hold the cattle in that area until we make the final clearance.'

'We'll get on it,' called back Gordon. 'You stay up there and advise us.'

Mark acknowledged the order. With him able to see the whole picture and direct operations the men worked more eagerly, knowing their job must be nearing an end. Mark relaxed a little. It was going well. His thoughts flew to Glenda and the diamond ring he had placed in a drawer before he left on this mission.

'Keep on the same track but aim ten yards to the left,' he called out. 'You should find the final clearance easier for the last twenty yards.'

Gordon called out his acknowledgement. The other two cowboys whooped at the prospect of rest.

The sound of hammers and picks rang out in the clear air.

Mark straightened, eased his back and flexed his legs.

An unearthly scream rent the canyon. A thud and an ominous silence followed, leaving a crumpled body to mark a place of death among the rocks of a Colorado canyon.

42

As she was crossing the room Glenda glimpsed a movement outside. She automatically crossed to the window.

Cat, who was reading, noticed her mother's action and asked, 'Who is it, Mama?'

'Four horses but only three of them being ridden. The fourth has something tied on its . . .'

The room was suddenly charged with a sense of deep shock. Cat jumped to her feet and in a few strides was beside her mother just as words poured from Glenda's lips.

'No! Oh, please God, no! No . . . not again!'

Her cry resounded through the house.

Cat stared out of the window. A group of slow riders . . . Mark's horse, a covered bundle tied across its back.

Cat was beside her mother, grasping her, giving her support against the grief that was overwhelming her.

'Mark?' Cat queried what she was seeing, not believing it, yet knowing the truth – the lifeless form was his.

Glenda had moved towards the door. Cat quickly grasped her hand and went with her.

Gordon took the reins of Mark's horse and the eight cowboys continued to escort them to his house. Gordon's bowed head slowly turned and gave Glenda a nod of condolence as they passed. Word spread through the Circle C ranch like a devouring prairie fire and everyone, dazed by the news, gathered in silent disbelief.

Zalinda sized up the situation quickly and came to join Gordon. A few words of explanation about the way Mark had died passed between them. In a moment she was with Glenda and Cat. Zalinda knew words of comfort would be useless at this moment but nevertheless she reassured them they were not alone; the whole of Circle C shared this loss.

Cat felt her mother tremble as they watched Mark's body eased from the back of his horse and taken inside by four broad-shouldered cowboys.

Zalinda quietly asked Glenda if she wanted to follow them. She nodded. Cat took her mother's arm.

Gordon led the way into the house with so many memories of times he and his friend had spent here together, laying plans to become the owners of one of the largest ranches in Colorado. Was the Circle C's future threatened by Mark's untimely death?

Mark had been laid on his bed, wearing the clothes in which he had been brought home. The traces of rock and soil on them hid a body broken by his fall. The shock hit Glenda hard. Silent tears streamed down her face.

Zalinda stood aside, allowing Glenda to mourn in her own way. Zalinda too grieved for a man she'd respected in many ways but mostly as her husband's friend. She knew she would have to be strong and help Gordon when the realisation of the scale of his loss hit him.

Later that day Zalinda informed the doctor of the tragedy so that he could write a death certificate and, together with her, lay out the body in preparation for the mourners who would pay their respects until the day he was buried.

Four days later Mark was laid to rest in an area of the Circle C set aside for such a purpose.

'You and Catlin cannot be on your own tonight,' Zalinda insisted. 'You both must continue to stay with us for as long as you like.'

'I seem to be too numb to think ahead,' said Glenda sadly.

'Take all the time you need,' said Zalinda, a statement that was backed whole-heartedly by Gordon who had met the loss of his friend and partner stoically while drawing on the strength of his wife. Her support was a prop for them both and they willingly let that spill over onto Glenda and Cat.

But mother and daughter knew they could not remain under the shadow of a friendship that was helping them deal with the tragic loss. Life had to go on. Everyone had problems but they put them aside. Cowboys' wives kept their meetings but respected Glenda's need for quiet until the time was right. Even the children learned to respect Mark's memory and mourn the loss of their friend.

The day after the funeral, Gordon decided he would deal with his friend's belongings. It was a simple task for he found in a drawer only one bequest – a small package on which was written, 'For Glenda'.

He took it with him as he left Mark's house. When Gordon walked into his home he was pleased to find Zalinda, Glenda and Caitlin waiting for him.

'Finished?' asked his wife.

'Yes. What little there was has been dealt with. It will be collected tomorrow.' His words caught in his throat. 'It seems an end not only to a life but to a vibrant personality who should still be with us.' He recollected himself, realising it was no use bemoaning their loss. 'Glenda. It's meant for you.'

'Me?' She took it from him, looking surprised. She removed the wrapping paper to find a small box. On opening it she gasped at the sight of a ring. A central diamond was set with three smaller diamonds to each side. Mark must have been saving up his money for a while to pay for this, she thought. For a moment there was silence. She was suddenly aware that a ring like this could only have been bought in New York all those weeks ago yet he had not shown his true feelings for her until their last goodbye. Now it was all too late.

'Oh, Mark! If only . . .' The tears had started to flow.

'Were you going to marry him?' asked Cat.

'I don't know. He never asked me.'

'It looks as though he was going to,' said Zalinda.

In a few moments, when it became obvious that Glenda wanted to drop the subject, the others let it go. But it rose again when mother and daughter went to bed.

'Would you have married him, Mama?' asked Cat.

Glenda's face was filled with regret and a trace of guilt. To have accepted a proposal from Mark would have felt like a betrayal to John. And yet . . .

'The truth is, I don't know,' she confessed. 'But I would certainly have considered it. He was a fine man.'

*

Lives were in turmoil. The devastation caused by Mark's accident and the severest winter for many years had to be put right. Recognising her husband's dilemma Zalinda quietly suggested to Gordon, 'Mark would have expected you to get on and rescue the Circle C from ruin. You owe it to him to do that. Aim with the accuracy of an arrow hitting its target.'

'I know what I must do but first we'll have to find the cattle to form the nucleus of a new herd and that won't be easy. It will take time to achieve that again.'

'You've done it once, there's no reason not to do it again.'

'And maybe face a winter as deadly as this one? Is it worth it?'

'Am I worth it?'

He took her in his arms and kissed her. 'You are worth so much more . . . and then all of it again and again and again.'

'If you think that then you'll do it. You can and you will.' Zalinda kissed and held him, promising love through the testing times to come.

43

Glenda saw the strong sunlight streaming into her bedroom. How long was it since she had seen that? It seemed to be calling her to a new life. But did she want one? No. She wanted the old one. But which one? She shook her head. The truth was, she could not regain either of them. John and Mark were gone and would not want her to mourn and be miserable. She must face a new future and come out better for doing so.

'Good morning,' she said brightly when she saw Zalinda and Gordon having their breakfast. 'The sun is glorious after that testing winter. Is it here to stay?'

'The signs are good,' replied Zalinda.

'Are you are going riding?'

'Yes. I'll help with any cattle that need to be brought into the pens.'

'Then I'll change and help too.'

'There's no need, if you don't feel up to it.'

'I want to keep busy,' replied Glenda. 'I want to help.'

'Then you shall,' said Gordon. 'Ride with Zalinda.'

'And so will I,' said Cat, who caught her uncle's under-lying instruction to look after her mother.

He left the table to glance out of the window. 'Tom's getting the men organised. I'll have a word with him; tell him he has three other riders to employ.' With that Gordon was hurrying from the room.

'Good morning, Tom, you're in good time.'

'You know me, Boss. Don't believe in hanging about if there's a job to be done. I think we're in for a very unpleasant one, so the sooner this is out of the way the better.'

'Right. I have three more riders for you: Zalinda, Glenda and Caitlin,' said Gordon. 'They insisted on working with us. Let them help the riders who are dealing with bringing loose cattle to the pens. I reckon they'll be pleased to be back in the corrals and will be easier to handle.'

'They're good horsewomen so I reckon they'll manage the lone critters. But I'll keep a couple of men working with them, just in case.'

'Sounds good,' said Gordon. 'You have the rest of us well organised.'

'Thanks, Boss. Let's hope we've seen the last of the freezing weather for this year.' Tom wheeled his horse around and galloped away. He cast his eyes over the whole assembly. Satisfied, he made the signal for them to start for their allocated areas.

They rode off in high hopes but the sight of circling buzzards left them with no illusions about the scale of the devastation they faced. Time and time again stock running before the thunderous wind had come up against fences that held them back. In panic steers and cattle had flailed and struck each other in their attempts to get through the living barrier that was holding them back. Wherever the cowboys rode, it was the same story. Animals piled high, unable to save themselves, having to wait until the cold agony took them away into the comfort of death.

Any survivors were rounded up, fed and taken into care or, where possible, allowed free range but kept under daily supervision. The dead animals had to be disposed of chiefly by fire, a task the cowboys abhorred though they put their personal feelings aside for the sake of the Circle C. The smoking pyres did not augur well for the ranch's future.

The losses had been greater than anticipated. Even Zalinda, who had tried to keep everyone's spirits up, was beginning to agree with Gordon's gloomy view of the future.

'I must tell everyone here to look for jobs elsewhere, with my blessing. They should take any opportunity that arises.' Gordon's attitude disappointed Zalinda but she knew he had to be practical about the situation; she would support him in whatever he did. They broke the news to Glenda and Cat at breakfast the next morning.

'You are the first to know,' Gordon concluded. 'I would be grateful if you kept it to yourselves until I have broken the news at a ranch meeting. To give me the chance to summon them all, we'll have it in two days' time.'

'This is terrible news,' said Glenda. 'What can I say? Sorry is not strong enough. I just wish there was some way I could ease things for you. I know Cat will be feeling the same.'

She nodded. Her eyes were full of tears as her dreams of life on the ranch lay in ruins.

Glenda saw her daughter's disappointment. She wanted to reach out and comfort her but knew the gesture would be too much for Cat to bear with composure.

'Gordon and I have much to consider,' said Zalinda. 'We must decide where our future lies. Until we make a decision you are more than welcome to stay with us or else remain in the house Gordon built for you. You don't have to rush into making up your minds.'

44

'Oh, Mama why did this have to happen?' asked Cat. 'Just when everything was going so well for us here … How strange to think that Ros doesn't even know.'

Glenda smiled weakly. 'Yes, I'll write to her within the week but for now we mustn't sit moping. There is still a whole world out there with new places in it for us. We just need to claim them.'

'I thought I had claimed my place,' said Cat sadly.

'Would you still remain here if you could?'

'Yes, and I was certain while Mark was alive that he would have tempted you to stay.' Cat thought too of Ahote and the bond they had shared. She had always hoped it would have led them to become more than just friends. But had he now deserted her? The Indians were still nowhere to be seen.

'You must not let me influence your decision,' said Glenda. 'It is your life and if you wish to rear horses you can still do so even if the Circle C no longer exists. Just follow your dream.'

'But that will not be easy if Uncle Gordon and Zalinda are not here at the ranch.'

'Let's wait and see what happens. We'll know in two days.'

It was mid-morning when the ranch hands and their families gathered to hear Gordon's decision on the future of the Circle C. The buzz of hope alternating with doubt fell away when he and Zalinda walked into the barn. They read nothing good in his expression. He had a brief word with Tom then turned to face the cowboys. Silence settled over the gathering.

Gordon cleared his throat. 'This last winter has been hell for us all. I for one would not wish to live through it again. I must be frank with you. It would not be fair of me to allow you to cling to any hope that we can continue where we were before the weather turned so deadly. It has torn the Circle C apart. After the last few days we now know our cattle losses are far greater than we had anticipated. For me to replace them fully would be financial ruin. We have looked at every angle and can see no way ...'

A distant rumbling sound drowned out his words. The noise continued. The onlookers exchanged glances of disbelief. Most of them had heard similar sounds before, but now ... and here? The uproar drew nearer and nearer and the earth resounded beneath their feet.

'Cattle!' The word was on everyone's lips.

The cowboys followed in Gordon and Zalinda's wake rushing outside to verify the unbelievable.

They poured out of the building and stood in amazement. Almost two hundred longhorns were pelting forward with

Indians manoeuvring each side of the herd while others ahead were forcing it to slow down. At the right moment they split the herd into two, and urged them into two large corrals. The ranch hands watched in awe at the skill of the Indians.

With everything under control the chief brought his riders to a halt and watched proudly as they formed up behind him.

Gordon and Zalinda hurried to greet him, their faces joyful. Chief Ouray dismounted and with a broad smile opened his arms to his daughter whose eyes were filled with tears of joy. He hugged her to him.

'Thank you,' she whispered. She had no need to say more – all her joy and relief were expressed in those two words. A thousand cattle plus the few hundred Gordon and the men had reclaimed would be enough to keep them solvent for the year ahead. Then they would build on that, and build again.

Her father smiled his love for Zalinda then turned to Gordon and took his son-in-law's outstretched hand.

'If I read correctly what you have done, all of us at the Circle C owe you an everlasting debt of thanks,' said Gordon.

Chief Ouray, waving this away, smiled and said, 'You owe my people nothing, we are only returning what is rightfully yours. No doubt you are curious, so let's you and I walk a little. My ageing legs need stretching.'

'Very well,' Gordon agreed. They signalled to their respective parties to take a break.

'You most likely wondered why we moved our camp earlier than usual. I sensed a change in the wind and knew the spirits of my ancestors were telling me to seek shelter in the foothills. The sky signalled great trouble ahead. I said nothing except to order my people to break camp. I led them to pastures in a secluded valley we had never visited before. The Great Spirits were guiding us, but first they told us to take sufficient cattle from the open range to ensure our own survival and the Circle C's. I took only cattle wearing your brand. We found the sheltered place from instructions handed down over generations and it was good. We survived the storm that destroyed so many without a single loss.'

'A miracle,' said Gordon.

'Call it what you will. I believe that my ancestors wished the Circle C to survive, for the sake of both our peoples.'

'It will not be easy to keep going after all we've lost,' said Gordon, 'but together we can do it. Please, move back on the land that you rightfully occupy and, in thanks for your actions, I will add more to your holding.'

The Indian chief bowed his head. 'You are a generous man, Mr Gordon. My people will sing your praise forever. I will go now and announce your generosity to them.'

45

Ahote, after helping to settle the cattle, rode into the ranch, looking for his friend. He halted his horse. 'Where is Mark?' he called to Zalinda. 'He wasn't with Gordon or Chief Ouray when I saw them.'

Zalinda placed her hand on his horse's neck and said, 'I have bad news, Ahote.'

Cat came up beside her but did not speak.

He turned his eyes to Cat and, alarmed by the great sadness he saw, asked, 'Tell me what is wrong?'

Zalinda went on to explain the loss of their beloved friend.

Cat reached up to take his hand but Ahote immediately jerked the reins to put his horse into a gallop. Cat was brushed aside.

'Let him go,' said Zalinda. 'He needs to mourn in his own way.'

Dear Ros,

I do not know if your Scottish newspapers reported

the terrible winter we have had here. I have never experienced anything like it. There were extremes of frost and blizzards that kept us inside for at least two months. Some of the townfolk did not survive, even Lily who ran the store, do you remember her? The freezing conditions are only now beginning to yield to warmer weather. It almost destroyed the cattle. Uncle Gordon has lost more than three-quarters of his herd and there are still more that may not survive. However the Indians, who as usual had moved their encampment for the winter, we knew not where, appeared two days ago as if from nowhere with the makings of a new herd. Suffice it to say they have saved the Circle C from ruin.

However I have worse to tell you. Mark fell to his death while trying to rescue some cattle trapped in the mountains. Everyone on the ranch was devastated, but, needless to say, this has hit Mother hardest. I think you and I had detected a certain closeness between her and Mark, but it had evidently grown into something much deeper. She did not know until after his death that he had bought her an engagement ring. This tragedy will affect her future, just when I thought everything was looking bright for her.

Hopefully when the winter finally lifts mail will start to reach us again, so please write soon. I hope all of you at Pinmuir, and Aunt Fiona, are well.

Your loving sister,
Cat

Ros opened the letter and read Cat's words with astonishment and grief. She had wondered why the number of letters had dropped off but had expected it was the Scottish weather that had held things up. But for them it had only been a normal Highland winter, nothing like the one her family had been living through in Colorado. She was glad she had come back to Clive when she had.

Ros went to her writing desk and wrote to her mother, expressing sorrow at the death of Mark.

He was a fine man and how I feel for the loss felt by everyone on the Circle C, but especially you. I am sure you will miss him sadly. I sense there was a strong bond between you and I think my father would have been happy for you. Remember, you have shown strength and endurance in such a situation before, and I am sure once the shock fades, you will look to the future with hope once more.

Now I know that you will receive letters again after your 'big freeze' interrupted services, we can resume more frequent correspondence.

We too had a bad winter if not on the scale of yours. Our sheep are hardy and found shelter where they could. We lost a few but nothing out of the ordinary for a Highland winter. Clive and Tim kept checking those they could find and I don't know how they would have managed without the collies. Clive did not want to retire old Bob, his father's dog, whose legs were getting unsteady, but needs must. Bob now sleeps in front of the hearth, keeping Mrs Lynch company in the kitchen. You would have laughed at the way she objected to him at first but now she has grown to think of him as her own. Clive and Tim have constructed a new barn so that the sheep may take shelter nearer to the farm if they want to. They both have more ideas for developing the Estate, which I will write about in a separate letter when I have more details. It could turn out to be an exciting time for Pinmuir. Things are going well here.

Finally, may my love give you the strength to face the future without Mark, whatever it may hold.

Your loving daughter,

Ros

Glenda put the letter down. She noticed the sun trying to break through the clouds, and feeling she needed some fresh air, put on her well-worn coat. Zalinda watched from her window as Glenda walked in the direction of Mark's grave, knowing life would never be the same again for any of them.

On her return, Glenda decided to put pen to paper and wrote a brief note in answer to Ros's letter.

Dear Ros,

It was good to hear all your news after so long and we look forward to hearing from you again more often. The truth is, I am in limbo. I don't know what I want to do. It was all so easy when I had Mark. It is true we had a special partnership.

At the moment Cat and I are living with Gordon and Zalinda. As good as they are, and insist we are no trouble, we feel we should be moving back into the house that they built for us.

On the ranch Uncle Gordon has had to replace Mark with Tom Harley, so he and his wife have moved into

Mark's house. Tom is taking to the new job well but his wife Sara feels rather shy towards me. Everything has changed.

Cat still wants to develop her plans for horse breeding, so Uncle Gordon is going to contact an expert he knows who will advise her further now that Mark cannot.

I must go now.

Write soon,

Your loving mother

46

The evening sun touched the hills around Pinmuir with a delicate light that lent them an extra beauty and the mountains beyond a magic that dazzled Rosalind. The loch lay peaceful with only enough movement to flicker the water into dazzling diamonds.

She slipped her fingers between Clive's. Not a word passed between them but their touch spoke for them.

A few more steps then Clive stood still, released his fingers and, putting his arms round her waist, drew Ros closer. His lips met her willing acceptance and he prolonged the kiss until finally she let their lips part. Clive looked into her eyes.

'Ros McKinley, will you marry me?'

She threw back her head and laughed. Then, with tears of happiness welling up, she answered, 'I was longing to hear that. The answer is, yes, Clive. I will.'

Joy swept through them both, bringing passion in its wake that made them remember these moments all their lives. Happiness still filled them as they strolled beside the loch. Ros sensed the spirit of her father nearby.

'Let's go and tell your mother,' she said.

Clive kissed her on the forehead and smiled. He turned for home eagerly, pulling her behind him.

They quickened their pace, which broke into a run as they neared the house. Laughing, they swept into the sitting room. Their sudden entrance brought Jessie spinning round from the window where she had stood admiring Clive's latest work in the garden.

'What's got into you two?' she asked as her son embraced her and lifted her off her feet.

'I've just asked Ros to marry me and she's said she will!' He gave his mother a kiss on her cheek. 'Be happy for us, Mother.'

'I am! I am!' gasped Jessie, her tone expressing all the joy she was feeling. She hugged her son and when she turned to Ros and let her tears of joy flow they knew they had her approval.

Jessie produced a bottle of brandy. 'I've been keeping this for just such an occasion.' She called in Mrs Lynch to break the news to her. After their cook had expressed her delight she added, 'I'd like to arrange a special meal in celebration tomorrow evening. Just tell me how many might sit down at the table.'

'I think we can do that here and now,' said Ros. 'There will be we four, plus Aunt Fiona and Tim.' She glanced at Clive, seeking his approval.

He nodded and the arrangements were quickly settled. 'I'll see Tim now and get him to take a message to your aunt right away,' said Clive.

An hour later Tim returned with the news that the invitations had been accepted.

315

'I wish both your fathers had been here to witness your happiness,' commented Jessie, sadness in her voice.

'They will be in spirit. I felt it when we were walking by the loch today,' Ros assured her.

Jessie nodded then asked, 'Have you decided on a date?'

'Not yet. It will depend if my mother and Cat, and maybe my uncle and aunt, can manage it.'

'We'll work out a schedule and then ask them for possible dates,' suggested Clive.

'I'll write to Mother and Cat tomorrow with the news of our engagement and see what might suit them.'

Dear Mama,

Yesterday Clive asked me to marry him and I said yes! Your approval would crown my happiness. Please, please approve. We have thought about dates, which can only be finalised after we have seen Rev. Kintail, but we are looking ahead to, say, six months' time so that you and Cat can make all the necessary arrangements to be here. We can't have the wedding without both of you.

We will also invite Uncle Gordon and Zalinda, and hopefully they will be able to say yes too.

No more for now.

Your excited daughter,

Rosalind

She wrote a similar letter to Cat, adding, 'Knowing your desire to stay in Colorado, I hope you and Ahote are remaining good friends but perhaps by now you have your eye on a handsome young cowboy working on the Circle C!'

*

316

In Colorado mother and daughter opened their correspondence at the same time and expressed delight at the news. 'We will be going, won't we, Mother?' exclaimed Cat. 'We *must*. Ros wants me to be her bridesmaid.'

'I wouldn't miss it for the world, and nor will you.'

Cat hugged her mother.

'We'll have to be careful with our money but we should be able to manage it. I'll be able to assess our financial situation properly once we are at Pinmuir and have seen the accounts. But don't let's worry about that now and spoil the happiness of the occasion.'

'I wonder if Uncle Gordon and Zalinda have received their invitations,' said Cat.

An hour later they arrived and were shown into the sitting room. Glenda thought they looked a little solemn but made no comment. She offered them coffee but they refused.

'We have had a letter from Rosalind with an invitation to attend her marriage to Clive of whom we heard when she was with us.'

'Good,' said Glenda. 'I am so happy with their decision.'

'We are flattered that they want us there but sadly we won't be able to attend,' said Gordon.

'Oh, no!' said Glenda.

'No!' protested Caitlin.

'Sorry, but we cannot afford the time away from the ranch after the problems the freeze caused,' Gordon told them. 'I must be here to see that the recovery is handled in the right way. I believe we can survive but it will take time and need to be carefully supervised. We have not been able to get enough done so far to leave Tom on his own. He is a good man but there are still things he needs to experience before he can maintain Circle C as a top ranch.'

'Then get somebody in who has the experience so you can come to the wedding,' said Cat.

Gordon gave a wry smile. 'It wouldn't work, Cat. Tom would be hurt and it might push him into resigning. I don't want to lose him; he's shaping up to be a man who, in the future, could bear sole responsibility here. He is good with the Indians, who have settled in again; I don't want that putting at risk. So I'm afraid our answer to Ros's invitation will have to be no. I've suggested Zalinda goes but she says she would not feel comfortable in a strange country without me.'

Zalinda raised her hands to Glenda and Cat. 'Please don't try to persuade me. I know it would be a delight to share your wonderful day but I can't leave my husband. After all, he has made me a ranch manager now.'

Glenda's nod of understanding was replicated by Cat, who added, 'Although I know she'll be disappointed, Ros will understand.'

47

The days passed and the wedding was a major topic of conversation between Glenda and Cat. Glenda was happy for both her daughters. They all had learned much by living in America and with that knowledge she knew Ros and Cat would be all right, but what did life hold for her? The problem of her future began to weigh heavily on her. Bereft and bemused, she had only her daughters to consult but did not want her troubles to encumber them.

First, she had to decide where she wanted to be. She had no doubt that Gordon and Zalinda would want her to stay and live in the house they had built for her and her daughters; the friends she had made and who had taught her new skills would want her to stay, but Scotland drew her. She recalled the purple heather, the mists that curled round the mountain-tops, the laughter of a tight-knit community and the Scottish voices as they sang with the local fiddlers and pipers. But then she remembered the occasional barn dance where Mark and she had laughed at his dancing antics. Now it was the beautiful prairies with their backcloth of the

Rockies that beckoned her. Both good days and hardships were recalled until she realised that she had better focus her mind on doing some work. After all, John's plan had been that they should come and help Gordon. She felt it was only fair to both her daughters that she should have made up her mind about her future before the wedding. She had not done so as yet but there was still time.

In the coming days possible solutions came and went in Glenda's mind until one morning her determination to make a choice was so strong it could not be ignored. To be sure, she would think the alternatives over once more; observe the loved ones here in America and remember the family back home. Without fully realising it, excitement crept into Glenda's mind as the answers became clear to her.

'What am I going to do about my bridesmaid's dress, Mama? Can I take one of the dresses Uncle Gordon bought for me in New York?' asked Cat the next day.

'Yes, but just in case Ros wants you dressed in something else, I think it will be best if you go early. Say a month or two before the wedding, depending on when you can get a passage.'

'It's sounding as if you are not going with me?' queried Cat.

'I have things to see to here, and after all that has happened I'd like some time to myself. You can be more of a help to Ros, deciding on dresses for you both.'

Train times to New York were studied, passage on a ship from New York was booked, and this information was conveyed in a letter to Fiona, who offered to meet Cat when the ship arrived in Liverpool.

When the time for her to leave was nearly upon her she went to say goodbye to Gila in her stall. As the horse nuzzled her she sensed someone behind her.

'Are you ready to go?' asked Ahote.

Cat smiled. 'Yes, I think so. But I would so like to have a last gallop on Gila before I leave.' She stretched out her hand to him. 'Come on, let's ride together.'

They rode at a leisurely pace before breaking into a thundering gallop. Cat knew Ahote's horse would outpace hers so urged Gila to a breakneck speed. They ran neck and neck, hooves beating a thunderous tattoo on the firm ground. Ahote noticed that Gila was going to overtake his Palamino so pulled the stallion up sharply, making the horse rear and dust cloud the air. Cat turned Gila around, almost slipping from the saddle.

'What's wrong?' she cried. Ahote's face was full of rage that sent a chill running through her.

'You stupid woman!' he shouted. 'Even our Indian squaws know a mare should never be ridden so hard unless it is in danger. You know I am the best horseman on the ranch. Do not mess with me, Cat.'

She was shocked by the way he was staring into her eyes and for a moment silence hung between them. Suddenly Cat was pleased to be going away. She kicked Gila into a trot and headed back to the stable.

On the day of her departure from Colorado Glenda accompanied Cat to the local station. They were informed it was on time and should arrive in ten minutes. Glenda, like every other mother, issued last-minute advice to her daughter, but Cat was not listening, still dwelling on

Ahote's criticism of her. She was hurt he had not said goodbye.

She looked at the station clock. It ticked away precious moments of her life. Then a distant rumble grew louder and louder. The train would be here at any moment. She flung her arms around her mother's neck. Over her shoulder she saw the face of an Indian brave.

'Ahote!' she whispered. Her mother caught the note of relief in her daughter's voice and released her hold on Cat.

Ahote walked towards Cat and took her hand in his. 'Don't forget me when you are away. Come back to me.'

Caitlin smiled, touched his cheek and said, 'Wherever we are, our spirits will be bound together. So you see, Ahote, I have to return to you.'

She made her goodbyes to her mother and boarded the train for New York with a lighter heart. She watched the two people who loved her best leave together.

48

It was a warm morning in the Highlands and an expectant air hung over Pinmuir House.

'Welcome, Aunt,' Caitlin greeted the arrival of Fiona. 'This is exciting.'

'So the first fitting of the wedding dress should be. Have you the pictures from the magazines I loaned you?'

'I have them,' put in Ros, and ran to the window on hearing a trap pulling up outside.

'Mrs MacNicoll the dressmaker is here.'

Ten minutes later a pale mauve corded silk dress was laid out on the bed for them to see.

'It's beautiful,' Cat enthused. 'It will really set off the colour of your hair, Ros.'

Mrs MacNicoll smiled. 'Your sister chose the colour for that reason. Now she needs to tell me of any embellishments or changes that are required.'

Ros reached for the fashion pictures and discussed some trimmings she had seen there, with Mrs MacNicoll and her aunt.

Once tucks had been pinned in place and the trimmings finalised, other fittings were arranged. Suddenly feeling weary, Ros sighed and said, 'I wish Mother had been here.'

'Have you heard from her recently?' asked Fiona.

'We received a letter only three days ago,' said Cat. 'I'll fetch it for you.'

A few minutes later she read it out.

My dear girls,

I hope you are enjoying your time together and I am sorry I am not yet with you for the wedding but I hope to see you soon.

Life at the ranch is recovering well. Uncle Gordon has bought more cattle to swell the herd. Some of those the Indians saved have now calved. This all promises well for a cattle drive next year, even though the herd will be a smaller one than we've had in the past. Time will lead to expansion.

Tom relishes his job and Sara is now fully settled; Gordon made a good decision.

Both he and Zalinda send their love.

Gila and Ahote miss you, Cat.

All my love,

Mother

'Where can Mama be?' There was a snap of annoyance in Rosalind's voice. 'Aunt have you heard anything since we had this letter?'

'No,' replied Fiona.

'But she promised!' There was irritation in Ros's attitude

324

as well as her tone. 'She knew I wanted her here for the last fitting of my wedding dress! Where is she?'

'I've never known her to break a promise to do something,' said Cat.

'It looks as if she's going to break this one.'

'Don't take on so,' said Cat, trying to calm her sister. 'And don't get wedding nerves now. You've three weeks yet.'

'But she might still be in America for all I know,' moaned Ros.

'You don't believe that,' rapped Cat.

'I may as well. If she cared, she'd be here by now, helping me!'

'We'll do that,' said her Aunt Fiona. 'Mrs MacNicoll will have plenty of time if there are any further adjustments to be made. You must have your wedding dress just right so that you delight Clive. Now go and put it on.'

After a few minutes Ros appeared in her wedding dress, followed by the dressmaker.

'Are you having your hair up or down?' asked Fiona.

Before Ros could reply, Cat interrupted, 'Oh, you must have it down, Ros.'

'I'll have to have it that way! I've told you before, I'm wearing a lace veil with an orange blossom headband,' she snapped.

'Then you definitely need a slightly darker ribbon on the bodice,' said Fiona. 'Don't you think so, Mrs MacNicoll?'

'Yes, I do.'

Ros, who was standing close to the dressmaker, was startled. Mrs MacNicoll had not spoken!

Before Ros could make any query the door steadily opened, drawing everyone's attention.

Glenda walked in!

'Mama!' Ros ran and hugged her mother as if she would never let her go. 'Where have you been?'

'I promised I'd be here, didn't I? So here I am.'

Before she could say any more, Cat and Fiona gathered round, and laughter and chatter were ringing through the room.

Glenda held up her hands. 'Stand back, Ros, let me look. You are gorgeous and that dress makes you glow. I couldn't have made you look any better if I had been here earlier. Clive will be so proud of you.'

Cat put her arm around her mother's shoulders. 'It is wonderful to have you here, Mama. Ros was beginning to feel on edge.'

'I will leave you now,' put in Mrs MacNicoll. 'I should not intrude on this wonderful reunion. If it is all right with you, I can return the day after tomorrow?'

'That would suit us very well,' said Ros.

Mrs Martins was called to escort the dressmaker out, whereupon Glenda said, 'Thank you, Jessie, for keeping the timing of my homecoming a secret.'

That evening when mother and daughters were relaxing after dinner, Cat said, 'This is just like old times. We will remember this when we are back in Colorado, won't we, Mother?'

Glenda gave a little smile. 'I love both of you and *never* forget that. It has taken me a lot of thought to decide what I want to do with the rest of my life. I still had not made up my mind when I stood with Ahote on the platform and watched you leave, Cat. I am lucky enough to have lived in Scotland and Colorado, but it is the Highlands that have won my heart and, with no disrespect to Mark, I am making plans to settle here finally, to be near the man I first loved and who is still bound up in my heart.'

Her daughters looked at each other, rose from their seats and together hugged her, saying, 'Wherever you are, Mama, be happy.'

'I will. I am sure, Cat, you are going to be a very successful woman with the help of Gordon and Zalinda, and you are lucky enough to have found a true soulmate in Ahote.' Then, turning to Rosalind, she said, 'Be happy with Clive. I am relying on you both to take care of Pinmuir and the land I love. There is much for us all to sort out. I promise I shall not interfere in your lives, but if ever you need me, remember I will always be here.'

Acknowledgments

I must say thank you to my family, who have always encouraged me to follow the wonderful life of a writer. The horizons are far and wide and contain so much magic. I consider myself lucky to have walked there and met so many interesting and wonderful people whom I would never have known if I hadn't put pen to paper.

There are always those who make a special impact on the publication of a book.

I can still hear the words of encouragement my late wife Joan gave me when I stepped on to the rocky road to a writer's life. That encouragement has been kept up by Judith, one of my twin daughters, who reads every manuscript as I write.

Geraldine, her twin sister, prefers to read a book when it is finished, before it goes to my publisher. Anne and Duncan are always keen to show interest and carry that on beyond publication.

I must, as always, thank Lynn Curtis who was involved in the birth of Jessica Blair and has copy-edited every Jessica Blair title. Thanks, Lynn, for that and for your friendship.

And thanks to all the Piatkus staff, past and present, who have looked after my writing in the topsy-turvy world of publishing, especially Dominic Wakeford, my editor.